DAD CAMP

DAD CAMP

A NOVEL

EVAN S. PORTER

DUTTON

DUTTON

An imprint of Penguin Random House LLC
penguinrandomhouse.com

LIBRARY OF CONGRESS CATALOGING-IN-PUBLICATION DATA

Names: Porter, Evan S., author.
Title: Dad camp : a novel / Evan S. Porter.
Description: [New York] : Dutton, 2024.
Identifiers: LCCN 2023036291 (print) | LCCN 2023036292 (ebook) |
ISBN 9780593474402 (hardback) | ISBN 9780593474426 (ebook)
Subjects: LCGFT: Domestic fiction. | Novels.
Classification: LCC PS3616.O768 D33 2024 (print) | LCC PS3616.O768 (ebook) |
DDC 813/.6—dc23/eng/20231106
LC record available at https://lccn.loc.gov/2023036291
LC ebook record available at https://lccn.loc.gov/2023036292

Printed in the United States of America
1st Printing

Interior art by Grace Han

BOOK DESIGN BY KRISTIN DEL ROSARIO

For my dad, John

DAD CAMP

SUNDAY

One

If we don't win this girls nine-to-eleven softball game, it might actually be the end of the world.

Well, my world anyway.

I'm leaning against the chain-link backstop just next to our dugout on the third-base line, fingers gripping the metal for dear life, the late-summer sun beating on my neck, which would be sweating from the nerves even if it were January. Number 9, a girl named Isla, is up at bat, and the count doesn't look good. One ball and two strikes. We only have one out left, but I feel, let's say, *pretty good* about who's coming up in the lineup.

If we can make it there.

Number 9 takes a ball—2–2 now. At twelve, she's the tallest and biggest girl on the team, by far. She's here only because of a late birthday and a clerical error, so everyone assumes she's our secret weapon. Every week, parents of kids on the other team sit up with a nervous energy when she steps into the batter's box. Little do they know that she's utterly, undeniably terrible. She hasn't quite got full control over her fast-growing frame yet. Her stance is elbowy and awkward, like a baby ostrich learning to run. Great girl, great kid, but she's more effective as psychological warfare than as an actual player.

So . . . we might be in trouble.

The pitcher winds up and launches a fastball. Number 9 swings hard and, miraculously, gets all of it, driving it deep into left field. A shocked "Oh!" escapes my throat.

"Go, go, go!" I shout as she drops the bat, sounding like a drunk guy at a bar who bet way more than he could afford on this game. She takes off for first. The ball just gets over the outstretched glove of the fielder, and 9 takes second. A bad throw skips between an infielder's legs, and, just like that, she's on third.

This is the part where the team behind me should be going nuts, but I steal a glance over my shoulder, and our bench is a sea of disinterest. Girls snapping selfies. Tying their baggy jerseys up into cutesy side knots. Chatting lazily, bodies turned completely away from the action. I've never had as hard of a time getting a team engaged as I did this year, with this age group, with these girls. But no time to worry about that now.

There are two outs, a runner in scoring position, and Avery's up.

She jogs to the plate, adjusting her helmet over brown hair sticking out in two braids on both sides. She's never cared about game-day hair before, but this season's hottest look, apparently, is pigtails, and Avery has adopted them along with the rest of the team. She wears her signature eye black, smeared like war paint all over her face. I catch up with her and pull her aside.

"So it all comes down to this," I say in my most ridiculous movie-trailer voice.

"Yep," she says, tightening her batting gloves, mostly ignoring me. Par for the course lately.

"We're all tied up. All we need is a base hit to bring Isla home. Just give it a little nudge into the gap." I point out a gaping chasm between two infielders. "And we walk off as champions. Think you can do it?"

Avery scoffs. "Dad . . . ," she starts.

"It's *Coach* Dad out here."

"I'm not calling you that," she says, tightening her batting gloves again, apparently unhappy with their snugness. "And I know what to do."

Now, here's the thing. It might sound a little cocky, but Avery and I have won more than our fair share of little plastic trophies that read *Number One!* or *Great Job!* She eats high-stakes scenarios like this for breakfast, and I mean that almost literally. Over Lucky Charms most mornings, she makes me quiz her on situational play. The more convoluted, the better. So she does, in fact, know what to do.

But there's always the chance that something goes wrong. A millimeter can be the difference between a home run and a pop fly, the difference between a joyful romp around the bases and Avery furiously bludgeoning the dirt with her bat. Today of all days, I'd much prefer the former.

I've got something I need to tell her, and she's not going to like it. At all. So, naturally, I've put it off until the absolute last possible second, which is right around as soon as this game is over. If I don't want my head bitten off, I need her in a good mood. If we lose? Who am I kidding—she won't let that happen. I'm sure of it.

(Please, God, don't let us lose.)

Avery brushes past me and settles in at the plate. I give a signal to number 9 at third, waving my arms in the air like a crazed chimpanzee, flicking the tip of my nose, then folding one leg up like a flamingo. She stares back blankly from underneath the brim of the batter's helmet for what feels like an excruciatingly long time.

"What?" she finally says aloud.

I'm really not sure how I could be more clear. We've practiced these! (I think.)

I sigh, then gesture animatedly toward home plate. Now she nods, finally getting it.

The pitcher winds up and delivers—and to my surprise, Avery doesn't appear to be aiming for a controlled line drive through the gap. She cocks back and uncorks a wild, Paul Bunyan–like swing instead.

And completely misses.

Number 9, who took off for home the second the pitch took flight, skids to a stop, confused, and runs back to third.

"Avery! Just lay it down!" I yell.

She glares back at me.

"Or, you know, trust your judgment or whatever. Woo!" I clap pitifully.

The pitcher reloads. Another perfect pitch, and another huge swing and a miss from Avery. The count is 0–2. It's not unlike her to come out aggressive and get behind like this. She has the skill to come back, and she knows it. Which is exactly what gets her into trouble sometimes.

I know what's more than likely about to happen, but it doesn't stop me from chewing what's left of my fingernails right off and spitting them out into the dirt as I watch. Seconds later, though, I'm proven right.

The pitcher adjusts her headband, digs her feet into the mound, and fires off another. Avery cocks back, not letting up, only this time she absolutely *crushes* it. The ball rockets into deep center, way over the outstretched gloves of the hapless fielders.

The team parents erupt in cheers from the bleachers, while the girls casually look over to see what's going on, mostly unenthused. I even spot a subtle eye roll or two—*There she goes again.* For years, Avery has stood out from her teammates, but they all used to look up to her for her prowess on the field. This year has been . . . different, to say the least.

Avery throws her arms up triumphantly and tosses the bat, then jogs the bases. Two runs score. We win.

Moments before she stomps on home plate, I position myself a few feet away and crouch down, arms wide, for a customary congratulatory hug, like we've shared so many times before. I see her running toward me down the baseline, and for a moment I can see all versions of her at once. Four-year-old Avery, who forgot to drop the T-ball bat and carried it around the bases; six-year-old Avery with the batter's helmet drooping over her eyes; nine-year-old Avery, who was finally big enough to tackle me to the ground in a fit of giggles. Beaming, I ready myself for the embrace that's been the highlight of my week for as long as I can remember.

It's a little un-coach-like, I admit, but it's one of the few fatherly indulgences I allow myself when we're out on the field. Back when I was in Little League and *my* dad was the coach, he bent over backward not to treat me any differently from the other boys, to the point where it felt like he was actively ignoring me. I spent years working my ass off in hopes of getting a wink or a warm pat on the back—anything—before I finally gave up and dropped out of sports altogether.

Avery speeds up, sprinting home to secure the win. But instead of us colliding into an epic hug, she whizzes past me, with a small, unintentional (I hope) shoulder bump, which sends me careening backward onto my ass.

From the dirt, I watch as Avery skips over to the bench, beaming, hands up and prepped for an avalanche of high fives. None come. Most of the girls are already abandoning the dugout like a sinking ship, jogging to the infield for a few robotic handshakes with the losing team. Quickly, their attention turns to the nine-to-eleven boys, who just finished up a game on a field catty-corner to ours. They approach each other in packs, eager for the rush of unpracticed flirting but not yet ready to go without backup. The boys and girls throw Gatorade on one another. Giggles ring out. In the dugout, Avery gets a couple of half-hearted *Good jobs* from the stragglers as they shoulder past her. And then she's alone, shoving her equipment into a worn batting bag.

My heart aches for her, her face so clearly yearning for a little recognition and love. Selfishly, though, I can't stop thinking: *I'm right here.* But at least we won. That'll mean something to her.

I always hate this part, even the winning, because it means the season is over. I'm suddenly more aware of the rust flakes still stuck to my hand from the chain-link backstop, the rich copper color of the baseball diamond, the smell of popcorn coming from the snack bar. And I'm cherishing it, of course, now that it's too late. These seasons are finite, and once they're gone—they're gone.

Before I can catch up to Avery and tell her how proud I am of her, she slings her bag over her shoulder and zooms off toward the parking lot.

I stay awhile and shake hands with a few of the parents, who congratulate me on a championship season.

"That's some daughter you've got," they say. And they're right.

But eventually, my smiling muscles begin to ache under the strain of forced pleasantries, and I know it's time for me to slip away. The small talk and schmoozing with other parents has always felt like a bit of a chore, an unfortunate side effect of spending all this time with Avery, and now I'm looking forward to a long break from it.

Speaking of Avery, she waits near the parking lot for me to finish, a brooding, impatient look plastered on her face. I squint to see if there's even a microscopic clue in her body language that she might be in a good mood. There is not.

"John?" a man's voice calls out. I stop and turn around.

"Hey . . . Jason," I say, recognizing my old friend's glasses and bushy beard after a moment or two. I'm cornered out in the open like this. At the grocery store, I'd be able to duck down another aisle to avoid the awkward small talk, but here, I'm trapped. "Long time, man."

"So this is how you spend your Sundays now?"

"Apparently so. Your girl on the los—" I catch myself before the word *losing* falls out of my mouth. "The other team?"

"My son, he's doing flag football." Jason gestures to another field across the way, where a group of jersey-wearing boys are tackling one another violently, apparently missing the point of the flags.

I glance over at Avery, who's getting more and more annoyed as I make her wait, twisting the toe of her cleat aggressively into the dirt. I'm squandering the mere droplets of goodwill gained through our victory.

"We've missed you at the meetups," Jason states, letting it hang in the air like a question, the silence demanding an explanation for why I haven't hung out with *the boys* in a while.

"Guilty." I laugh. "But hey, listen, I've got to—"

"What's it been, a few years now, yeah?"

OK, a long while.

"Guess I've just got my hands full doing the dad thing right now. Speaking of—"

"I don't see why you can't do both," he says, continuing to bulldoze past my attempts to eject. "We'd love to have you back. Anytime."

"I'd like that," I lie. "You know, if I can ever conjure up some free time."

"Your girl's gotta be starting middle school, right? Don't worry, you'll have all the time in the world soon."

I chuckle politely, allowing the laugh to wind down into a wrapping-up sort of sigh. Mercifully, Jason seems to finally take the hint. He lets me go with a hearty "Welp!" and a half hug, and I jog over to the car.

There's no sign of Avery now. Evelyn, my wife, is waiting for me in our daughter's place, leaning against the car in yoga pants and a tank top with matching headband and holding an icy Starbucks drink.

"You know, eventually you're gonna have to tell the other moms you're actually a career woman who prefers a sharp pantsuit," I say.

In our little suburb, things are done . . . a certain way. The moms stay home to coordinate playdates and volunteer for about thirty-five school events a month, while the dads are typically scarce, off on business trips or in the office *circling back* on how much *bandwidth* someone has for a *deep dive* into some new *action items*. Either that or on the golf course. Evelyn and I both work, which doesn't make us freaks, per se, but definitely puts us in an uncomfortable minority. While other moms were here at the field early, staking out the best seats, supplying individually bagged snacks, Evelyn had to rush over after a morning of catching up on emails at home. She's a corporate recruiter, so for her there's really no such thing as "office hours."

"Eh, this getup disarms them, gets me more gossip and info. For example"—she takes a sip of her drink to build the suspense—"Avery's new teacher, Mrs. Bates? Total hard-ass. We're talking *hours* of home-work."

"Fantastic," I grumble, already imagining Avery in a prison jumpsuit, stuck studying in her room and only coming out for meals and bathroom breaks. But no sense in borrowing tomorrow's prob-lems. "So, how was your morning?"

"Oh, you know, I just love being glued to my laptop on a Sunday and showing up late to my daughter's game. Feels great."

"And how's Avery?"

Evelyn sighs. "She's in the car."

"Please tell me she's in a fantastic mood after hitting a walk-off homer to win the championship?"

"You know her. She's already thinking ahead to soccer. I'm guess-ing you still haven't told her?"

I sigh and shake my head.

"Are you really sure this is a good idea?" she asks. "She's growing up and freezing us out a bit, yeah, but it's normal. I'd hate to see you force something and have it blow up in your face."

"Thanks for the vote of confidence."

Evelyn places a loving hand on the small of my back.

"Good job out there today, Coach," she says. Then, "If it'll make you feel better, I'll let *you* round the bases later on."

"The guy's already coming around to put them away in the equip-ment shed, so . . ."

"No, I mean . . . Never mind."

She plants a tight-lipped kiss on my cheek and walks around to the other side of the car, and it occurs to me that I just whiffed on the biggest softball of my long career.

In my defense, I've got a lot on my mind. As soon as I get in that car, I've got to tell Avery what's going on. It's not actually bad news. Not to me anyway. There's even a chance she won't react so poorly, that I've built this up in my mind needlessly and it might actually be fun.

OK. Deep breaths.

In the car, I stall for a while, recounting big moments from the game, cranking up a cheery pop song I think she'll like, offering to stop for ice cream, trying everything I can to get a positive reaction out of Avery—and failing—before Evelyn finally elbows me in the ribs and eyeballs me to get on with it.

"We're going on a trip," I announce suddenly and a little too loudly.

"Spring training?!" Avery squeals from the back seat. She's been asking to go for years.

"Not exactly. Guess again."

"The beach? Are we going to the beach?!"

"Keep guessing."

She slumps back down, the brief moment of excitement vanish-ing from her face and slipping out the open window, my expectation management a spectacular fail.

"Ugh," Avery relents. "When? Like, winter break?"

"Tomorrow, actually."

"What?!"

I look over to Evelyn, hoping for a flitter of emotional-support eye contact, but she's staring out the window. *Hey, this is your thing, don't drag me into it,* the back of her head seems to say. I take a long breath and finally say this: "We're going on a retreat. Just you and me. For a week. And before you ask, yes—you have to."

Over her stunned silence, I explain how I've heard about this placed called Camp Triumph and how, one or two weeks a year, they offer special retreats for dads and daughters like us.

"It'll be awesome," I assure her. "We'll go canoeing. We'll make fires and eat as many s'mores as you want. There's literally no way it won't be fun. It's like every summer camp I loved as a kid, except we get to do it together. What do you say?"

Judging by my excited tone, you'd have thought I was taking her to Disney World on a rocket ship made of Sour Patch Kids.

I don't mention that I found out about the place after googling *11-year-old suddenly hates me,* or that this is my last-ditch effort to make us friends again before she starts middle school and forgets about me forever. I don't say that I know the timing is bad but booked it anyway. And I don't acknowledge that I knew she'd hate the idea from the get-go.

So when she shouts, "THIS IS SO UNFAIR!" and "ON MY LAST WEEK OF SUMMER?!" I act totally surprised.

Because as unfair as she thinks I'm being, I am absolutely sure this is the right thing to do.

She needs her dad right now, whether or not she's willing to ad-mit it. She'll see.

MONDAY

Two

The only thing separating us from Camp Triumph, and a total rejuvenation of my relationship with Avery, is a couple hundred miles of rural road.

She dragged her feet, but Avery's now loaded in the passenger seat. Our bags are packed. The car is gassed up and fresh off an oil change. I'm doing final checks, and then we'll hit the road to enjoy five days of intense (in a good way . . . probably) father-daughter bonding. We'll roast marshmallows around an open fire. Learn to shoot arrows. Sleep in log cabins under the stars. There is one downside, I guess, and that's that we won't have the whole place to ourselves. A bit of forced masculine small talk is inevitable with the other dads, but I've gotten pretty good over the years at ducking most of that. Otherwise, the whole week is about one thing and one thing only: Avery. And me.

There's just one problem: Avery's not currently speaking to me.

"We got the sleeping bags and pillows. We packed swimsuits,"

I say, rattling off from a packing list I printed from the camp's website as I stand in the driveway. Our ancient graying mutt, Fred, lays panting in a shady sliver of driveway up against the house. "We remembered bags for laundry and extra socks."

By *we*, of course, I mean *I*—Avery made it pretty clear she wouldn't be lifting a pinkie in preparation for this trip as a form of protest. And, credit to her, she didn't. I eventually got her in the car by threatening to dress her myself, like a scarecrow, and carry her out here over my shoulder. I could tell she believed I might really do it, and even though she's eleven now and it might have cost me a herniated disc, I definitely would have.

"Bug spray? Did we pack bug spray?" I say through Avery's open window. She doesn't respond, of course, just retreats further into her hoodie and fiddles with her phone. It's a cheapo, highly restricted thing with a few games and messaging with approved numbers only. No social media, despite her near-daily requests. Evelyn and I resisted the cell phone milestone for as long as we could, not fully comfortable with the idea despite Avery's pleading, but eventually we caved. Texting proved to be a logistical game-changer, not to mention a ton of fun—when she used to text me back, anyway.

Suddenly, a hand appears in front of my face, holding a multipack of Off!

"Honestly, what would you do without me?" Evelyn quips.

"I don't want to find out." I look down at my watch and realize we were supposed to leave twenty minutes ago, and we need to get on the road. Dads love getting on the road.

"Did you pack her book? She needs to finish it before Monday," Evelyn asks.

"She's not done?"

"Hasn't even started," Evelyn says, her voice low. "Can you believe that?"

Truthfully, I can't. We've never once had to coerce, bribe, or harass Avery about her summer reading. For years, it's been automatic, her reports outstanding, like the rest of her schoolwork. I look into the sky, as if speaking directly to the heavens: *Can't just one thing stay the same?*

"Shit," I say.

Evelyn shoots me a disapproving look as my *Shit* wafts directly into Avery's open window.

I switch to a whisper. "I mean . . . shit. OK, where is it?"

"I don't know."

"What do you mean, you don't know?"

Now she shoots me another look that needs no explanation. Evelyn's ability to know where everything we own is at any given moment borders on psychic. She knows this, and she wants her props when she uses it to save our asses. But the second I start counting on that superpower a little too much, she takes it away, the way you might snatch a lollipop away from an ungrateful child.

Rather than push it, I decide to ask Avery instead.

I lean down to the small opening in the passenger window. "Avery?" I say.

She's curled up like a potato bug, a fortress of hair covering her face.

"Where's your Narnia book, for summer reading? We need to bring it."

She says nothing and shifts her gaze away from me. I look at my watch again. Time ticking away. It's 6:56 now. Google estimates a two-hour-and-forty-seven-minute drive. Check in starts at 10:00 a.m.

One missing book. Two women who probably know where it is. None who will tell me. There's a word problem in here somewhere.

If there's any traffic whatsoever, or any unexpected pee breaks, we'll be late. And that's not the start to the week I'm looking for. There's too much on the line.

I let out a growl and sprint back into the house, up the stairs, and into the wasteland of Avery's room. Every surface is covered in clothes. I miss when it was toys, and stray puzzle pieces, and crayon drawings on brightly colored construction paper. Now it's just a maze of dirty athletic socks, field-stained shorts, and various jerseys, with a pair or two of jeans hanging off the door like Spanish moss.

A cursory search of the floor yields nothing. It's not under the covers. Not, God forbid, on the actual bookshelf. So I walk to Avery's desk, though right now it more closely resembles an ironing board than a working surface. I swipe a few loose socks away, but still no book.

But then something catches my eye. The desk drawer, running the entire length, has a note attached to it. It reads, in bold, aggressive lettering: **KEEP OUT!**

That's . . . strange? I briefly forget about *The Lion, the Witch, and the Wardrobe*, and now I'm much more intrigued by the Drawer. What could she be hiding in there? Drugs? *Oh my God. She's on drugs*, I think. It would explain the changes in her. The attitude. The slacking on her homework. But then I remember that I can still barely get Avery to choke down bubble gum–flavored cold medicine. I'm just reaching out to open it up when I catch a glimpse of my watch again: 7:02.

Jesus. This is a can I'll have to kick down the road. The universe must decide I've suffered enough for one morning, because I catch a glimpse of a small lion just peeking out from behind Avery's floor-length curtains: Narnia. I grab it and hustle out of the room, nearly tripping over a soccer cleat.

In a flash, I'm back outside, and Evelyn's holding the driver's-side door open for me.

"We'll be back on Saturday," I tell her. "Please, promise me you'll take some time for yourself."

"I will."

I lean in for a kiss goodbye, and she offers me a cheek. I take it.

Then she places two hands around my face and looks deep into my eyes. "I love you, John," she says, not in the casual *Love ya* kind of way we so often say it.

"Love you, too."

And on that, I swing myself into the driver's seat and hit the gas. I haven't put the car in gear yet, so the engine screams, but we go nowhere.

"All right, we're here. That was fast," I say, faux-unbuckling my seat belt.

Avery rolls her eyes.

Irritated with my stupid joke, I clunk the car into reverse and back out of the driveway until—

"Dad, stop," Avery says.

So I do. "What's wrong?"

She pokes her head out the window. "Mom?"

Evelyn jogs over. "Everything OK?"

"Just remember to take care of Fred," Avery says.

"I think I can handle it." Evelyn laughs.

Avery loves that damn dog. All kids want one, beg for one, promise they'll do all the feeding and pick up all the poop. But Avery really does it. For years and years she begged us for a little sister, and when that never happened, I guess she decided a dog was the next best thing. We felt like we owed her that much at least.

"Yeah, but remember he needs his medicine at the same time every day. And sometimes he'll eat better for you if you soften up his food with a little bit of water."

She's so tender and thoughtful when she says this, about our crust-covered dog who does nothing all day, that I find myself strangely jealous of him.

"OK, I've got it."

"And he needs walks, too, don't just let him out in the yard."

Evelyn leans in and places a kiss on Avery's forehead. "Have fun with your dad."

I let go of the brake and we start moving backward, away from the house again, and I'm pretty sure when we hit the main street and I put us into drive, I can hear her mumble, "Fat chance."

• • •

They say complete silence—the true absence of all sound—would drive a person insane.

Avery and I are currently putting that theory to the test.

We're stopped at a red light and, without the road noise, it's so torturously quiet in the car that I can hear a faint buzzing sound in my ears and nothing else. That little hum that reminds you Earth is still spinning, even though it feels like time has to come to a full stop.

"It's gonna be a long drive," I say to Avery, and she startles when I break the silence. "We might as well talk."

She leans even harder into the passenger-side door, almost willing her body to dissolve straight through it and get away from me forever.

"You're upset about soccer tryouts. You have every right to be," I say.

Yeah, there it is. The elephant in the car. Avery has been begging to join the travel team this year. It'd mean practice four nights a week, overnights in hotels for special games and tournaments, and a much, much higher level of competition. It's not like the leagues she's done before, the ones that have gobbled our Saturdays and Sundays—and one or two evenings a week—for years. Sure, they took up a lot of time. But I never considered it a waste because we were doing it together, which is exactly why I always signed up to coach. But I can't coach in this league—I'm horribly underqualified—and I won't be able to chaperone every overnight trip. I don't know if I can stomach all this extra time away from her.

Anyway, you don't just pay $15 and pick a jersey number. Only the best of the best kids in the county can play for this team. And the tryouts are today.

We were supposed to be there.

"They couldn't get enough girls; it happens. It's a big commitment, and not every parent is OK with it. It's a lot of time away from your kiddo."

"But that doesn't make sense," Avery says, among her first words of the day. "How can there just *not* be a team?"

I know my story won't stand up under scrutiny, so I decide the best thing to do is change the subject as quickly as possible. Try to cheer her up, if I can.

"So whadya say we stop at the next gas station and you can get an extra-large ICEE. Or an ice cream. Or whatever you want. I'll let you get a Red Bull if you promise not to tell Mom."

"I can't believe this," she huffs. "My last week of summer. You know April is back from vacation and her pool has a waterslide? I could be there right now, but *noooo*. You know Kayla's parents are taking her to *Malibu* this week?!"

And just like that, I miss the silence.

This attitude represents uncharted waters. Avery has been pissed at me before, but usually it's her fault, not mine. A tantrum or over-reaction to a minor grievance where it's easy to respond with a template like, "I'm sorry I [took a lick of your snow cone without asking], but you can't just [throw yourself on the ground and cry for forty minutes]." And when the tears pass and the tiny but furious rage subsides, we hug it out and the whole thing is over.

But this is bigger, lingering. I've done something, though I don't know what. Everything I say is wrong. Even the most mild of greetings provokes a venomous response. Every single thing I try seems to make things worse.

I suddenly spot an opportunity in the form of a red VW Beetle pulling up next to us on the highway. You almost never see them anymore, so I take it as a sign from above, a generous offering. This is it. My chance. This is her favorite game, and she's never, ever let a Beetle pass us by without playing. Not even once.

Immediately, I shout it out—"Punch buggy!"—and launch a playful jab in the direction of her arm. But she's faster than she used to be. She jerks her body forward like lightning, leaving me swiping at the air, but—*THUNK*. In what I'm choosing to believe is enthusiasm for the game and not extreme effort to avoid my touch, Avery miscalculates and inadvertently smacks her face right into the dash.

"Oh God!" I shriek. "Are you all right?" I nearly swerve us right off the road trying to place a comforting hand on her back, which she throws off.

"DAD!!!" comes squeaking out her nostrils.

Oh God, please don't let her be bleeding, please don't let her be bleeding. I'd never be able to live it down. She still brings up the time I pinched her thigh in the car seat when she was three. If I gave her a bloody nose, she's going to write this on my tombstone.

She pulls her hands away from her nose, slowly, bracing herself for a waterfall of blood.

None comes. *Thank you, deity in charge of interstate highways.*

"I am so, so sorry, Avery. Are you OK?"

She mumbles something. A nasally jumble of words as she clutches her nose again.

"Did you say *ice cream*? You ready to stop for that ice cream?"

"I said *ice*," she says. "Just ice."

At least she's finally talking to me.

• • •

By the time I return to the car, carrying a cup of ice and an assortment of checkout-land candy to use as a shameless bribe, Avery is asleep. Quietly, I climb in the car and get us back on the road. She's got her arms tucked in super close to her body, cell phone vise-gripped in one hand, and I can see her shiver a bit as we drive. The AC vent is pointed directly at her, and it's sweltering out, so I've got the air blasting. I kick it back a notch or two, then reach over and close her vent. Her body relaxes immediately, like someone's just thrown a warm blanket over her. I turn on one of my favorite playlists—all sappy, ooey-gooey songs about a father's love—and set it to a gentle volume.

I drive, and I think about the message on the Camp Triumph website, the one that popped up after my credit card had processed:

Leave with a stronger and more fulfilling bond than you arrived with, guaranteed, or your FULL tuition refunded!

Looks like we're going to put that guarantee to the test.

Three

We pull off the highway at an obscure exit. The sign that's supposed to list the hotels and restaurants at the exit is completely blank. This place doesn't even have one of those shitty fast-food joints that turns out to be inside a gas station.

We take a long rural road for a few miles before we spot the sign, CAMP TRIUMPH, carved gloriously into what looks like the wall of a log cabin wedged into a boulder. I turn in, and we follow a dirt road through some winding woods as roots and rocks jostle the car. Eventually the trees part, and we come to a gigantic open field.

Avery peers out the window with genuine curiosity, taking in the sights while she rubs the sleep from her eyes. A crew of gangly teenage counselors in bright orange vests waves us past with wands, and we drive until we reach a pebbly parking lot next to what looks to be the camp's head office, joining a small handful of other cars.

We park, and I get out first, stretching my legs in the sunshine. It's immaculately quiet here. Only a few birds chirping in the nearby woods. Somehow, the tranquil nature sounds take the sting out of Avery's prolonged silence.

"Howdy!" a high-pitched voice yells from about two feet away from me.

My heart stops, and I spin around to find a squirrelly-looking man dressed vaguely like a Boy Scout, head-to-toe khaki and way more pockets than could possibly be functional. He's in his fifties, I'd guess, with thinning hair, glasses, and a look about him that suggests he might blow away with the next strong breeze.

"I'm Dennis, the director here. Welcome to Camp Triumph," he says. "I am *grateful* to have you here."

His unusual emphasis on the word *grateful* throws me. "Uh, thanks. I'm John." I motion to my daughter, who's very slowly dragging herself out of the car. "That's Avery. We're really looking forward to this."

Well, I am anyway.

"Of course, the Collins. Or is it the Collinses? We've been waiting on you to arrive. You're the last and—"

He stops on a dime in mid-sentence. Avery has moseyed around from her side of the car and shown her face—swollen, red nose and all.

"Sweetheart, are you all right?" Dennis says.

"Oh, that," I jump in to head off his concern. "Don't worry, that's . . . that's from me." Nope, that doesn't sound good. Rephrase.

"I mean I hit her. Well, no, I tried to hit her, but don't worry, I missed." Worse. That was way worse. Try again. "Sometimes she hits me, too! It's a game we play."

Why are words so hard?

Dennis sits in stunned silence until Avery throws me a lifeline. "We were playing Punch Buggy, and I jerked my head forward and . . . It was just an accident."

"Oh." He exhales, visibly relieved. "I didn't know people still played that." Then, looking at me: "Because of the punching."

The judgment in Dennis's eyes burns hot, and I'll admit, this is not the foot I wanted to start off on. But still, Avery piping up enough to spare me from a Child Protective Services investigation is a good sign. And I realize just how low the bar for good signs has fallen.

"You had me worried. But now I have to say I'm *relieved*."

There it is again, the strange emphasis.

"Now, just a couple of things to go over with you," he continues, eyes locked on me. "First things first, there's no technology allowed here. None whatsoever. Before you settle in, I need you to put your cell phone and any laptops or tablets into that box."

He gestures to a wooden cube sitting on the wraparound deck of the main office building.

It's painted yellow with a black frowny face on the front.

"If anyone needs you, they can call the camp, and we'll pass on any messages. Think of it as a throwback to the summer camps of your parents' and grandparents' youth. It'll be fun! And besides, you two both deserve each other's full and undivided attention this week."

"No spam calls for a week? Sign me up!" I laugh, elbowing Avery in the ribs jovially.

"Ow?" she squeaks.

I turn back to Dennis, red-faced. "I promise I'm not doing this on purpose."

His eyes narrow, and he clears his throat, determined to soldier on. "It is, however, highly encouraged that you write to someone back home this week and tell them how things are going! Helps make the whole experience feel more real, I find. And besides, what's summer camp without letters home?" He laughs quietly, and when we don't join in, he winds it down into a little sigh—a technique I recognize as him being ready to exit this interaction. "Anyway. I will need you to drop those phones before you head to your cabins."

"You've got to be kidding me," Avery snaps.

"She loves kidding," I tell Dennis. "It's her favorite." I really don't want him thinking Avery and I are a walking disaster. Nonetheless, he gives me a supposedly reassuring pat on the back.

"It should also go without saying that this is a dry campus." Then, under his breath: "No alcohol under any circumstances. Let's see, what else . . .

"Here's your welcome packet, schedule, map of the camp, things like that," the director says, offering me a stack of papers. Still side-eyeing me.

I take it and he doesn't let go immediately, and I have to tug a bit to get him to loosen his grip.

"The cabins are right along this trail here, about a hundred yards into the trees. You're in"—he checks a sheet attached to his clipboard—"cabin number four. So go ahead and get settled, then meet the rest of the group for a late brunch here in about half an hour."

I nod and reach into the car to pop the trunk, but Dennis still has more to say.

"Now, all I need from you is the parking fee, and we'll be on our way."

"The parking fee?"

"It's just five dollars per day. But you'll get a dollar off if you pay for the week upfront!"

What is this, the parking deck next to an aquarium? I already paid an outrageously high tuition just to get us here at the last minute, and now this? But I don't argue. I'm already on thin ice with this guy, and the last thing I want is for him to send us packing—which, by the way, is a weirdly prominent warning all over the website. Apparently they reserve the right to boot you out of here any time, for any reason, without a refund. So even though I know I'm being scammed to pay for parking in the middle of nowhere, I reach into my wallet and fork over the twenty-five bucks. Dennis makes a big show of handing me one dollar back, then thanks me and turns to leave.

"I'm so *happy* you're here," he says as he walks away, but not in a cheery welcoming way. More like the way you'd greet a friend who just unwittingly walked into his own intervention.

I turn around and there's Avery, furiously typing on her phone.

"All right, all right," I say. "Hand it over."

"One second."

I've been around long enough to know that *one second* can go on forever if you let it, so I decide to rip the Band-Aid off, and I snatch the phone from her.

"DAD!"

"I get it, OK? But we're in this together."

Wouldn't that be nice.

• • •

With Avery huffing her way down the dirt path toward the cabins, suitcase kicking up dust behind her, I grab my bags, lock the car, and quickly pull out my own phone. There are a few missed calls waiting for me on the notification screen, but I ignore them. I send Evelyn a quick text, and I feel a wave of homesickness as I type out how I miss her already and will talk to her in a week. How am I supposed to know what to do without her in my corner? Evelyn has a way with Avery; she just does. As my daughter and I have grown further apart, the two of them have become closer and closer. It fills my heart, really, even if I'm sometimes jealous. Evelyn tries to help me, feeds me vital information, offers advice, purposefully leaves enough space for me to have time with Avery. And things are *still* so rough between us. For the first time, I realize that I am completely alone in this.

Gulp.

I hit Send, turn off my phone, and dump it into the sad-face box, which I realize has a thick padlock holding it shut. My phone falls in and clatters against a few other devices inside. To be honest, I'm relieved to be rid of its incessant buzzing. Avery's goes in next.

Then I jog and catch up to her a little ways down the path. "I'm sorry this trip got off on kind of the wrong foot."

She doesn't respond.

"I know I sprung it on you, and then I—well, you know, your nose and everything. So I realize I have no right to ask you—but will you just please promise me that you'll try? Try to have a good time?"

The path leads us right into a group of about a half dozen cabins, all raw wood and green shingles. In front of us, the cabin closest to the trail looks lively—bodies shuffle around inside, and voices emanate out. Avery pauses for a second, scanning the cabins.

"Which one do you think is number four?" I ask her.

"Probably the one with the big four on it."

Ah. Now I see it.

Inside number four, it looks, feels, and smells like summer camp circa 1999. Wooden bunk beds lined with prison mattresses. Cobwebs in the corner. The aroma of damp logs. A wet towel hanging in the corner.

If I'm honest, it doesn't quite match the pictures online. The gallery on the website had a nostalgia to it, like the photos had been run through one of those yellowy Instagram filters that made you yearn for a simpler time. But now that we're here, I realize the photos were just naturally that color because they were taken in the nineties.

Or before.

The space reminds me a little of the cabins I stayed in at camps like this when I was a kid. But only a little. Mostly, it's just shitty.

What surprises me most, though, is that the cabin isn't empty. We've arrived in the middle of the melee for free beds. Suitcases litter the floor, opened, clothing strewn everywhere as two girls mill about, hardly noticing us.

"Oh," I mutter, my heart sinking. "Kinda thought it'd be just us in here." I realize I must be sleeping with a bunch of dads in another cabin somewhere around here. I'm sure that'll be a real hoot.

The website wasn't really clear on this, either. I had been looking forward to late-night chats with Avery as we both drifted off in the evenings. Waking up and seeing her face first thing every morning. Speaking of her face, I scan hers and I can tell she's surprised, too. Maybe even a little intimidated, though she would never admit it.

One of the girls, the younger of the two, sits cross-legged on the floor riffling through her suitcase. She's got round cheeks, glasses, and tight, immaculate braids held together with those gumball hair ties, and she chucks pants and sock balls and sunscreen bottles aside until she finds a small plastic case, opens it, and pulls out an inhaler. She takes a deep puff.

The older girl is tall, with dark hair worn straight down her back like a waterfall and bright blue eyes. I only get a glimpse of them as she studies her suitcase, situated neatly on the bed, and gently removes exceptionally folded items one at a time and places them aside with military precision.

No one notices us.

"Hi," I say.

Both girls look and offer limp waves.

"This is Avery."

"Dad," she sighs. "I know how to introduce myself."

"I'm Erica," the younger girl says, bouncy and energetic.

"Jessie," says the older girl, formal and rehearsed, like she's responding to roll call at boarding school.

I nudge Avery forward a bit into the middle of the cabin. "Why don't you ask where they're from?"

She throws her suitcase up onto a top bunk—an impressive throw, to be honest. I lay my suitcase down on the lower bunk so I can hoist myself up and peek above the rail, where Avery has climbed and now lies facedown onto the mattress.

"You gonna be OK?" I ask her. As sad as I am not to be sharing a cabin with her, I'm just anxious about leaving her alone with a bunch of girls she doesn't know.

"No, please stay," she starts. "How will I remember my name or how to make basic conversation if you're not here?"

OK. Point taken.

Suddenly, I hear the cabin door slam shut. I look around but don't see anyone until I glance down, and there she is, a third girl, standing inches away from me. She's younger than the other two, and quite a bit smaller. Straight midnight-black hair and a gap between her front teeth.

I kneel down to her level. "Hi, what's your name?"

She locks eyes with me and reaches for the bed, grabs my suitcase by its handle, and drags it slowly off the edge until it crashes to the floor, never breaking eye contact.

"*My* bed," she says.

"Oh . . . right, no I wasn't going to . . ."

Her gaze is unwavering.

"The dads' cabins are back a little farther," Jessie, the oldest girl, offers. In other words, *scram.*

"And that's Tam," says Erica.

"Hi, Tam," I say.

Tam says nothing.

I hate that Avery and I aren't bunking together. I hate that I just paid that ridiculous parking fee and drove three hours just to hang out with a bunch of dads I'm sure to have nothing in common with. I could have done that at home, in my own neighborhood, for free. But despite all my hating, the girls are all staring at me, clearly waiting for me to leave.

"I guess I'll go get settled, and, Avery, I'll see you at brunch in a few?"

She waves an arm at me in acknowledgment, and the other girls all watch me leave, the screen door slamming shut behind me.

I walk slowly through the rest of the cabins outside. If I'm being honest, I'm in no hurry to meet the other dads.

• • •

"Good, you're here. I think you're the last of us," says a bearded man as I walk into the dads' cabin, a carbon copy of the one I just came from. He's in exceptional shape, sleeves hugging muscular arms as he unpacks his suitcase on his bed in the same Marine-like manner as—I'm guessing—his daughter, Jessie.

He extends a massive paw, and I endure a long and brutal handshake, along with a nagging feeling that he's *trying* to make this painful, like some twisted show of dominance. "Ryan," he says, "and you should be John, if the roster they gave us is accurate."

"It is," I say.

"Lou," says another man, forcefully interjecting himself between us. He shakes my hand, too, and tries to finish the job Ryan started, though he fails to generate the same crushing power.

Lou and Ryan are, physically, complete opposites. Where Ryan is action-figure jacked, Lou is rail-thin—but less "I run marathons" and more "I'm awake at weird hours and don't keep a normal meal schedule." Lou's completely covered in faded ink, sleeve tattoos wrapped all the way to his wrists, with slightly unkempt hair to complement a face full of stubble.

"And that's Booker," they both say in unison before sharing a surprised glare, pointing to a third man in the corner. He's sitting on his bed, hunched over a laptop, holding his cell phone high in the air with one hand. A clean-cut, polo-wearing dude with neatly trimmed hair and no evidence that he's ever skipped a day shaving his face.

"There's a free bunk above him," Lou says. I look around and confirm that it's, in fact, the only free bunk. Then, leaning in so only I can hear him, Lou adds, "Good luck with that."

"Good, good, this is good. Finally got a signal," Booker says to no one in particular. "Nobody move."

Ryan clears his throat. "We're due to meet in the chow hall in about ten minutes. If we unpack quickly, we should have a few minutes left for a round-robin get-to-know-you session. Two truths and a lie is always efficient, but I'm open to other formats."

Lou cuts in. "I say we get to know each other first." Then, clearing his throat and dropping his voice an octave: "There'll be plenty of time to finish unpacking later."

"'Only put off until tomorrow what you are willing to die having left undone,'" Ryan says. "Picasso."

"I think I can rest in peace knowing my underwear never made it out of my suitcase."

Ryan offers another retort, but I walk away and leave them to bicker. I had imagined I'd walk in on the middle of a friendly but opinionated group conversation about cryptocurrency or interest rates or car engines or, God forbid, politics—I've been to enough neighborhood barbecues and children's birthday parties to know when you get a group of dads together, the conversation will always veer toward one of those eventually.

Typically, I don't stay in these conversations long. Most of the time, you'll find me in the bounce house tossing small children around or mainlining cake. I've learned how to tread water when these topics come up, usually citing the headline of an article I didn't read or asking a few pointed questions before ejecting to go play on the tire swing. But somehow the dick-measuring contest happening here is worse.

I walk over to Booker's bunk, and he doesn't look up at me.

"Mind if we bunk together?" I say.

He offers a distracted grunt. "As long as you don't narc on me about the laptop."

"Wouldn't dream of it," I say, tossing my suitcase down onto a free corner of the floor, kneeling down, and zipping it open.

Booker finally looks up at me and says, "I'm not an asshole, by the way. I'm just trying to finish one thing up, that's all."

Right. Mustn't forget to send those spreadsheets while you're supposed to be spending time with your daughter.

"No, of course not," I say.

From my suitcase, I pull out my trusty pillow, vacuum-sealed in a small plastic bag, and watch it balloon back to life. Then, I climb the child-size ladder to the top bunk and have to hunch over to keep from smacking my head on the ceiling. A high-stakes game, to be sure, because I'm almost certain I can see a few rusty nailheads poking through the roof. On the bed, there's a small stack of papers, folded into thirds, sitting upright as if greeting me. And a Camp Triumph–branded pen. And a prestamped envelope. Dennis's aforementioned letter-writing materials. For now, I shove it all aside, lay my pillow down on the wafer-thin mattress, and clamber back down.

I dig into my suitcase and pull out a wooden box, a little bigger than a shoebox, stained and carved by yours truly. It's thick and heavy and, thankfully, it's managed to survive the trip without any obvious damage. This is our Adventure Box.

I built it years ago when Avery was little. The seeds of the idea, though, started even earlier, when she was just a baby.

The specifics are a blur, because at the time I was so sleep deprived and, honestly, depressed, that all I wanted was to wish time away. There was the initial excitement of setting up the nursery, counting down the days, bringing her home for the first time. But quickly I realized that having a baby wasn't glamorous at all. I desperately wanted the nighttime wailing and feedings to end, the colicky screaming, the soul-sucking cycle of laundry and dishes. I desperately wanted Avery to get older and be "easier," whatever that means. And one night, around a crackling backyard firepit, I found myself dumping it all on some friends who were older parents, whose kids were where I wanted Avery to be. You know, self-sufficient. "Easy." I was fully expecting the usual bullshit—"Enjoy these moments!"—but my friends actually surprised me, and reframed the sentiment in a way I've never been able to forget:

They ambushed me with math.

Your time with your children is frighteningly finite, they said. Assume they live at home with you for eighteen years. When they're school age, they spend most of that time in a classroom, right? So by the time they become truly functional, interesting human beings, you might have thirteen summers where they're all yours. And once middle school starts? All bets are off. Chances are they'll want to spend more time with their friends than you (the word *more* being optimistic, at best—you'll be lucky if they even acknowledge your existence at that age. I had been warned). And that's doubly true for high school, which also comes with their first jobs, dates, internships. When you're all done with subtraction, you have a window of something like five summers where your kids are home and are both old enough and young enough to actually want to play with you. And the baby phase? The plodding, monotonous grind that, at that point, defined every waking second of my life? So short it doesn't even register as a blip on the abacus, so to speak.

Something about that got through to me. The raw numbers were hard to ignore, and I thought about it every single day until I built this box. The box itself isn't much. Just a heavy wooden rectangle with a questionable stain job and Avery's and my initials etched into the bottom. But the inside, that's what makes it special. For five-plus years, we've been filling it with little trinkets and tokens from fun things we've done together. Adventures we've taken.

They started small, when Avery was small. A pine cone we found in the park. A cool rock. And when she got bigger, so did our adventures. The fishing hook she caught her first fish with. A badge the airline gave her when Evelyn and I took her on her first flight. Eventually the box started getting full, and the tradition evolved. The past couple of years, we've done so much together, it's been impossible to put everything in the box. So the night before school starts, and the summer is officially over, we both pick our favorite adventure token we've been saving. And we give it to each other, like a gift, and we put them in the box. Last year, the night before her first day of fifth grade, she gave me the most incredible drawing she did of the night sky when we took a three-day backpacking trip together. I had no idea it even existed, and now it's in the box. I gave her a little key chain stuffed animal I spent about forty bucks to win for her at the midway at Six Flags.

This summer, there haven't been a whole lot of adventures. But there's still time. There has to be.

Suddenly, a loud air horn blares outside and interrupts my train of thought.

"Time to move out, men," Ryan announces.

"Yep, let's get a move on," Lou adds.

For fuck's sake, these two. This is going to be a long week.

Three and a Half

Avery is three and a half years old, and I'm sitting on a park bench watching a merry-go-round, well . . . go around. Giraffes and gorillas bobbing up and down, and a few adults sitting on those boring benches that don't move.

She's not on the ride, no. Avery is at day care. A cute little colorful house just a few minutes from our home where she plays with blocks and, judging by the rate of illnesses in our household, licks the floor all day long. She's happy there. But now that I think of it, it's her last year. Soon, she'll start pre-K, which is sort of kindergarten lite, where she'll start following the real school schedule with proper lesson plans and all. She'll be giving up nap time soon and she'll be expected to stop pooping her pants and all of those other things that come with growing up (for some of us, at least).

But I'm not just some weirdo sitting in a park by myself. I'm waiting for someone. And it's not really a park at all, well, not a regular one. It's a place called Happy Hills Amusement Park, and I'm here to interview for a job.

Fine, I'll say it: a dream job.

A chipper college-aged girl in khakis with a walkie-talkie clipped to her belt and a signature Happy Hills pink polo walks up to me.

"John?" she says. "We're ready for you. You can follow me."

I stand and catch the eye of a little boy about Avery's age holding tight to a lion on the merry-go-round; he tentatively lets one hand go and waves to me. I wave back. And then I follow the girl through the park and into an office of some kind, tucked behind a row of concession stands.

A suited woman in her forties or so greets me with a "John Collins?" and a powerful handshake. "Great to meet you."

Happy Hills is one of the best and least-known amusement parks in the country. No one's heard of it, and it never makes those online lists of must-see tourist spots, but they have incredible rides. A small but fierce selection of roller coasters. Tons of tame up-and-down or spin-you-round types for the littles ones. And the park is spotless, the staff so damn friendly. It's the Chick-fil-A of amusement parks—without the homophobia. But while people like me who live relatively close by love that it's somewhat undiscovered, apparently the top brass don't. And that's why they're looking for someone to bring their marketing efforts into the digital age. Case in point: their website still has a hit counter and a guest book.

Challenging, in a good way? Yes. Fun? Duh. Great pay? Cha-ching.

The bright pastel colors and cartoon characters that adorn every square inch of this place are misleading, because the interview process has been a beast. Five rounds so far. And now here I am, one of the final candidates, ready to meet the CMO.

But first, before I can sit down across from her desk, my phone vibrates in my pocket. I pull it out to make sure I ignore the call before the buzzing drives this woman crazy and costs me the gig. But I immediately recognize the number on the screen as Avery's day care.

"I'm so sorry—I have to take this really quickly."

• • •

An hour later, Avery and I are curled up under a blanket on the couch watching a nonstop queue of kids shows on Netflix, a puke bucket stationed on the coffee table in front of us. Just in case. We're pretty good at this routine by now. It feels like the seventy-fifth time this year she's come home from day care sick in one way or another. These unexpected interruptions used to break me, send me hurtling into spirals of stress and anxiety. These days, I've gotten a lot better at coping with the chaos. You might even say I've come to love it, along with everything else about being a dad. After about nine or ten short episodes of random cartoons, I feel her twitch. I look down, and her eyes are closed; she's fast asleep. I have to pee, so I take this opportunity to try to slip away, carefully peeling back the blanket to make my escape.

"Daddy, stay," she says sleepily, never opening her eyes. So I do.

Eventually, she's feeling a little better, so we get up and we go outside for a walk. It's sunny and the sky is clear and I can tell immediately the bright weather is putting a pep in her step. At some point during the walk, she stops and kneels down, examining something in the grass.

"Daddy! Come see!"

She shows me what she's found. A rock.

"Whoa!" I say, in the way that parents do.

"No, look!"

She turns it over, and there's a funny face painted on the rock in bright red.

"Huh, look at that."

"Can I keep it?"

"I don't know, someone must have painted it and put it there."

"Because they wanted me to find it!"

"OK," I laugh. "Sure, why not?"

"We have to keep it forever. You have to *promise* me we'll keep it forever."

"I promise. We can keep it forever," I say, figuring she'll forget about it halfway home and never bring it up again. Or maybe I'll find it in the dryer two weeks from now. But the second we get through the door at home, Avery scurries off and finds a shoebox. She places the rock inside and hands me the box.

"Put this somewhere safe," she commands.

Mommy's working late, so it's just the two of us. Before we eat dinner, Avery falls asleep again on the sofa, wiped out from the ups and downs of the day and the demands being sick is placing on her body. My phone rings again as I'm stirring a pot of mac and cheese.

"Hello?"

"Hi, John." It's the CMO. "I hope everything worked out OK today with your daughter. She feeling any better?"

"She's coming around. Thanks. And thank you for understanding today."

"Listen, we know you've got a lot on your plate right now, but we really like you, so just give us a call when you're ready to reschedule that interview. OK?"

"Will do," I say.

I never did call them back.

Four

The dining hall—I refuse to call it the chow hall, this is summer camp, not the Marines—is a long log building tucked away behind the pool, shaded by ancient pine trees and covered in moss.

I walk in expecting a sea of faces. But there's hardly anyone here. A few dads and their girls have spread out to various tables—the ones you'd see in a middle school cafeteria—barely filling in a quarter of the space. The clang of kitchen workers somewhere behind the buffet line should be background noise, but with so few bodies in here to dampen the sound it's almost overpowering. I walk to join Ryan and Lou (there's no sign of Booker) at a corner table. Avery's there, too, among the other girls. The four of them sit surrounding a cup, filled to the brim with brown liquid, all staring at it like it's a glowing space orb. Erica leans in and sips from the straw poking out, makes an exaggerated puking face, then erupts in laughter.

"It's absolutely disgusting!" she yelps, and they all laugh. "You all have to try it."

Erica pushes the cup toward Avery, who shakes her head.

"I don't think so."

The girls begin to pound the table and chant, "Do it! Do it! Do it!"

"I don't want to play." Avery crosses her arms, refusing to give in.

Tam, the smallest in the group, reaches over and gently pokes her. "If you go, I'll go."

Avery rolls her eyes, huffs out a "Fine," holds her nose, and takes a long pull from the straw, then nearly gags as she swallows.

"I don't get how anyone could drink that." She retches.

"Is that one of those things with every different kind of soda mixed together?" I ask, approaching the table.

"No, it's Diet Coke," Erica says. "Adults are gross."

I feel attacked.

"My turn!" yells Tam, and she grabs it. She can barely reach the straw and, in reaching for it, tips the entire cup into her lap. Tears well up behind her eyes, and Avery springs into action, snatching heaps of napkins from the center of the table and blotting at Tam's clothes.

"Hey, it's OK"—then gesturing to the empty cup—"you're better off wearing it than drinking it, trust me."

Tam laughs. Avery has always had a natural way with much younger kids, and every time I see it, I ache for her, just a little. She would have been an amazing big sister.

Lou snatches up Tam, exasperated but clearly well-practiced at handling spills and messes. "I got it from here." He sighs, and he carries her away to the bathroom for cleanup.

The other girls chip in, sopping up the soda off the floor with paper towels.

"Hungry?" I say to Avery.

She nods, and we walk toward the food line together.

"You know, when I was your age and I went to a camp like this, meal time was the best part of the whole week."

"That's . . . great."

"Yeah. They had all this amazing stuff like chicken-patty sandwiches. Unlimited soft serve with every meal. And the counselors would do these hilarious skits while we ate. It was the best."

Avery gives a mildly amused "Mmm," as we step up and survey the buffet. It smells like . . . food. I'll give it that. But boy, it sure isn't easy on the eyes. There's steam coming off a tray of indistinguishable mush that might be scrambled eggs. I think the reddish strips are bacon, but the consistency is way off. It honestly looks like someone shat yesterday's McDonald's breakfast into some metal dishes and called it a day.

I feel duped. The meals on Camp Triumph's website looked downright mouthwatering. I figured they were heavily digitally altered, or at least posed and lit to look their absolute best. But the photos online don't remotely resemble what I'm seeing in front of me. That food looked like it came from actual chickens, pigs, and cows. The slop Avery and I are about to ladle onto our plates looks like an alien's best approximation at human food.

This sucks, but I'm not about to let Avery know that I think it sucks. So I scoop some yellow stuff onto my plate with a smile.

"Mmm, look at this," I say.

"Look at what? What is it?"

"Scrambled . . . eggs?" I squeak, my voice involuntarily adding a question mark.

"Are you sure?"

No, I think. "Yes!" I say. "Try some." I gesture for her to hold her plate out, and she does. I load it up with a little bit of everything, including the saving grace, a stack of honest-to-God pancakes.

Who cares if they're more gray than golden brown?

"Dad, I don't know about this stuff," Avery says, faking a gag as we walk back to our table. We sit, and she immediately begins prodding the items on her plate with a fork, the glob of eggs jiggling back and forth like Jell-O.

"Dig in, we've got a big day coming up," I say, as I shovel a portion of what I'm guessing is hash browns into my mouth. The potatoes, if they were potatoes, could have been good, bad, moldy, filled with worms. I'd never know it. All I can taste is salt.

I gasp aloud and grab my water and chug.

"You OK?" Avery asks me.

I compose myself. "Yeah just . . . this camp food really takes me back."

"If you say so."

Now Avery's going for a bite of potatoes, and I suddenly realize that I cannot, under any circumstances, let her taste them. In my effort to hype her up and get her excited about something, anything, I've completely forgotten that the illusion will go out the window as soon as she puts a single bite of this crap in her mouth. She raises the fork to her face and, without thinking, I slap the potatoes, and her utensil with them, right out of her hand. They go flying under an empty table to her right.

"Dad! What was that for?"

"Sorry . . . thought I saw a fly on your fork. Why don't you go get a clean one?"

She rolls her eyes and grunts and gets up. As she walks toward the clean plates and silverware, I inhale bites of everything on my plate. The eggs are foul. The bacon? Too tough. The sausage, like the potatoes, is suspiciously salty. Only thing left is the pancakes. I cut off a corner from my stack and hold my breath and put the fork in my mouth. They're . . . not bad?

They're not bad! Not bad is good enough for me. I give Avery the rest of my stack and quickly scrape the rest of her food onto my own plate, moments before she returns and sits back down.

She notices the switcheroo immediately.

"What's this?" she asks, regarding the stack of pancakes and nothing else on her plate.

"I just thought we'd skip the whole 'Eat your protein or no dessert' argument for once. Just enjoy the pancakes."

She smirks. "Thanks."

On that, she takes a bite, chews and ponders for an excruciatingly long second, and says: "Mmm. Not bad."

Not bad. That's exactly what I wanted to hear. Something quasi-nice. A warm feeling tingles in my belly, and I'm hoping it's love and not the faint beginnings of food poisoning.

Before I can bask in my small win, the air horn sounds off in the distance again; our cue to meet up for the next activity.

"Jeez, already?" Avery says, swallowing a bite of food. "Where does the time go?"

• • •

We assemble on the field—the big green one we passed on our way in—where Dennis is waiting for us. He's standing by a white folding table littered with "Hello My Name Is" stickers and one black marker.

There's a small mass of people—probably a dozen pairs of dads and daughters in total. Certainly fewer than the photos from previous years suggested. Everyone's jostling for the single marker and sticking name tags to their shirts, smeared and crooked.

A few girls are running around, playing tag, high-pitched squeals ringing out, freshly cut grass flying into the air. There's an older girl with them, egging on the chaos. She's tall—impressively so—in a red Camp Triumph T-shirt, with hair piled into a bun on top of her head. Their counselor, I figure. She oozes unmistakable camp counselor slash lifeguard confidence, the kind that only exists in teenagers who spend their summers with a bunch of young kids who think they're the coolest person in the entire world.

Avery hangs by my side.

"Go. Play," I say.

This week is all about the two of us, but I'm not an idiot. She doesn't get a lot of time with her friends, and it wouldn't be the worst thing in the world if she wound up getting along well with her bunkmates.

"You don't have to talk to me like I'm a dog. *Avery, sit. Avery, fetch*," she mocks.

"All right. No treats for you, then."

"I'll go get us name tags," she huffs, stalking off toward the table.

"Wwwwwwwelcome, campers!" a voice calls over the din. It's Dennis, and he's got a megaphone, which seems like a little much considering there are only about twenty of us, in total, and he's standing about five feet away. It's cranked up way too loud, and he doesn't bother adjusting it.

"I'm sure you all have a lot of questions about the schedule for the rest of the week, and I promise you we'll get to all of that," he says, each word that echoes out of the megaphone stinging like a nail driven into my temple. "I'm just as *anxious* as you all are. Look, I'm actually shaking!" He holds out a jittery hand. "But first, before anything else, let's have a little fun!"

With the help of assorted teen counselors, Dennis divides us into groups with our cabinmates. Avery makes it back from the table just in time to join in, slapping my name tag onto my shirt for me.

My fingers are crossed that it says something silly, like Poop Head or Fart Face. Sadly, it just says John.

We're instructed to stand in a tight circle in alternating dad, daughter order. Avery is at my side and next to her is the towering Ryan and Jessie, then Lou and Tam, then Booker and Erica. The groups are told to lock hands across the circle. I reach out with my left hand and I grab Lou's right hand, and I reach out my right hand and I grab little Tam's left hand. Everyone pairs up, forming an incredible tangle of arms in the center of our circle.

"*Human knot, oh yeah*," Jessie says in a silly, singsong voice, dancing in place.

"Jessie," Ryan snaps. "Get your head in the game."

She nods, serious again, instantly straightening up. "Yes, sir."

"You know this game? Want to fill the rest of us in?" Booker asks. "I've gotta get back to the cabin, so if we could get out of this quickly, that would be great."

"That's . . . kind of the idea," Lou points out.

"Where do you have to go?" Erica asks her dad.

"I, uh, have to go . . . *potty*," Booker says.

Dennis blows an air horn, our cue to start untangling.

"No one move," Ryan commands. "We need a plan."

But Tam and Avery and Erica aren't listening, each ducking under arms, twisting, climbing over various limbs, and contorting in ways only underdeveloped bodies can.

"Guys, we have to communicate," Ryan says. "*Guys!*"

"Avery," I say, "you're all knotted up with . . . Jessie, right?"

Jessie nods, and I point at someone's arm with my foot.

"Duck under here."

"I've got a plan," she says, ignoring me and scurrying under Lou's legs.

A meek voice cries out, "Help," and there's Tam, tiny little Tam, buried under a mass of flesh, her face barely visible.

"Lift her up, we can use her to get us untangled," Ryan says. "Think of her like the free end of the rope."

"Sweetie," Lou says. "I just had the most amazing idea. We're gonna lift you up and through to untangle everyone, OK?"

Tam nods, Ryan grunts an aggravated harrumph, and we all hoist our arms upward, and Tam elevates off the ground just enough to shimmy down in the middle of the arm circle.

Ow, ow, ow. Something suddenly hurts as my wrist twists to an unnatural angle. I try to turn it back but Tam's small hand is clamping down on my own like a vise grip.

"What's the policy on adjusting your grip?" I ask aloud with a wince.

"Absolutely not," and "That's fine," Ryan and Lou answer simultaneously.

"If you break your grip, you lose the game," Ryan says.

"If you don't flip your hand around you can't form a proper circle at the end," Lou responds.

Booker chimes in with "It feels like we're more tangled than before. Erica, you OK, baby?"

Erica, oblivious to the bickering, is having an excellent time. I'm not sure she's trying to untangle anything, but instead she's gone limp, letting herself get swung and twirled around by the hands like a marionette, giggling uncontrollably all the while.

"I'm gonna try something," I say, and I duck under the briar patch of limbs, where Tam is hiding out, and I try to pop out the other side without losing my grip, but now I'm face to crotch with Booker, and stuck there, so close I can count the teeth on his shorts' zipper.

Suddenly, Booker's phone buzzes in his pocket.

"Uh, you gonna answer that?" I say, tilting my face as far from his crotch as I can manage.

"Answer what?" says Erica.

"Nothing, baby."

"OK, everyone," Ryan says, trying to regain control. "We all need to take one step backward so we can see where the tangle points are."

Jessie immediately complies and backs up a few inches. Erica's still swooping and looking dizzy now. Avery has been working feverishly this whole time but is hopelessly engulfed in arms somewhere in the center of the circle, and I can't even see Tam at all.

Suddenly, some of the tension in our human knot releases and we all tumble to the ground like scattered bowling pins. Booker has let go and backed out of the circle.

"Guys, I'm sorry, but we're getting nowhere and . . . well . . . I really gotta go," he says, catching Erica's suspicious gaze and adding, "to the bathroom." He sprints off toward the cabin, but not before he murmurs quietly to me, "Cover for me, will ya? And keep an eye on Erica."

And then he's gone, the rest of us standing there like a bunch of buffoons.

I gotta say, this group is not what I expected. Far from it. I had imagined being surrounded by playful, engaged dads, smiling and doing their best, overjoyed to soak up quality time with their girls. Instead, the whole place feels like some kind of dad rehab center full of troubled men, a museum of parental failures.

A group of dads and daughters across the field from us lets out a cheer, and applause rings out from the other groups, then that air horn again, signifying that the contest is over and the cheery group won. And more important, we lost.

Ryan storms off, and Lou lets out a dramatic grunt. Avery scrapes herself off the ground, and I offer her a hand to help her up, which she ignores.

"We gave it a good effort," I say.

"Yeah, that was a real blast," she says.

I tread carefully here because Avery is known for legendary tantrums when she loses. She's just lucky she got a boatload of talent to go along with her major competitive streak—because, thankfully, she doesn't lose often.

It's been a while since I've seen her have a major episode, but I know she's barely holding it together as it is, and I can sense the storm brewing.

"Take a deep breath. It's just a silly game."

"Dad, I'm fine, I don't even care," she says.

"Good, good, just keep repeating that."

"Ugh," she says. Her new favorite word. But I can't help but notice the lack of visible rage on her face. No beet-red cheeks. No bulging forehead vein. Maybe she really doesn't care; and that worries me even more than a potential meltdown.

"Great job, campers!" Dennis chirps through the megaphone. "If your team didn't win, don't worry—you're about to get another chance."

He instructs us to further divvy up into teams of two to four people. Dads and daughters, all dads, all daughters. Doesn't matter as long as we break out into smaller groups.

"When you're ready, come grab a sheet from me. It's got all the items you need to find, plus a few clues that might help you find your way. Think of this as a fun way to get to know the camp!"

"Did you want to pair up with me or . . . ?" I ask Avery. I'd been privately looking forward to the scavenger hunt, a chance for the two of us to get away from the rest of the group.

She looks back and forth between me and the other girls, dread weighing her face down like I've just asked her to choose between cleaning the toilets or eating a bowl of creamed spinach for dinner. She slowly shuffles over to stand near Erica and Tam, giving me my answer. But then Tam, without warning, sprints to Lou and grabs his leg like it's her favorite teddy bear.

"Can I go with you?" she pleads.

"Come on, we talked about this. It's good practice, right?" he says, shooing her toward the others. "It'll be OK, I promise."

She pouts and clings, but he gently nudges her back over to the girls, and she eventually complies.

"Jessie, come on, then," Ryan grunts.

"Actually, is it OK if I go with them?" she says, pointing meekly at her cabinmates.

There's a brief flicker of hurt on Ryan's face, but quickly his expression turns to stone. "Fine," he says. "Men, let's group up."

No objections from me or Lou, so I guess we're a trio now. We grab the scavenger hunt list from Dennis, and I watch the girls—Erica and Jessie laughing and running off to find the first item, Tam meekly struggling to keep pace, Avery reluctantly pulling up the rear.

Five

The first day at Camp Triumph is finally over, and I am absolutely exhausted.

To close things out, the entire camp gathers around a large fire. Stars twinkling above. Hand-chopped logs popping and hissing inside a rock firepit. Avery's squatted next to me, attacking a s'more, bits of graham cracker tumbling off the edge of her napkin, as the rest of the campers settle in around the flames, flickers of orange lighting up faces I haven't put names to yet.

The scavenger hunt hadn't exactly been the peaceful stroll through the woods Dennis advertised it as, so the relative quiet is more than welcome. The hunt had seemed simple enough at first. A big rock with an inscription in it to find. A five-hundred-year-old tree. A couple of basic landmarks like the boating shed and the ropes course.

I guess this "journey through history" was supposed to make me fall in love with the camp, but instead, it—and the excruciating time spent listening to Ryan and Lou bicker—just left me wondering if I'd made a big mistake by bringing us here.

I started to wonder if it was too late to get our money back.

"I'm so glad you're all here," Dennis's voice booms, interrupting my train of thought. He's standing in the center of the circle, one foot propped up theatrically on the edge of the firepit. "We have so much work to do together, and we'll get started in earnest in the morning. But before we do, I want to hear from each of you."

I don't know what he's going to say next, but I can tell I'm going to hate it.

"I want each man here to stand and speak a goal into existence. Into the universe. I want to hear what you hope to accomplish this week and how far you're willing to go to become a better man. The man I know each and every one of you is capable of becoming."

Yep, I hate it.

I don't know about the other guys here, but I didn't sign up for some kind of spiritual journey to achieve self-actualization. And I don't see why I should have to lie about it. I'll just tell the truth—which is that I'm here because I miss my daughter. I miss having adventures with her. And what could be more of an adventure than a week of summer camp together?

And suddenly the first dad slowly raises a hand—a stout, hairy man, with a small daughter who's dressed about six years too old; ripped jeans and a stringy tank top in stark contrast to her baby face. Her shirt says only one thing, in aggressive lettering: the word *FUCK*.

"Yeah, I got something to say," he says in a deep and powerful voice. Truly, just incredible gravitas—a real Sam Elliott type. "I reckon this is one of them, what do you call 'em, safe spaces."

"It is." Dennis nods.

"Good," he bellows, then he takes a deep breath, and his voice cracks now, transforming into a mere squeak. "Because I don't know that I can hold all this in any longer."

"It's OK," whispers Dennis, like he's comforting a dog in a thunderstorm. "Let it out."

"I guess I'm here because . . . I haven't always been *there*."

He chokes back the beginnings of a sob. This is going to be a long night.

"Yep, I'm your classic absentee dad. A real piece of crap, all right. Piano recitals. School plays. Little League games. I've missed 'em all. And not because I'm doing something more important, or because I don't want to be there."

"Then why?" Dennis prods. "You're here now. You're safe. Keep going."

"My therapist says I'm afraid I'm not good enough for her, says I'm afraid I'll turn into my own dad. For him, absent would have been an upgrade." He heaves, decades of suppressed emotions tumbling out of him in waves. "Can't screw your kid up if you don't even try, right? But look where that got me." He gestures to his daughter, staring up at him with a face full of over-applied mascara. "No offense, love."

The man turns back to the group, finally regaining his breath. "But we're here, and I'm ready to keep doing the work. I'm ready to finally be the dad she deserves."

The rest of the group offers applause and murmurs of encouragement as the man takes a seat. I don't even have time to process that roller coaster of a speech before Dennis calls the next name: mine.

"John," Dennis says, and lays his gaze on me. "We'd love to hear from you next."

OK, I did not expect to have to follow that, not directly, not without a chance to regroup, but here we go.

I stand. "I'm John, and this is Avery," I announce, laying a hand on Avery's shoulder—she gives a small smile, teeth and lips caked with chocolate.

"And in terms of a goal for this week, well . . ." I pause, stalling a bit, scanning faces that all look like they expect me to match the raw honesty and emotional depth of the last dad. "I saw on the website that we might go waterskiing? I'd love for Avery and I to both stand up on water skis. I guess that would be pretty cool."

And I sit back down.

The group stares at me. One guy in the back claps politely but stops quickly when no one else does.

"Is that really all you want to say right now?" Dennis says.

"Um. Yeah. I mean, we just want to have some fun. Is there something wrong with that?"

Dennis kneels down next to me, marshmallow breath wafting straight into my nostrils. He places a friendly and warm, if firm, hand on my knee. "John, your answer makes me feel"—he pauses, considering an internal thesaurus—"*disappointed*. It's OK if you're not ready; it really is. But you're never going to get where you want to go if you don't figure out what's holding you back first," he says. "Don't worry, though. I'm going to open you up. Before the end of this week, I'm going to crack you wide open. I promise." For some reason, I gulp.

"Now," he says, with a quick tug on his shirt, straightening it out. "Who wants to go next?"

Not a single dad raises his hand.

Finally Dennis picks someone out, and the man stands and speaks, but I'm too busy drowning in a sea of humiliation to hear anything.

"You're in trouuublllleeee," Avery whispers.

"Shut up," I say with a playful elbow nudge.

She smiles and licks some s'more residue from her fingers, and she looks like a little kid doing it—happy, happyish anyway, like she's suddenly forgotten or just grown tired of her aggravation and general disdain for me, how I forced her to come here and miss the end of her summer break.

But it's hard to enjoy the nice moment. Looking around, we're surrounded by seriously flawed fathers with tons of work to do. In my cabin alone, there's a guy who cares only about being the most alpha dude-bro on the planet—two of them, actually—and one of the most neglectful workaholics I've ever seen. It's painfully obvious that Avery and I shouldn't be here, and here pretty much sucks anyway.

I don't need to be cracked open. I don't need to be fixed. There's nothing wrong with my relationship with my daughter, we just need a little vacation, a little adventure, for Christ's sake. It's becoming increasingly obvious that we won't find that at Camp Triumph.

I let Avery finish her s'more. Because as soon as this godforsaken campfire is over, we're getting out of here.

• • •

"We're leaving," I whisper to Avery as the campfire comes to an end and the group disperses.

"Why?"

"I thought you'd be happy about that."

"I am, I guess. When are we going?"

"Now."

"What a humongous waste of time."

"You're telling me."

"You gonna make it up to me somehow?"

"Maybe. We'll . . . talk about it. Meet me by the car in ten minutes."

I'm well aware that *maybe* means *yes* to kids, and I don't really have any good ideas for how to buy her off, but I can't deal with it right now. Avery scurries off with the rest of the girls, back toward the cabins, and I jog to catch up with Dennis. I pull him aside gently, into the shadow of a huge pine that blocks out even the dim starlight.

"Listen, Dennis . . ."

"John."

"I just wanted to give you a heads-up that I don't think Camp Triumph is right for us. So Avery and I are going to take off tonight."

Sorry if I scared you off back there, I imagine him saying. I picture him turning back into the smiley Boy Scout who greeted us warmly when we arrived. But that doesn't happen.

"Not right for you? What does that mean?"

"I think I maybe misunderstood what this is all about."

"And what is it about?"

I shuffle my feet, trying to think of the right way to phrase this without insulting Dennis, the camp, and every single person here.

"Well, some of the other dads . . . they're in rough shape, right? They're either totally absent, or they have some other kind of broken relationship with their daughter. And that's not me and Avery."

"It's not?"

I laugh to hide my irritation at his questiony way of speaking. He's like a little riddle-speaking bridge troll.

"No, she's . . . you know, she's at that age. She's just going through a phase is all. And I guess what I was really looking for was a light-hearted week, something fun where we could just forget everything else and enjoy each other's company again. You know?"

"And you don't think Camp Triumph fits the bill?"

"No offense, but it seems like . . . you know. Like therapy. Or a boot camp or something. Anyway, it's just not what I'm looking for, and I'm hoping you'll be able to refund the bulk of the tuition. And the parking fee."

"Sure, I'd be happy to."

"OK, great."

"Just as long as you admit you're not being fully honest."

It's all I can do not to shove a finger in my ear and wiggle out the earwax; I can't believe what I just heard.

"I'm sorry?"

"Just admit that you have work to do as a father and you're scared to do it. And I'll cut you a check right now."

"I don't think you heard me before. This is all just a misunder-standing, us being here."

"Come on, John, drop it. Let's get real."

OK, that's it. This guy is officially pissing me off. And I don't even care if I don't get the money back at this point, though I'm not sure Evelyn will agree if I show up in the middle of the night tonight a thousand dollars poorer than I left. But damn it, this is about prin-ciple.

"All right, you want to get real? This place is a scam, and you know it. You get these men here and get them feeling like they're not good enough—and most of them, maybe they're not, but that's beside the point because all you do is use that to bleed every last cent out of them."

"We have to make a living, that's true. Doesn't mean we don't help people." He's calm and measured despite my agitation. "It *hurts* me to hear you say that."

"OK, that right there? Not helping. Why do you always talk like that? You sound like a cult leader."

"Putting a name to your emotions is a good thing, John. Being able to say them out loud is a good thing."

"It's fucking weird!"

"You're right. It's much better to do what you do, bottle it all up, keep it inside, only smuggle small amounts of your real feelings out every now and then, disguised by jokes."

I am angry. I am enraged. I am furious.

"You don't know the first thing about me. You don't know how much I do for my daughter, for my family. What I've given up. I'm a good dad, damn it."

"Then why are you being so defensive?"

Another fucking question. I glare at him, and though I can barely make out his face in the dark, I can see the smugness clear as day. How can someone so chipper just flip a switch like that? He must not be a dad himself, must not understand what it's like. You know what they say. Those who can't do, teach.

"Fine, you don't want to evolve or grow as a father, heck, as a man? That's on you." He sighs, sounding suddenly weary. "But don't pretend it's anyone else's fault. And don't be surprised when this 'phase' doesn't end. Ever. There are plenty of guys here who want my help, so I'll send you a check in a few days. Congratulations, I am now *ambivalent* toward you." He swipes his hands together, as if washing them of me. "Goodbye."

He stomps off, then stops to say, "Oh, but I'm keeping the damn parking fee."

And then he's gone. I scoff out loud, as if there were anyone around to hear me be offended.

Still, there's a part of me that knows Dennis is right, that I might be waiting a long time for this "phase" to end, for things with Avery to magically fix themselves. Which is exactly why I'm so afraid of her starting middle school. She's already signed up for math club on Tuesday afternoons, drama on Thursdays, and she's been bugging us about the Spanish club lately, too. Plus, we let her try this wilderness-survival day camp earlier in the summer, and now she's obsessed with it and wanting to join *their* after-school program.

And then there's the little matter of her fifth-grade teacher and guidance counselor calling me and Evelyn in for a Very Serious Meeting in the middle of last school year. Avery's grades were excellent, she was excelling in sports, and she was off the charts in her standardized testing. They wanted us to consider moving her up a grade, and I nearly went into cardiac arrest. We decided to table the idea until Avery got settled in middle school, but if it's really the best thing for her, we won't be able to ignore it forever. If she skips a grade, of course, she'll be home with us for one less year—a thought that causes me immense dread.

With all of that unresolved, when exactly am I going to fix this, if not now?

But there's no time to think about all of that. It's past 9:00 p.m., and we need to get on the road to even have a prayer of getting home at a decent hour.

I rush back to the cabin and hastily throw my things together. On my way to the parking lot I spot Avery's counselor doing a sweep of the grounds with a flashlight. I grab her and explain that we're leaving and could she please help me get my phone out of the locked box.

"Dennis said it was OK?" she asks.

"More or less," I say, looking up, the top of my head at about her earlobe level.

"I'm Megan, by the way," she says while leading the way to the office.

"John. And thanks."

Outside the office, she guides me over to the box and undoes the lock with a spin of the numbered dials. It pops open, and she lets me riffle through for mine and Avery's.

"So did he give you his *You're just scared of doing the work* speech?"

"How'd you know?"

She chuckles. "He's become a bit more intense the last year or two. He's under a lot of pressure. But . . . there's a method to his madness, I swear. And this place, it's really not so bad. I think you'd get a lot out of it."

There's a deep sincerity in her voice that makes me want to believe her. But then I remember the gruel from the cafeteria and the obnoxious parking fee and the skin-crawling afternoon spent with my cabinmates.

"Thanks," I say, meaning it. "But we're going home."

When I get back to the car, Avery's waiting for me, bags in hand. I throw them in the trunk, and we're on our way, ten yards down the long drive, now twenty, approaching escape velocity and leaving this place behind us for good.

Then, a loud *POP*. Avery yelps. I throw an arm across her chest, a makeshift human seat belt.

The *flub-flub-flub* of a flat tire.

I ease off the gas, and we roll to a stop.

For now, at least, it looks like we're not going anywhere.

Six

I pop the trunk and throw our bags out into the dirt and pull up the cover to the little hidden compartment inside the rear of the car. It's been eons since I've opened this flap, but to my relief, the spare tire is still in there.

There, but certainly far past its prime. The ragged doughnut is as old as the car itself, which is to say about twelve years. Never once have I looked at it, checked that it's in good shape, or otherwise acknowledged its existence. Yet here I am, in my hour of need, just expecting it to be there for me. Frankly, it borders on abuse.

Despite my neglect, I'm sure it'll do. The tire feels firm to the touch and good enough to use in a pinch, which is now. I hoist it out of the compartment and lay it down on the road.

"Dad, what's going on? Can you fix it?" Avery says, watching me intently.

"In theory, yes."

"In theory? That can't be good."

She's right to be pessimistic. The spare tire might be in decent shape, but I don't see a jack or any of the appropriate tools for changing a tire in here.

I'm in a remote area at a camp for dads, and I don't even have the tools to change my own tire. This is an absolute nightmare, and I can, under no circumstances, allow one of them to see me in such a state.

Racking my brain, I try to remember where I might have put the tools. My old car had a set, the sporty little fuel-efficient sedan I used to drive around. I made a point of checking regularly that I'd be prepared for a roadside emergency back then. Changed my wipers, checked tire pressure and wear at a regular clip. I even had one of those Sharper Image multitools that lets you cut your seat belt and break open a window in the event you drive your car off a bridge and into a lake—which, right now, compared to this, isn't sounding so bad.

From there, we traded in the sedan for the SUV right around the time Avery was born. More room for a stroller in the back, a better fit for the bulky car seat. Extra cupholders. All that stuff. It made sense. And I *think* the tire-changing tools made the switch with me? But that's about where I lost track of them. Long weekends of washing the cars in the driveway and doing yard work and catching up on errands before spending the night out with friends turned into chasing the baby around for fourteen straight hours. Grabbing naps at every possible opportunity. Tedious mornings spent in doctor's office waiting rooms. More days than I'd like to admit of not wanting to get out of bed, not wanting to face what the day might hold.

"Soooo," Avery says, hauling me back from the depths.

"Sooooo, I'm working on it."

"Doesn't look like you're working. Looks like you're just standing there."

"You could give me a hand, you know."

"OK. What can I do?"

She's got me. There's nothing she can do because there's nothing I can do. Maybe if I just distract her for a few minutes.

"I need a long blade of grass, a chestnut, and the whisker of a squirrel."

"Funny," she deadpans. "Are we going to make it home or not?"

"Yes. Probably. I just have to make a call."

I whip out my auto insurance card and call the number on the back. It's been a while, but I'm pretty sure there's some kind of road-side assistance service attached to our plan. After waiting through an excruciatingly long menu of choices, I mash some buttons on my phone and manage to connect to an associate. She asks for my name and address to verify my account, then transfers me to someone else who asks me the same. This happens three different times before someone who sounds suspiciously like the first person I talked to tells me it will be about a two-hour wait for the nearest tire service to come out.

I'm not sure what to do. Avery's looking at me with this forlorn face, like she might physically die if I don't get her home this instant. It would likely be after midnight before we can get on the road, at the earliest. And is it even worth it, then?

"Don't tell me you don't know how to change a tire," a voice says from the shadows. And it's Ryan, because of course it is.

"What are you doing out here?" I ask him.

"Just walking. And thinking. Looks like you could use a hand."

"You know, someone broke in and stole my tools a few weeks

ago," I say, even though he didn't ask. "Hadn't got around to replacing them yet."

"They did?" Avery asks.

"Anyway, we're fine. Don't worry about us."

Dads love telling people not to worry about us when we're clearly drowning.

"I've got everything you need in my truck," Ryan says. "Wait here."

I slump against the car. It's emasculating being bailed out like this—it just is. It shouldn't be; we should be more evolved than this by now. But any guy who's ever been helpless and stuck and in need of rescuing from another man, especially in front of the women in his life, will tell you it's an awful feeling. A rock-in-your-stomach type of feeling leftover from a time when we carried around big wooden clubs.

"Well, that was lucky," Avery says.

"Yeah. Lucky."

In a flash, Ryan comes roaring back in his oversized truck. He doesn't even bother asking me for help, permission, or my opinion on anything. He just hops out, hoists his tools out of the truck bed, grabs the doughnut, and gets to work with the speed and precision of a NASCAR pit crewman. I'm humiliated, but at least Ryan's the only one here to see my shame.

And right on cue, other dads start to pop out of the woodwork, out on late-night walks of their own, or maybe responding to a fatherly sixth sense drawing them to a situation in need of supervision. Here's another one, holding a flashlight, and now aiming it over Ryan's shoulder while he works. Here's another, grabbing the tire gauge from Ryan's toolbox and checking the pressure on my remaining tires.

"Oh, I can do that," I offer, but he ignores me. "Yeah, but you go ahead. Thanks."

I recognize a few of the faces from earlier, but no one speaks to me or asks my name. Like wild animals, they're simply drawn to the smell of a project, compelled to offer help and condescending remarks about the state of my car.

"Pressure's fine on the other tires but long overdue for a new set," one says to no one in particular, as if I can't hear him.

"Wipers are in rough shape, too."

And "Don't love the trade-in value on this model," as if there's something I can do about that now.

Another dad saunters along as the crew is finishing up and helps Ryan load the jack back into his truck. A few others gather in the shadows and simply watch the proceedings.

I stand by uselessly, put on trial, physically feeling the Man Points as they leave my body.

And then, the job is done, and as quickly as they emerged, they're all gone back into the night.

"Thank you," I say when Ryan's done packing up, checking his handiwork. The incident has rocked me to my core, but still, I'm genuinely grateful. What? It's a thing.

"Anytime. But I hope you're not planning on driving all the way home on the doughnut."

"It's not too far, it should hold up."

"This thing?" Ryan says, giving it a kick. "Maybe eight years ago. It's lost a little air. Seen better days."

He's probably right. He's definitely right. But I'm not about to admit it.

"If I were you, I'd at least wait until morning. See if you can get a shop around here to put on a real tire. If you want, I already checked out most of the major mechanics around here, just in case. Be happy to share my list."

He checked out the mechanics around here *just in case*? What kind of person is that well prepared?

"We'll be all right, thanks."

"Suit yourself. Night," he says, effortlessly lifting himself back into his truck, slamming the door, and peeling away.

I turn to Avery. "Ready to go? For real this time."

"I don't know," she says, biting her lip. "Are you sure we should drive? He didn't seem to think so."

"I thought you were dying to get out of here?"

"He just seemed really sure."

"*I'm* really sure."

"But he was . . . more confident."

I sigh.

"Dad, maybe we should call a mechanic in the morning like he said."

For some reason I soften when she calls me Dad. "OK, OK. And we agree we'll get out of here first thing in the morning?"

"Sure."

I guess one night won't kill us. Driving down the highway in the dark on a doughnut just might. And I know that, and I'd like to think I wasn't really going to do it just to save face. But I've got so little face left, who really knows what I might have done.

"Avery?"

"Yeah?"

"*Lo siento*," I say.

She stares back, blank-faced.

"*I'm sorry*. For bringing us here. You're really gonna have to brush up on your Spanish."

"Oh, right, the club. Yeah, I decided I . . . don't want to do that anymore," she says with a stammer. "Are you mad?"

"Why would I be mad? You've got a lot on your plate. Totally makes sense," I add. Truthfully, I'm taken aback. She's been adamant about this, and it's extremely unlike her to just drop something so suddenly, at least without a good reason.

"So is there a specific reason or—" I throw out there, not quite able to let this go yet.

"See," she huffs. "You're mad."

"I'm not mad! I'm just asking! What, it's illegal to ask questions now?"

"Isn't it enough to know that I don't want to do it?"

And now *she's* mad, and I know I have to prevent this from escalating by any means necessary.

"Of course it is. But now it's extremely obvious that you're not telling me everything and you know I just can't"—I poke her playfully—"let"—another poke—"that"—another—"GO!"

She laughs and swats me away.

There's something there, something under the surface. Not even I'm dense enough to miss that. It makes me think of the other loose thread, the secret drawer in her bedroom. But now, as if she can see my wheels turning and decides to interrupt before I interrogate her further, she hugs me. Well, not a real hug, but the way kids hug you once they reach a certain age. Where it's more like they're allowing you the honor of hugging them. Avery leans her body into me, arms at her side, and by doing so grants me permission to give her a quick squeeze.

At this point, I'll take it.

"Night, Dad," she says. And then she walks away, back toward the cabins.

"Good night, Avery."

TUESDAY

Seven

I wake in the morning with a dull and mocking pain in my lower back. Could be the mattress so thin you can see an impression of the wooden slats through the fabric. Could just be another day in my thirties.

I peer over the edge of my top bunk and take stock of the cabin—Ryan's bed is empty; he's up and gone somewhere already, sheets tucked tight with hospital corners sharper than his obnoxiously chiseled jawline. Lou is here, dressing himself on the edge of his bed with a series of aggressive yawns. Booker, directly underneath me, remains sprawled and unconscious, a leg and a half hanging out from the covers.

The sun coming in at a low angle through the windows is blinding, and I realize I have no idea what time it is. Staring down from my perch, I spot Booker's contraband phone as it lets out a buzz, sitting directly on the hardwood floor next to him. The screen lights up for a few seconds, revealing an avalanche of notifications—seventeen new emails and two missed calls if I read it right. The time is 6:38 a.m.

Suddenly, reminded that I've got my phone, too, I check it. A string of missed calls and one new voice mail from a number I recognize but wish I didn't. I've been ignoring this caller for days. A bit longer won't do any more damage.

I shimmy down from the top bunk and land on the floor, softly so as not to wake my bunkmate.

"Morning," Lou says in my direction.

"Morning."

Unsure of what to say to each other, we trade yawns.

"What a night, huh?" I finally come up with, and he grunts in agreement as he ties his left shoe.

Now that he's fully dressed, I think Lou is about to leave, but he doesn't. He just sits there and stares ahead for a moment. The silence is enough to make my skin crawl, and even though I'm leaving as soon as I get a cup of coffee in me—so it doesn't really matter if I get to know Lou or not—I have to break it. I know very, very little about this man, so I lead with an easy icebreaker—talking shit.

"Can you imagine bringing your work with you to a place like this?" I gesture over my shoulder at a sleeping Booker as I slip on my own shoes. "Kind of defeats the purpose, right?"

"Yeah, pretty crazy."

"Never did find out what you do, speaking of," I say through another yawn.

Lou sighs. "You know those big silver buttons you push at crosswalks? Yeah, I install those."

"Oh . . . uh. Cool."

"There's more to it than that, of course. I also test them, to make sure once they're in they don't actually do anything."

"Ah. I get it," I say, realizing that he's screwing with me. He smirks.

I wait for the real answer, but none comes. "So"—riffling through my suitcase for my toiletry bag—"what do you actually do?"

"Does it matter?" he says with a hint of irritation. "So what if I'm a professional nap coach or an alligator groomer? Like what is this obsession with what people do for a living?"

I don't think I was obsessing. I certainly wasn't trying to.

"Whoa, didn't mean to strike a nerve," I say, taken aback. "It's just one of those vanilla conversation starters, you know, like *How are you?* No one actually cares. I didn't mean anything by it."

"Sorry, sorry," he says, waving me off. "Just . . . I thought I could get away from all of that way out here. You know. Just all be dads together and not sit around comparing and competing. So far, though, it's just been more of the same."

I know what he means. I hate it, too, the way people try to tie your identity to what you do for work. Like Lou, I like to think of myself as a dad first and foremost.

"Just something that's always irked me is all," he says, rising, filling the silence. "Must have woken up on the wrong bunk of the bed," he adds with another smirk, walking toward the door.

"Hey, I'll trade ya," I say. "Mine's got a rusty nail waiting to stab you in the forehead if you sit up too fast."

He laughs and walks out. A few moments later, I throw on some shorts and join him, leaving Booker asleep in the cabin, phone buzzing away. I'm not even sure if Avery is awake yet, so I might as well grab a shower before we hit the road.

I follow a dirt trail to the bathrooms, housed in a long and leaf-covered building with a noticeable sag in the middle of the roof, and "enjoy" a lukewarm shower. There's a hairy brown spider nestled in the upper corner of my stall, and I watch it carefully as I scrub. The white grout between the tiles is yellowed and greened from years of use and a lack of cleaning. None of this surprises me because, again, this place is awful.

Then the air horn sounds off in the distance again, waking up the stragglers and calling us to breakfast. It breaks my concentration, and I take my eyes off the spider for a moment. When I look back, it's gone—aaaand now so am I.

I get dressed back at the cabin, which is completely empty now. It's as good an opportunity as any for me to google around a bit and find a mechanic nearby. A single phone call later and I've got a bead on a shop that even has the tire we need in stock. They can have us on the road in under an hour if we get there soon.

In the dining hall, Avery's at the very end of the bench, waiting patiently for me to show up and extract her from this hellhole. Ryan and his girl, Jessie, sit across from each other, and I take stock of their plates—perfectly balanced, high-protein camper fuel. Loads of eggs and lean sausage with a heaping portion of fruit for both of them, plus a slice of what looks like whole wheat toast. They eat like prisoners, in silence, scarfing and protecting the borders of their plates with a free arm. I watch as Jessie steals a longing glance over at an unguarded plate of sugary, prepackaged muffins someone left behind.

"Jessie," Ryan snaps, "eat up."

"Yes, sir," she says.

Lou and Tam sit side by side. She's got a little bit of everything on her plate—protein, fruit, but also a waffle with a deep lake of syrup threatening to flood the entire meal.

Lou slices her sausage into pieces, and she says, "Can you make them smaller?"

He does.

"Smaller, please!"

And he slices and slices.

"Can you make a funny face on my waffle?" she asks him, and he considers this.

Ryan shoots a glance over at them, which Lou clocks, and he says to her, "Not right now."

"But you always do it at home!" she whines. "Just a little one."

"I said no, OK? Here, you need more sausage," and he gives her one of his links and begins slicing that one, too.

Erica's here without Booker, and since she's completely unsupervised, her plate is a kid's dream. A stack of waffles so high you can barely see her face behind it, syrup and butter oozing off the side. That's it, that's the plate. Not a fruit or whole grain to be found. Living her best life.

Booker scurries in, breathless and disheveled, says "Good morning," with a smooch on Erica's cheek, and joins us just as I'm sitting down. He's either not aware or just doesn't care that she's mainlining sugar to start the day. He's already back on his cell phone— holding it under the table so no administrators see, as if we're in high school.

"Dad," Avery says to me under her breath. "You ready to go?"

"What, not in the mood for a nutritious breakfast before we hit the road?"

"This stuff? Yuck. No, thanks."

"Hey, it looks downright edible today," I say, just realizing this.

"Yeah, you're welcome," Lou says through a mouthful of waffle. "I visited the kitchen last night after 'dinner.' If you can call it that. Gave a few tips. Made a few adjustments. No biggie."

"Seems like a biggie. I'm almost considering grabbing a plate," I say.

"I mean it's just frozen junk and stuff out of jugs. But the preparation was all off. I just gave a little guidance is all."

"Are you a chef, or just a breakfast enthusiast?"

"Both."

"Dad . . . ," Avery says, kicking my foot under the table.

"Right. We better get going," I say to the rest of the table, most of whom aren't aware I'm talking to them. "We're not staying after all, so . . . Good luck to all of you."

Lou offers a small salute, Ryan the subtlest flick of his brow, Booker a barely audible grunt, and the other girls a meek but well-synchronized wave, and then we're off. Avery and I briefly go our separate ways to grab our bags. I tell her to meet me in the parking lot in a few minutes, and as I'm hoisting my luggage down the cabin steps, I feel a sudden twinge of something. Regret maybe. Like I'm leaving a project unfinished, and for the wrong reasons. I think about what Dennis said. About how I was scared that I might actually have to confront some uncomfortable truths on this trip, how I might have to face the fact that Avery is growing up whether I like it or not and if I can't come to grips with that, I really will lose her for good.

There is one more thing to do before we leave, though, and I've just remembered, so I drop my bags (gently, the construction on the Adventure Box leaves a lot to be desired) and pull out my phone again. I need to call my wife, and I'm not sure how I should be feeling about it. She resisted at first, being the unstoppable type A personality she is, but I hounded her relentlessly before we left to *please* take some time for herself. To rest. If anyone deserves a break, it's her. Telling her I'm about to cut her week off short? I can't imagine that going well.

On the other hand, I miss her. More than I thought I would, if I'm being honest. It's been one night. One strange and shitty night. But even if the bed in the cabin had a functional mattress and proper headroom, it still wouldn't have had her. On some level, us seeing each other day in and day out for years straight without spending any significant time apart had me thinking maybe a little vacation would be refreshing. But maybe what I really needed was a break from everything else.

I pull out my phone to call her, but there's that tiny voice mail icon on my screen. Like a little telltale heart, it tricks my brain into thinking it's gigantic, swallowing the whole face of the phone, so much so that I can barely make my way to the menu to dial home. I can't take it anymore, I have to listen. Reluctantly, I hit Play.

"Mr. Collins, this is Coach Johnston with the Ambush. I've been trying to get a hold of you, and we just can't seem to connect, so let me give you an update and you can get back to me at your convenience," a woman's voice says. "I know your daughter, Avery, had expressed interest in coming to our tryouts."

The tryouts, that, as far as Avery knows, had been canceled.

"Well, hopefully you got the word and didn't show up to the field yesterday. But we decided to push the tryouts back two days, until

Wednesday. Despite the slow start, we just keep getting more and more sign-ups and we just needed a little more time to organize everything."

My heart sinks like a rock. No, something bigger. An anvil. A hippopotamus. A planet.

Yes, I lied. A little white lie that, admittedly, spun a bit out of control.

The tryouts *were* canceled due to lack of interest. They really were. And my God, was it a relief. I was genuinely bummed for Avery, but I went ahead and, idiotically, got my heart set on being her coach for one more year on the regular old pedestrian soccer team.

And then, suddenly, overnight, there was magically "sufficient interest." I got the email, full of exclamation points and *Great News*, practically dripping with confetti, a few nights before we were supposed to leave to come to Camp Triumph. I could have canceled our trip, could have swallowed the deposit. But I admit, I panicked a bit, I wasn't ready. I was sure I wouldn't have to be. Not yet.

I lied, and even though I was disgusted with myself for it, I broke her heart by failing to tell her the Great News.

She'll find out eventually, one way or another. I know that. But maybe it won't hit so hard after we have a great week here together. Besides, she can always try out next year. One year to her is nothing. To me, it's everything.

These are the sorts of things I told myself. But the voice mail isn't over.

"Anyway, I keep hearing buzz and rumblings about this Avery Collins. She sounds like she's really something, and I can't wait to see what she can do. I hope you get this message in time. You know what—if I don't hear from you, I'll send one of my assistant coaches by the house on Wednesday morning, just to make sure. Like I said, I'm excited to meet your daughter, and I'm not going to take no for an answer!" She laughs. "Anyhow, call me if you have any questions, and looking forward to seeing y'all on Wednesday."

Great. So now, on top of everything else, this hotshot travel team soccer coach has already heard of Avery and she's just waiting to be wowed by her. Does that make her a shoo-in to make the team? Ah, who am I kidding . . . she was always a shoo-in. And if we go home now, there's no way I could keep the rescheduled tryouts from her, even if I was despicable enough to try.

Not with the coach literally coming to our doorstep to recruit her.

I drag myself to the parking lot with all the urgency of a sloth, buying myself time to figure out what to do. What I'm feeling. When I finally reach the car, Avery's already waiting for me.

"You ready to go?" she asks.

I don't really see any other way out of this. It's stupid, I know. But I have to admit something. I don't even like sports that much. Really. It's been decades since I've played, and I remember almost nothing, though I've picked up what I can from books that end in insulting words like *Dummies*, *Idiots*, or *Morons*. And I certainly don't have a passion for strategy—things like infield shifts in softball or attack formations in soccer. I don't enjoy, at all, dealing with asshole parents who think their daughter is God's gift to youth sports. I do it for the kids, the girls. Even the aloof ones, the distracted ones, the way-too-cool-for-this ones. I love all of them, I really do.

But most of all, I do it for my time with Avery.

The five years or so I've spent coaching Avery's teams have given me some of the greatest joys—and the absolute best celebratory hugs—of my life. Does it make me so bad if I'm just not quite ready to give that up? Am I the worst person in the world for wanting just one more year with my only daughter? Soccer is and always has been something we do together. It belongs to both of us, not just her. And while she'll get another chance . . . I never will.

Plus, there's still the Adventure Box of it all. Without this camp, Avery will spend the last week of summer continuing to ignore me, we'll have nothing to give each other for the box, and our tradition will die a whimpering death.

"Dad, hello? Are you ready to go?" Avery says again.

"I changed my mind," I say. "We're staying."

• • •

Walking in to the main office, I find Dennis and hand him my phone. Avery's, too. He smiles smugly and drops them into the box.

I get Avery's frustration—how could I not? She certainly gave me an earful of it while I was trying to explain why I decided we needed to finish out the week. It's her last week of summer, and she'd rather be anywhere else in the world than stuck here. With me. And, to twist the knife, even though she's been mildly distracted, I know she's still absolutely crushed about the travel team, the thing she's been dreaming of and chasing for years. Which, of course, is completely my fault.

There has to be some positive outcome here, where one day she'll look back on this camp and be glad we went—even after I tell her the truth about the tryouts. And I *will* tell her the truth. Eventually. I've just got to make all of this worth it somehow.

Starting now, I've got less than a week to try.

Eight

What I really want to focus on now is calming Avery down so she doesn't murder me, but before I can get the steam to stop coming out of her ears, we're all herded over to the main field for the first activity of the day.

Dennis, now drowning in an oversize Camp Triumph T-shirt, cradles his beloved megaphone as we arrive. He's flanked by the counselors, including Megan.

"OK, campers," his voice cracks. "Time for rise and shine!" He blows an air horn. Why does he have a megaphone *and* an air horn?

There's a tangible grumble from the dads, clustered together on one side of the field, and a buzz of excitement from the girls on the other side. I spy Avery among the gaggle, off to the side really, and pantomime a sarcastic "Yay!" She stares directly into my soul with the considerable venom of an angry preteen.

"Let's start with jumping jacks to wake our bodies up. Ready? Go!" shouts Dennis, and the girls explode into the movement while the dads, circles under their eyes and many still sipping coffee from cups smuggled out of the dining hall, putter to life like a lawn mower starting up for the first time of the season.

Well, except one dad—Ryan, next to me, bursts into jumping jacks, form perfect, achieving exceptional altitude on every jump. I give it a good effort next to him, but these are harder than I remember. There was a time that I worked out every day. I even saw an ab one morning when the light hit my stomach just right. But that . . . that was a long time ago.

In between jumps, I joke, "Is it . . . just me . . . or did someone . . . turn up the gravity?"

Ryan shoots a side eye at me and keeps jumping.

"I might be . . . a little out of shape," I explain, stopping briefly to get the huffing and puffing under control.

"Better save your breath, then," he says.

"Now arm circles, everyone, arm circles! Wake those shoulders up . . . to the front . . . and now to the back!" Dennis shouts.

I swing my arms in the tiniest, laziest loops I can muster.

"I don't know how you manage to stay so fit. Is Jessie your only kid?" I ask, as if that would explain why Ryan has the time and energy to maintain his physique. I don't know why it matters. Avery's an only child and, well, look at me.

"Oldest of five."

"You're kidding."

"Look, I decided a long time ago I wasn't going to be one of those dads who throws out his shoulder picking up the baby or something; it's pathetic," he says while swinging his arms, not out of breath at all, not even a little bit. "I decided I was going to keep my body strong."

"Totally," I say.

I try not to recall the time I bruised a rib putting Avery down into her crib after we put it on the lowest setting, all the times I had a sore back from leaning over the bathtub or tossing her into the air in the pool, and, yes, even the time I quite literally damaged the ligaments in my shoulder after a long day of holding baby Avery when she was home with an ear infection.

"And the media encourages it!" He's getting worked up. "*Oh, the dad bod is the new six pack,*" he whines in a mocking tone. "Gimme a break."

"All right, all right, everyone down for push-ups! Use your knees if you have to. A strong body is a happy body!" The megaphone crackles.

I drop down, and I'll be honest, I'm trying to keep up with Ryan even though I'm completely overmatched. I don't know why; I know that it doesn't matter, that your physical fitness has nothing to do with the kind of dad—the kind of man—you are. But I can't help but be a little intimidated. A little in awe. The dude's a stud—a grating, annoyingly macho one, I'll admit—but I can't figure out how he's pulling it off. I have one kid, one older and fairly self-sufficient kid, and I feel like I'm drowning. And this man woke up early for a three-mile run through the woods on vacation.

"Well, it's impressive that you manage to find the time," I say, straining. "Kudos."

"I tell every dad I meet, if you have time to watch TV before bed, you have time to work out," he says.

This guy. He's arrogant and obnoxiously commanding, a true alpha if there ever was one. But somehow, some way, it seems to work for Jessie. She hangs on Ryan's every word. Yeah, he's tough on her, but she'd follow her dad anywhere, and you can see it in them instantly. Something tells me Ryan doesn't stay up at night wondering whether his daughter likes him enough. I'm even more envious of this than the biceps.

I started off hot, push-up wise, but I'm fading fast. My shoulders and chest are on blazing fire. I'm falling further and further behind Ryan, who is 100 percent not aware that we're competing.

"Allll right, campers, on your feet. Time to work out our funny bones with some camp songs!"

I hop up off the ground with vigor, or try to, but my ascent is slow and jerky. Most of the rest of the dads match my speed, and a loud chorus of groans rings out into the morning air.

I try to get into our off-key rendition of "Camp Granada," but I can't focus. All I can think about is how I'm going to turn this thing around, with day one of camp already over and the clock ticking on day two.

According to the schedule, later today we've got the first official dad-and-daughter activity on deck—archery. That's if hell's national anthem ever ends and if I don't collapse in a heap. But unfortunately we're not going *right* to the range.

First, there's something called "men's group."

Something tells me that's not going to be a whole lot of fun.

• • •

Still sweaty from the five minutes of physical activity, I join my cabinmates as we're splintered into groups. While other groups of dads splay out in the grass and find quiet nooks across the camp, Dennis instructs Booker, Ryan, Lou, and me to head for a building we haven't visited yet, nondescript and tucked quietly behind the dining hall. Inside, it's all drop ceilings and bland beige walls. The main room is

large and empty except for generic blue carpet and a few long portable plastic tables. At the front, there's a lectern on a small raised
platform—this must be where the camp does talent shows, though I
pray I won't have to see or, God forbid, participate in one this week.

A handful of chairs are positioned in a circle at the center of the
room, and I'm already thinking of excuses to get me out of here.
Diarrhea? Heart attack? Dennis sits in one of the chairs and beckons
us inside. We all join him with some hesitancy.

"Men," he says once we've all taken a seat. "Welcome to group."

For some reason, I think he's about to bow his head and start
praying. Evelyn had warned me that the camp might have some weird
Christian undercurrents, you know, with words like *purity* and *obey*
being thrown around in strange contexts. But so far that hasn't been
the case.

"Charles Dickens once said, 'The more man knows of man, the
better for the common brotherhood among men.'"

I had expected a Bible verse, so I'm pleasantly surprised.

"I know you're all eager to spend time with your girls this week,
and you will. But you're also going to spend time with your fellow
dads. Your brothers. And, by extension, yourselves."

We all look around at one another.

"Because iron sharpens iron, as the expression goes. And I believe that by learning from one another, all of you can become better
men by the end of this program. And better men make better fathers.

"Now," he continues, "two quick housekeeping items before we
get started. First up—how are your letters coming?"

We all shuffle uncomfortably in our chairs, the sound of procras-
tination.

"I'm positive you noticed a pen and paper on your beds when you arrived. Use them! If you find in these sessions that there's something that's too hard to say out loud, write it down. Share your wins and losses from this week or, better yet, something even more meaningful with someone important to you. I'm not going to say it's mandatory, but . . ." He chuckles. "Well, you'll see."

I haven't given it much (or any) thought yet, but if I know Dennis, I know I'm not going to be able to weasel my way out of it. Who would I even write to? Friends I haven't spoken to in months? Evelyn, who I never stop speaking to?

"And number two, the big event at the end of the week will be the father-daughter dance. Everyone at the camp will attend, but my challenge to you for the week is not to take it for granted. Court your daughter, so to speak. I want you to ask her for permission to take her to the dance when you feel you've truly earned it. Think of it as a way of gauging how successful this week has been for the two of you."

This one doesn't catch me by surprise. I saw the photos of dances from years past on the camp website, dads and daughters in prom clothes, laughing and dodging bits of falling confetti. Those photos were a big part of what made me pull the trigger on this camp in the first place. I wanted desperately for it to be us in those pictures.

Dennis stands, scans each of our faces, and turns to leave.

"Uh, where are you going?" Ryan says.

"Like I said, you're going to learn from each other. Not from me." He laughs. "I'm going to check in on the other groups."

"So we just . . . talk?"

"Oh!" He smacks his forehead. "No wonder you're confused. I forgot the cards."

Dennis scurries into a back storage area, things clattering around, muttered obscenities amid banging and shuffling sounds. We all stare at one another, no one daring to speak. In moments, Dennis is back, with a small black rectangle in his palm.

"These will get you started. Ryan, why don't you pick the topic for today's session?" Without waiting for an answer, Dennis shoves the card box into Ryan's hands and turns to leave. "Have fun, fellas! And remember, be brave!"

And with that, he's gone. There's a palpable discomfort in the air, none of us quite sure what to do or how to start. But Ryan, in a very Ryan way, doesn't waste too much time before taking command. He scoots his own chair forward so we can all see him a little better and reads off the front of the box.

"'Man Cards: Discussion topics for enlightened masculinity,'" he announces. Then, a sigh. "Fantastic."

He opens the box and pulls out a card.

"'What beauty or strength do you see in your own heart?'" he reads. "Abso-fucking-lutely not." He tosses the card over his shoulder, where it bounces off the drywall and floats down to the floor.

Now, another. "'What's one secret you've never shared with anyone?'" He laughs. "We're joking, right? This is a joke. Has to be." He chucks this one and draws another. "'How are you . . . really?'" Ryan takes a deep breath to steel himself.

And one more now, Ryan reading it silently and nodding to himself, as if tasting a mediocre but palatable soup. "All right, here we go. Good enough, I guess." He clears his throat. "'What does it mean to you to "be a man"?'"

Booker opens his mouth to speak, but Ryan plows on. "I'll start. Look, it's simple really. Men are protectors and providers. We set the example and the standard for the people in our lives. But the *what* is easy. It's the *how*—that's the real test."

"So how, then?" Booker asks sarcastically, poking the bear. "Tell us how, wise one."

"It comes down to this: you just need to optimize every facet of your life and relentlessly work on improving yourself every second of every day. That's really all it takes."

Oh sure. Easy.

He leans in and continues. "People, other men, ask me what my secret is all the time, and that's it. I never stop working on myself. I attack my flaws aggressively. I've forgotten what the word *lazy* even means, that's how long it's been since I used it. I don't waste a single second of time and, if you want to be the best man you can be, neither should you."

Just the idea sounds exhausting. I don't like working on myself any more than necessary. I like the couch. But I'd be lying if I wasn't at least a little bit intrigued. I mean, the guy seems to really have his shit together. So maybe I should just keep an open mind here, go with the flow.

"John." He turns to me with alarming suddenness. "How often are you having sex with your wife?"

The flow has taken a sharp turn.

"Whoa, whoa, whoa," I say, holding my hands up in a *Let's pump the brakes* sort of gesture. "That doesn't seem relevant."

"I couldn't disagree more. Besides, we're all men here. Let's hear it."

"That's just . . . it's private, that's all."

Ryan doesn't break eye contact. "Twice a week? Less?"

I say nothing at first. But his eyes pierce mine like lasers, so eventually I decide I have to speak. I can't stand the pressure any longer. But what am I going to say? The truth? Not likely.

"I mean . . . on average, it really varies, I guess." I clear my throat, still unable to believe that I'm talking about this, or how on earth this is going to help bring me closer to Avery.

"And is it the sex you crave? Is it raw and animalistic and wild and everything you need as a man?"

Lou shrinks in his seat a bit, staring at the floor. Booker stands abruptly, mutters something about the bathroom, and disappears. I know it's this big cliché that men love to sit around and talk to one another about sex—*locker room talk*—but that hasn't been my experience at all. Exhibit A? This is about as awkward as I can ever remember feeling in my own body. Ryan never breaks his gaze, even though I'm willing with all of my might to be spontaneously swallowed up by the floor.

"Is it?" he repeats.

I mean, it's not. But that's not a bad thing! It's just not anything I've stopped to think about in a long time. I've come to think of sex kind of like mowing the lawn of your marriage. It needs to be done around once a week for maintenance. Sometimes more or less depending on the season. If you're feeling generous, you can count it as exercise, and when it's over, you're always proud of the work you put in and you're glad you did it. But this idea of a raw, animalistic fantasy? It just seems a little unrealistic after you have kids. Besides—I'm tired. Evelyn is tired! I feel like I'm supposed to want more, but I honestly don't. What Evelyn and I have is fine. Good, even. Shouldn't that be enough?

"Tell me about the last time. Go ahead, don't spare any detail."

"Can't we just *tell* Dennis we did the cards?" I say, stalling. "There's gotta be a board game or something around here we can play instead. Monopoly, Candy Land . . . Nothing manlier than Candy Land, I always say."

"I'll go," Lou interrupts, straightening in his chair.

I catch his eye briefly, with an expression like *Are you really going to do this? Because if you go, I'll have to go.* He clears his throat and begins. Traitor.

"My wife and I were both home one day recently; she was a little under the weather . . . I mean, we both were. Super sick. That's why we were both home in the middle of the day, I mean."

"Not starting off super hot, but go on," Ryan prods.

"So, anyway, Tam and her sisters were with my folks, so we had the house to ourselves, which never happens. And I remember us both lying there and looking at each other and immediately we just knew that we had to capitalize, even if we were feeling crappy. So we had this crazy, passionate sex right there in our bed. And somehow we just kept going, doing different stuff in different rooms all over the house. We fooled around in the bathrooms and in the kitchen, and I'm pretty sure the UPS guy saw us doing it in the living room at one point, but we didn't care. When we were finally all tapped out, I had completely forgotten that I was sick."

Ryan offers a fist bump, which Lou accepts. "Well done, sir," he says, then, "John? Don't think you're getting off that easy."

What could I possibly say? The last time with Evelyn was a sleepy, five-minute quickie with a sitcom on low volume in the background and both of us stinking from not having showered after two days of nonstop errands, housework, and Avery's sports. I'm certainly not going to talk about that and become some sort of a case study in failure, put on display in front of the group and dissected like a frog in high school biology class. But I asked Avery if she would try this week. So since we're here, I might as well try, too.

I guess I'll just have to make something up.

"It was the dead of winter," I hear myself saying, sounding more like the beginning of a fantasy novel than an erotic tale, and I've got absolutely no idea what words might come next. "Snow on the ground. Everything frozen. We got a . . . a hotel. Yeah, a hotel. Avery was with a babysitter. My wife, Evelyn, brought some—" Uh . . . what do you bring to hotel sex? Lingerie? Toys? "Toys. Like, a . . ."

For some reason the only toy I can think of is Mr. Potato Head, and I literally cannot get it out of my head to think of the name of any actual sex toys.

"Well, you know," I say, ejecting from that dead-end thread. "*Toys.*

"We ordered champagne to the room, and some chocolate-covered strawberries." We did? News to me. "And let's just say they sent up some plates, but we decided to eat off each other instead."

And now I'm thinking of a chocolate-covered strawberry rolling willy-nilly around on my stomach, landing on the floor, and tumbling under the bed, picking up lint and dust bunnies, and I'm not sure I could have picked a worse food for my made-up story.

"We threw the windows open so everyone could hear us," I add, for some reason.

"Damn," Ryan says. "Now that's hot."

"Yeah, yeah, it was hot. And the heat coming in through the window had us covered in sweat."

"I thought it was winter."

"It was," I blurt, completely carried away in my own crisscrossing lies. "But you know, climate change and all of that."

Ryan furrows his brow. Lou literally scratches his head like the perfect stock photo of a confused person.

But suddenly, I'm struck with a nugget of truth, because I think Evelyn and I did do something kind of like this one time. It was years ago, when we were a freshly married couple without a single responsibility in the world other than each other. And it was at home, not a hotel. And it was whipped cream, not strawberries. I had set it all up for her after a particularly rough stretch at work, knowing she needed the break. Candles, steaks grilled to perfection, a foot massage, and then . . . dessert, so to speak. And I remember it being one of the absolute greatest nights of my life. It still is.

"And it was one of the greatest nights of my life," I say, warm from the memory.

"Now that's what I'm talking about," Ryan says.

"But I still don't really see how any of this is relevant," I add, shaking myself back into the present.

Ryan sighs. "You guys don't get it yet, and that's OK. But it's all connected. Your masculine power. Your sex life. The respect other people give you, including your kids. You have to get your ship in order. You're the captain, damn it. Everything will fall into place once you realize that. It all starts with you, how hard you're willing to work on yourself."

Lou reaches out and snatches the deck of cards from Ryan, as if to put him under the spotlight. "So how about you? Let's hear about this perfectly steamy marriage of yours."

Ryan pauses ever so slightly. "My situation is different. I'm divorced now, or nearly so," he says, eyes down at the floor for the first time since I've met him, then quickly recovering. "I had poisoned that marriage by letting my standards lapse, by not being my best self. I admit it. It was too far gone, so I had to leave. I won't make that mistake twice."

"So when you say 'work on yourself,'" I chime in, "you mean, what, going to therapy?"

I had considered it at one point, long ago, not long after Avery was born.

Ryan gags. "Don't make me puke. No."

And it was the fear of exactly that kind of reaction that kept me from taking the plunge.

"It's honestly more than we even have time to cover right now. But I'll give you the basics," he says. "It's physical preparedness. Regular exercise, both cardio and strength. It's meditation and journaling and mastering your inner life. It's optimizing your sleep schedule so you're fully energized but never wasting time. It's dressing like you actually give a fuck and throwing out anything in your closet that you bought from a store that ends in *mart*. It's never, ever touching a video game ever again in your life and using your time in ways that are actually valuable. It's eliminating little weaknesses, like the luxury of a hot shower or using a bookmark to keep your place in a book. Shower cold. Use the brain God gave you. These things matter. They sharpen your body and mind. It's about building the life you want because you are a man, and gentlemen, *man* is a title that can be given and taken away. You have to earn it every single day."

He goes on like this for a while, giving us a mile-long checklist of things—quote-unquote—*high-value men* should do. According to the book of Ryan, a man's relationship with his romantic partner, specifically the quantity and quality of the sex, is the ultimate measuring stick to chart progress by.

It all sounds like good stuff. Getting into shape. Dressing well. Being more productive. But there's a vague threat behind it all that I'm not even sure Ryan is aware of. *You better do these things, or else.* Or else what?

When the session finally ends, I pull Lou aside on our way out.

"Hey, you were just bullshitting back there, right? To get yourself off the hot seat?"

"I may have exaggerated a little."

"Phew," I say. "Glad to hear that. I made my story up, too."

"Oh, I didn't make it up. I just might have embellished my own, uh, *prowess* just a bit. But we do have a pretty exciting bedroom life. And"—he looks around to make sure no one's listening—"it doesn't come from meditating and waking up at five in the morning, or any of that crap. It comes from putting in actual effort. You know, going on dates. Flirting with each other. Just, I don't know, trying. Even when it's hard."

"Oh," I say, feeling worse than before.

"Yeah, he's got it backward, if you ask me. I think being a better husband and father is what makes you a better *man*. Not the other way around."

He gives me a pat on the shoulder and walks off, leaving me standing there alone, wondering why I couldn't think of a wild romp with Evelyn that didn't happen twelve years ago.

Eight and a Half

Avery is five and a half years old and asleep in her bed. It's late, and I'm out in the garage. I've got the work bench set up, and off to one side is the shoebox we've had for two years. Now ratty and limp and peeling apart in several spots, it's also nearly overflowing with riches.

Most of it, at this point, is stuff we've found outside in the yard or in parks on long walks.

There are pine cones and heart-shaped leaves that have been reduced to crumbs by now, and there's a plastic army man we found abandoned on a playground. And there's the rock that started it all, smiling at me from the gap between the top of the box and the lid that won't quite shut anymore.

Which is why I'm building a new box.

Avery doesn't know yet, it's a surprise. But I'm almost done. It's a lot bigger, not so big that it can't be carried around or moved, but it should hold a lot more stuff. At least for a few more years. More like the size of a large jewelry box. And a little deeper. There's a hefty lid I've managed to attach with basic hinges, and it even latches shut. Right now I'm sanding it down to make it silky smooth before I put on the amber stain.

"I love it when you work with your hands," Evelyn says to me from the doorway.

"Well, enjoy it, because after this they're taking a much-needed vacation," I say, barely looking up.

"You coming in anytime soon?"

"Hopefully. Just a few more rough spots to smooth out, and then I can put on the first coat of stain."

"How long will that take?"

"Not sure. You can't rush art," I tease.

"Finish tomorrow." She pouts, playfully. "I miss you."

"I have to have it done tomorrow."

"Why?"

"Because I want to surprise Avery with it before she starts kindergarten on Monday. And we've got soccer in the morning, and then I know we have a few errands to do in the afternoon, so I'm not sure when else I'll have time."

"You can finish it Monday, give it to her when she comes home as kind of a celebration of her first day."

I chew on the inside of my cheek. That's not really what I had in mind, not how the tradition usually goes, but I'm trying to think of a nice way to say it.

"OK, OK," Evelyn says, reading my face. "Just a suggestion."

She turns and walks inside and closes the door softly behind her. I'm picking up on the fact that she's annoyed, but it's not like I'm out at a strip club or something. I'm just working on a surprise for our daughter. Is that a crime? I rev up the handheld electric sander and take a few passes at an uneven-looking corner of the box. But about twenty seconds later, the door opens up again and Evelyn reappears.

"I'm sorry," she says, very intentionally. "'If you don't ask for what you want, you can't expect to get it,'" she adds, quoting . . . someone. "So I guess what I meant to say before was 'Please come inside, I would really like to spend some time with you because we've been so busy lately and haven't had enough time for us.'"

I stop what I'm doing, place the sander down, and walk over to her. I meet her on the threshold of the doorway and wrap my arms around her waist. She's right. We have been busy—her at the office late, me rushing home early to cart Avery around from activity to activity—and we keep saying that things will "calm down in a few weeks," and they never do, and I'm starting to think that's just something you start saying one day and you never stop. Not to mention, I still don't think, after five years, we've fully adjusted to the routine of planning dates and babysitters and everything spending time together really entails.

"I should have just said that before," she says. "Sorry."

"Sorry I'm too dumb to take a hint."

She smiles, and I kiss her on the nose.

"Give me ten minutes to wrap up what I'm doing, and I'll find time to finish this tomorrow."

"You won't regret it," she says, throwing in a wink.

She goes inside, and I get back to work, more excited by the implication than a grown man has any right to be. But this goddamn corner won't even out. Pass after pass after pass with the sander and I think I've sanded it too much and now I need to go over the whole thing to try to smooth it out. I put on a little music, and I keep at it. I don't want to stop until this thing is perfect. Avery may only be five, but she has an incredibly perceptive eye, along with a total lack of a filter for ego-crushing criticism. But it's the thought of her face lighting up when she sees it for the first time that keeps me going.

I'm about halfway through putting a coat of stain on the box when I realize I've completely lost track of time. How many songs have played since I said I would be inside in ten minutes? Five? More?

I hurry in and wash my hands in the sink, then slink into the bedroom. It's dark, except for a handful of candles burning on our bedside tables. Our room smells like apple cinnamon. The first fall candles of the season. Next to the candle on my side is a full glass of wine. My eyes scan over, and there's Evelyn, in the bed. Asleep. Her glass is nearly empty.

I've got that feeling rumbling around in my stomach like I just got called into the principal's office. I fucked up, and I know it. I think about waking her up, at least so I can apologize. I don't deserve anything more. But we've got an early morning, and I know she has trouble falling back asleep, so I would only be making things worse by waking her up now. It'd be selfish, really, and I'd only be doing it so I can feel better. Right?

I blow out the candles, lie down in bed next to her, and fall asleep trying to decide.

Nine

WHISSHHH

We're back with Dennis now, at the "archery range," which is really just the other end of the big field. A few bales of hay have been adorned with paper targets, and Dennis demonstrates proper form and safety protocols, firing off a few arrows for good measure, the tall bow dwarfing his slight frame.

WHISSHHH, WHISSHHH

All three of his test shots sail wide of the target.

"Well, you get the idea." He sighs. "Remember, this is about working together. Dads, I want to see you at your best here—encouragement, patience, teamwork," he announces. "You're only competing against yourselves. Of course, there *will* be medals for the first girl and the first dad to hit a bull's-eye."

A few murmurs from the crowd, along with a general lack of enthusiasm. Screw 'em. I don't know about everyone else, but I'm here to win. And I know Avery wants to win, whether she'll admit it out loud or even glance in my general direction. Plus, the thought of snagging one of those medals has me salivating. I couldn't think of a better gift to give Avery for the Adventure Box if I had a thousand years to brainstorm.

Megan walks along the line of dads, passing out bows and sacks of arrows with the other counselors. Avery and I grab ours eagerly.

"So how was . . . ," I start, suddenly blanking on what the girls did while I was stuck making up erotic stories with a bunch of dudes I barely know.

"Ropes course."

"Right. How was the ropes course?"

"You know. Ropy."

"Making new friends at least?"

Avery looks over at the group of girls from her cabin, all huddled together, comparing their bows.

"I *have* friends. At home. And they're all probably wondering why I'm not texting back. Bet they all think I'm dead."

"Nah, if you were dead they would have seen it in the papers by now."

"The papers?"

"Never mind."

We inspect our weaponry. I'm no hunting expert or anything, but this stuff has seen better days. Not a straight line to be found on any of our arrows, and the bows resemble children's toys from the fifties. Not just that they're old-fashioned, but they literally look like they've been in use for about seventy years.

"Have you ever done this before?" she says.

"Of course." Thirty years ago, but who's counting? "Here, you start," I say, and I nudge her up to the shooting line. "Feet a little wider, good." I adjust her stance—going off what I saw from Dennis (yeah, I know he missed all three shots) and what I remember from elementary school (which isn't much), but it's all I've got.

"Pointer finger on top," I say, but she cuts me off.

"I was paying attention," she says, squinting down the range, locked in.

"All right good, looking good." I back up a little. "Now just—"

"Dad," she whispers, "stop talking."

Right.

She aims and launches her arrow with confidence. It whizzes through the air and lands limply in the hay, a few feet shy of the actual target. Avery sags.

"Hey, that was a good shot," I say.

"I stink."

I lift her chin up with a finger and say, "I know the thought makes you want to crawl out of your skin, but let me help you next time, just a little, OK? Now watch this."

I step confidently to the line, knowing that I've just written a check I'll certainly not be able to cash. Steadying myself, I scrape all the form pointers I can from the back of my memory, and I let my arrow fly. It feels good coming out of my hands, and it flies straight, and it sticks into the target with a *THWUMP*. It lands in the outer black ring, but hey—I'll take it.

I turn around to face Avery and gesture to myself like *Who's the man?*, but she's not even watching. She's looking a few groups down from us at Ryan and Jessie. They are causing a bit of a ruckus, drawing audible gasps from the crowd. I crane my neck to see what's going on, and there's Ryan, stepping up to shoot. He's brought his own gear, because of course he has. Instead of the loaner bow the rest of us are using, he's sporting some insane compound hunting bow straight out of a sporting-goods catalog. It looks like a sniper rifle had a baby with a medieval trebuchet.

He draws and fires a goddamn missile of an arrow, and it slices through the target with emphasis, nearly toppling the entire barrel of hay. A few *ooohs* and *aaahs* echo throughout the group. Dennis calls a halt to the action, walks down the course, and uprights the target. An impressive shot, but several inches off the mark.

"In a master's hands," I say to Avery, "the tools don't matter. Or something like that. There's an expression. Now this," I say hoisting the rickety loaner bow again, "*this* is what archery is all about."

I fire off another shot, and it sails right past the target.

"All right, so the tools matter a little bit. Hey, it's unpredictable, but at least it's the real deal. Believe me, I'd be doing a lot better if I weren't stuck with this crooked antique right here."

Avery giggles.

"What now?" I say.

I follow her gaze, and I spot Booker, finally present for once, using the same crap bow as me, straight *dealing* like he's Legolas—firing darts and lighting up the target with precision. He even looks cool drawing the arrow from the quiver. How come I didn't get an awesome quiver?

THWUMP, THWUMP, THWUMP. In seconds, a cluster of arrows forms around the center ring of the target. No bull's-eye quite yet, though. Booker lays the bow down on the ground and inspects it.

"Something's off," he murmurs. "I know my draw length is right, arrow weight seems good." He positions his hands just so, eyeballing different measurements of the bow, then picks up the arrow and balances it on a finger. "Of course. Weight distribution!" he finally announces, as if he's Sir Isaac Newton discovering gravity. He picks up his equipment, lines up another shot, and this arrow flies gloriously through the air and lands mere millimeters from a perfect bull's-eye.

"Almost." He grins. "Almost."

Erica, standing by and watching him with pride, smacks him a high five.

Feeling my face turn flush with jealousy, I decide I should say something supportive, something encouraging, but I land somewhere between *Nice shot* and *Nice job* and holler "Nice shob!" down the course at Booker. Avery cocks an eyebrow at me, and I can feel her perception of my IQ tumbling dozens of points.

THWUMP, THWUMP, THWUMP. Booker's on a roll, getting closer and closer.

Avery regards the bow. "Yeah, so *unpredictable*," she teases.

I throw her in a headlock, and she laughs and wriggles free.

"OK, here's the truth . . . No, I don't know anything about archery. I tried it once, and I sucked then and I suck now."

She looks up at me.

"You said *suck*."

"What?"

"Usually you say *stink, stank,* or *stunk*."

"Sorry," I say, slapping my forehead. "I'm all mixed up this week."

"I kind of liked it," she says with a smirk. "More authentic."

Avery steps back up to the shooting line, draws back, and fires off another shot.

It slices into the target, agonizingly close to the center. Heads turn to look at Avery as she readies another arrow. She picks up on this, everyone watching her, and I swear I see her scanning the faces of the other girls—all eyeing her with a strange mixture of awe and jealousy. Avery makes a slight adjustment and shoots. This arrow sails wide, landing in the grass somewhere, and the disappointed crowd returns to their own targets.

"Did you just miss that on purpose?"

"What? No!" she cries, a little too defensive.

"It looked like you pulled it to the right just before you shot."

"No, God! Sorry I'm not perfect all the time," she says, slumping into a seated position on the ground. I sit next to her.

"Sorry. Didn't mean to accuse you."

"Maybe I'm just not very good at this." She looks around, most everyone here failing miserably, arrows flying dangerously off-target everywhere we look. "No one else is, anyway."

"You're not like everyone else."

She looks almost hurt that I would say this. "Yes I am," she insists.

But she's not. Never has been. And, until now at least, she's always taken pride in that. I thought she would take my remark as a compliment.

"You were good at soccer right away, but maybe archery's just a different beast," I say, switching gears. No sense in riling her up any further right now. "I guess it's just ugly when you're learning. At least in soccer, you can run hard and be near the ball, and it looks like you're doing something. Maybe occasionally tackle someone."

She lets out a small laugh, and I nudge her playfully in the side until it becomes a bigger laugh.

"If you were a total beginner and walked right up and got a bull's-eye on your first try? That would actually be kind of weird."

Suddenly, cheers erupt around us, and we look and see that Lou is hoisting little Tam on his shoulders, lifting her up and down like he's at a bat mitzvah.

"My baby got a bull's-eye! My baby got a bull's-eye!" He catches my eye and yells to me, "First try, dude!"

"I'm just gonna shut up now," I say to Avery, who's busy smiling brightly and sending a congratulatory thumbs-up Tam's way.

Dennis jogs over and places the first medal around Tam's neck, so long it almost hangs down to her knees.

Avery gets up, and we take turns for a while, trading shots—she gets a little bit better every time, progressing rapidly the way kids seem to do with hardly any effort. But I can't shake this feeling that she's holding back and that she could be doing even better if she really wanted to.

Before too long, of course, Booker gets the other medal. The dads offer polite applause, mine just barely qualifying as a golf clap. Erica beams at him, her hero, and I struggle not to scoff out loud. Big deal. Anyone can ignore their kid and throw themselves into work; that's easy. Then what? You just show up at key moments like Career Day and the archery competition to show off? Still, the way Erica's looking up at him, the medal hanging off his neck, it sure seems like she doesn't mind. At the moment, anyway.

On the walk back I say, "Sorry we couldn't snag one of those medals."

Avery says, "Sorry that you were the worst one out there."

We share a laugh.

I want to squeeze her and tell her how much I love her and miss her, maybe wrap her up tight enough to completely absorb her so she can never get away.

But I don't. We just laugh and then walk in silence. I take one last look back over my shoulder, Tam walking off with her medal, Booker with his. I'm bummed. It should be us. It would have been the perfect thing.

Still, if this is my consolation prize, it isn't so bad.

But suddenly, Jessie's walking next to us, hovering close enough that I can tell she's looking to strike up a conversation, stealing glances over at us through the curtain of hair framing her face. She and Avery are pretty close in age. Therefore, I reckon they should be friends. I slow down a bit, falling behind, and quickly Jessie drifts over into my place, walking side by side with Avery now, as if we're Formula 1 racers jostling for position. I give them space, but of course, I'm listening in.

"That was pretty annoying, huh?" Jessie opens.

"So annoying."

They laugh.

"Yeah, I just couldn't quite get the hang of it." Avery shrugs.

"So what do you think of this place so far?" Jessie asks.

"It's OK. I'd rather be at the beach or something."

"Me too! When my dad said we were going away, this wasn't exactly what I had in mind."

"Where did you think you were going?" Avery asks.

"I dunno, anywhere. It's been an awful summer. We might be moving, so there are always people in our house looking at it or fixing things. It's just been shitty."

"Yeah. Same here—shitty."

Jessie sighs dramatically. "Wonder what super-fun activity they have planned for us now."

"Should we go find out, or should we hide out in the bathroom for a few hours?"

Jessie laughs and grabs Avery's arm tight. "*Do not* leave me, you have to promise."

Avery playfully shoves her away. "OK, OK."

They giggle and branch off toward the girls' cabins.

"Avery," I call out. "See you in a bit?"

She throws up a lazy peace sign over her shoulder and disappears.

Ten

Something wonderful happened today.

Something that hadn't happened in ages. Something so rare and delicate that I hadn't allowed myself to so much as whisper it in eleven years.

I took a nap.

While the girls cleaned up their cabins and launched into some kind of group-bonding activity, the dads were blessed with the gift of R & R, a chance to rest our old and brittle bones. Nothing on the schedule for the remainder of the morning, absolutely nowhere to be. When I got back to my own cabin, it was weirdly empty. I wondered where the guys were, but I didn't really care because, suddenly, something washed over me, a feeling that took me by surprise:

Fatigue without guilt.

When I find myself alone—you know, in real life—it's nice and all, but it's usually served up with a bit of heart-pounding anxiety.

The feeling I've done something wrong or forgotten to do something. There's a heaviness that drags me down. If I even think of allowing myself a brief eye break, the feeling becomes heavier and heavier, snowballing into a reluctant momentum that takes me . . . somewhere, anywhere. To wash a dish, pull a weed, tidy a surface, tighten a screw. It doesn't really matter as long as I'm moving. I can't remember sitting in a quiet, empty room and not feeling horrible about it at some level.

Until this afternoon.

I hopped into my top bunk at the cabin and pulled out the itinerary just to be sure, and there it was, scheduled from eleven to noon: *REST AND FREE TIME.*

Don't get me wrong, it took a minute to get going. It had been a while and, at first, I wasn't sure what to do with my body during a nap—should I get under the covers? Half in, half out? Should I throw my head under a pillow to block the sun, or should I let it wash over my face? But eventually I drifted away, and it was the most restful sleep I've had in years. My brain jumped directly into REM, bursting to life with vivid dreams.

I woke gently on my own about fifty minutes later to the chirping of birds outside the cabin window like a goddamn Disney princess.

It was awesome. No, scratch that. It was perfect.

Recharged, I moseyed over to the dining hall—I can't even remember the last time I moseyed anywhere!—and met up with Avery for a lunch of over-mayonnaised tuna salad on cheap rolls that come four dozen to a pack.

After lunch, we had one-on-one time. A few hours to do whatever we wanted to do as long as we did it together—the schedule said so.

There were plenty of choices, like Ping-Pong in the main building, swimming in the green-tinted pool (no, thanks), or tennis on the cracked and leaf-covered courts.

Avery said she wanted to kick the soccer ball around in the big field, and so we did, me silently wishing the entire time it wouldn't remind her of her grief over the soccer tryouts. It didn't, at least not that I could tell.

Now here we are, at the end of our first *full* day at Camp Triumph.

The sun's gone down over the field, and the staff has wheeled out a rusty old charcoal grill. Paper plates and SOLO cups crowd a plastic table. More of those stale rolls from lunch attract flies, buzzing excitedly in anticipation of the coming feast. Avery and I are the first to arrive, as Dennis, Megan, and the other crew are setting up.

Dennis hands me some tongs and a giant bag of frozen burgers and says, "You get to do the honors."

Slowly, the rest of the campers trickle in. I light up the charcoal grill with some effort (I'm more of a push-button gas guy), but I get it going before anyone's there to see me struggle—the last thing I need is a rerun of my flat-tire fiasco. And I lay the first round of burgers down onto the hot grates, still caked with crispy residue from the cooking efforts of previous dads, many moons ago, who once stood where I stand now. My spiritual ancestors, I think.

The girls run off as they arrive, forming a massive game of tag or some other running-and-squealing sport. The dads hover around the grill.

Dads love hovering around a grill.

"What do we got here, a Weber?" one says.

"Sure wish I had my Egg," adds another. "I miss my Egg."

"Those babies look about ready to flip," chimes in a third.

118

The pressure with all of them watching me is too much, I feel like I'm suffocating. But I manage to make some basic small talk with the grill crew and catch wind of a few dad names, like Steve, Mark, Jeff, and Bob.

Steve is a life-of-the-party type, quick with the dad jokes. *"Tongs a lot!"* he quips as I claw-machine a burger from the grill over to his plate.

Next to him and frozen in a perpetual eye roll is Mark, his partner. "Sorry about him," Mark says several times. "I told him he was more than welcome to stay home, that we don't have to do *everything* together, but he . . . insisted."

Jeff tells us he's an adoptive dad. "It wasn't easy," he says of the process. "It costs an arm and a leg, obviously. But there's all this other stuff, too. Drug tests. IQ tests. The blood oath."

I'm pretty certain he's joking, but I don't dare laugh until he throws in a good-natured wink to let us all know it's OK.

"Sorry, I just love the way people squirm and panic about the etiquette around this stuff." He chuckles. "Don't mind me."

Bob, a general contractor and a walking meme of fatherhood, complete with fresh white New Balance sneakers and a fanny pack, scolds me for overcooking the first batch. "A little crispy, don't ya think?"

Calm down, Bob, they're fifteen-cent Costco burgers.

And yet I relent, handing over the tongs to a Tim and grabbing myself a burger. I stand and watch the girls chase one another while I scarf it down.

Avery, to my surprise, is right in the thick of the game. She seems to be "it," chasing after everyone with an outstretched hand, trying to pick off a few of the slower, weaker girls. Avery lets out a monstrous growl as she chases after Tam, who squeals with delight and falls over trying to get away. Just as Avery's about to tag her, Jessie runs up behind Avery, taps her on the shoulder, and laughs hysterically, running the other direction. Avery gives chase. Now Erica pulls the same maneuver, a shoulder tap to distract Avery, and takes off. Avery's smiling through it all, relishing her role in the game, and the girls are laughing. It looks like the perfect picture of summertime. But again, as I watch the game, I can't shake this feeling that Avery's jogging. Going half speed. She could run circles around any of these girls if she wanted, but it looks like she doesn't want to. Maybe it's just to make the game more fun for everyone. If so, that's great. But I guess it just strikes me as odd because I've never, not once, not in her entire life, ever seen her half-ass anything. And today I've seen it twice.

"Hey, we're out of buns!" Jeff calls out, standing by the condiment table with a naked burger on his plate, helplessly looking for more rolls.

"Uh-oh, we're *rolly* in a *pickle* now," Steve yelps, eliciting groans and pity laughs.

"Someone? Hey! Buns?" Mark says frantically, I imagine to prevent Steve from making another bun pun. A murmur of concern ripples through the crowd. I look around and realize I just happen to be standing pretty close to Megan, who's keeping an eye on the girls, so I walk over to her.

"Not sure if you heard about the buns," I say.

"You know what's weird is we brought out the same number of buns and burgers. The math doesn't really check out."

"It's the girls," I say. "Kids love weird shit like plain buns with ketchup on them. I'll never understand it."

"That makes sense." She laughs.

"I mean, weird *stuff*. Sorry," I add. "I don't know if we're allowed to curse here."

"Do you mind checking the chow hall? Kitchen's open, and the rolls should be easy to find. I'd do it, but I can't leave them," she says, gesturing to the game of tag.

"You got it."

"And hey, maybe you can wash your mouth out with soap on your way back," she teases.

I smirk and head off toward the *dining* hall. Briefly, I consider turning back and clarifying that I wasn't flirting with her just now, despite the banter. She's twenty years younger than me, but I shudder to think how rarely that deters other dads here from shooting their shot.

I decide saying anything would only be weirder.

Inside the hall, it's completely dark, except for one dim light coming from the kitchen area. And some kind of white glow coming from one of the lunch tables in the far corner. I move a little closer, slowly, and I realize it's a laptop. And there's a person in front of it, hammering away at the keyboard.

"Hello?" I say in the human's direction. At least, I hope it's a human.

"Oh, hey. It's just me."

"Who's me?"

The figure reaches over and flicks a light switch, flooding the entire room with fluorescent white and nearly blinding me. After a few moments, my eyes recover and I see that the man is Booker, and he's got not only his laptop but also papers and a phone spread out on the table in front of him.

"You found my secret lair," he jokes.

Booker is smiling at me like I'm in on the joke, but I've had about enough of this guy. Yeah, Ryan and Lou are obnoxious in their own ways, but at least they're out there making some kind of effort. Booker may as well have just stayed home and ignored his daughter there instead. Would have at least been cheaper. Dads like him are out here giving all of us a bad name, and if I'm not careful, I might just tell him that right to his stupid face.

"What would it take to get you to bring me a burger? I'm starving."

"I'm just here for more rolls," I say, and I brush right past him through the swinging door into the kitchen and scour the countertops.

"So that's a no?"

I ignore him and root around, opening what looks to be a pantry. Inside is just random storage, stuff that must have been ripped out of the abandoned cabins. Piles of bedding and Tupperware full of hooks nearly tumble out before I can close the door.

"I'm kidding. Yeesh," Booker adds.

"It's not a good look, huh?" he shouts to me through the little pass-through where the cooks place hot trays of food. "Me, hiding away in here. I know how I come off. With all the work and everything."

"Hey, you do you," I say, trying as hard as possible not to engage. In the kitchen, I see everything but what I'm looking for. Bags of onions. Tubs of flour. Curiously, a case of beer on a lower storage shelf, hastily covered by an apron, which I take mental note of.

"What do you do?" he says to me.

"I'm in marketing."

It's an intentionally vague answer.

I work at a marketing agency, and I manage projects for huge brands, the kinds of brands you see on the sides of basketball shoes and in major grocery store aisles. Massive corporations so bogged down in red tape nothing ever gets done. I send an email, and before they can respond, the response has to be run up five different chains of command and approved by about eleven different teams. It takes months to get anything done. It's great.

Is it a challenge? Is it intellectually stimulating? I guess not. But I'm the one who picks up Avery from school when she has a fever, or takes her to the dentist, or plays hooky to get some things done around the house.

It's the perfect job. I mean, it's not a *dream* job, it's no Happy Hills. But it suits me, and another big change is the last thing I need right now.

"Got a card?" he asks.

"Not on me."

Why would I have a card? I'm getting more and more annoyed, and I can't find the bread anywhere. I'm considering just grabbing a pack of tortillas and calling it a day. Those seem to be everywhere, giving me an inkling some kind of taco night is in our near future. But at least, for now, Booker seems to have stopped talking.

Suddenly, though, he's next to me in the kitchen, holding a pack of rolls. His appearance nearly stops my heart on the spot.

"They were in the walk-in."

"Oh, thanks," I say, collecting myself.

"Happy to help."

Ah, come on, man. Don't do this. Don't do the thing where you're really nice to me so I have to be nice back.

"I'm an architect," he says, dropping the world's least-subtle humblebrag. "That's what I'm working on out there, I mean. They're building a new arena near where I live, trying to have it ready for the start of basketball season. Huge team working on it. *No days off* and all that," he says, trying and failing to sound lighthearted.

"I'm not much of a hoops fan," I respond, shifting my weight subtly toward the door.

He tries a different tack. "So, you like it? Being in marketing?"

Honestly, I don't understand the question. Like it? Like what? Does anyone *like* their work? It helps afford us a comfortable lifestyle, and I can take off at the drop of a hat to do something like this with my daughter, so yeah, I guess I "like" it. Besides, I've learned the hard way not to complain about gainful employment, especially employment that includes a beer cart on Fridays and quarterly company outings to things like laser tag and bowling.

"What are you crying about?" my dad said the one time I dared lament not being *passionate* about the work. "Rather work in a factory? A coal mine? Clean septic tanks?"

I shook my head, and that was the end of that conversation.

"Are you kidding? I hit the jackpot," I say, surprising myself with the enthusiasm in my voice. I worry Booker might realize I don't actually mean it, which would risk a much deeper conversation than I'm ready to have.

But he doesn't pick up on it, or if he does, he doesn't say anything. I guess this is the part where I'm supposed to ask him something about his job, but what I really want to do is get back to the cookout so I can dodge small talk with the dads there instead. So many people to ignore and so little time.

"Yeah, being an architect is—"

"Listen," I cut him off. "I don't want to be rude, but I really don't care about what you do for work or why you're doing it here instead of spending time with your daughter." I suddenly think back to what Lou said, about men and their obsession with talking about work. "We're here for harsh truths, right? I know I've gotten a few already. So I guess that's yours—you're not trying hard enough."

It came out a bit harsher than intended, and he's taken aback, clearly. It takes him a minute to find the words to respond, but when he does, it takes me completely off guard. "I probably deserve that."

Booker slumps his way out of the kitchen, the door swinging shut behind him, throwing in a "I'll let you get back to the cookout" for good measure.

The sad-sack routine almost works on me, and I do feel a little bit bad. I nearly follow him to apologize, but then I remind myself that there's only one person's approval I really need, and I'm not going to waste my time with anyone who can't help me get it.

Besides, there are a lot of hangry dads waiting on me.

• • •

I don't see much of Avery for the rest of the cookout.

She's busy getting tagged in tag, swiping helplessly at air while being the monkey in the middle, and snagging the occasional foot on the jump rope during double Dutch. I watch her for a while, chewing on my burger like Sherlock Holmes mouthing his pipe, trying to make it make sense.

Meanwhile, I'm pretending I have anything to say to the other dads, or anything even remotely in common with them. One halfway-decent day aside, my opinion of them, and this place, hasn't changed much so far. Maybe some of them have a few things going for them. Brains. Brawn. Lucrative careers. But I still don't think we belong here, Avery and me.

Eventually the charcoal grill fizzles out and people begin to disperse. The few leftover burgers, shriveled and hardened like hockey pucks, are tossed in the garbage. Floodlights that lit the field are shut off. Another air horn sounds off, alerting us that it's time to head to bed.

I walk over to where the girls were playing. Most of them are gone now, but Avery's still there. She's taking turns juggling a soccer ball with Megan, in some kind of playful competition to see who can keep it up in the air the longest. Suddenly, they break out into a spontaneous one-on-one session, Avery dribbling and trying to get the ball past Megan, who doesn't give her an inch, boxing her out with impossibly long limbs.

"That all you got?" Megan teases.

Avery furrows her brow and charges ahead with even more intensity. She takes a hard turn and lowers her shoulder, trying to bend around Megan, but Megan is way bigger—and Avery bounces off her and hits the ground hard.

I jog over, but there's no need. Megan helps Avery up, Avery with a huge smile on her face despite dirty knees and a fresh grass stain on her clothes.

"Talk about a clash of the titans," I say. "Not too many people out there who can keep up with Avery."

Megan laughs. "I play water polo at State, so yeah, I guess I'm no pushover."

"Hey," I call out to Avery, who's dusting herself off for another go. "We should probably head back."

"Aww," she whines. "Can we have a few more minutes?"

"It's OK," Megan says to me, panting ever so slightly. "I can walk her back to our cabin in a few."

I had imagined doing that myself, getting a proper good night instead of a dismissive wave while I stand here like an idiot, getting ravaged by mosquitoes. But I guess Avery is finally having a good time, and I'm not about to look a gift horse in the mouth.

"Sure thing. Night, Avery. I love you."

She doesn't respond, because she's on defense now and Megan's charging hard at her with the ball.

I walk back alone.

Waiting for me on my bunk, though I swore I had tucked them aside, are the papers and pen. Dennis's nasally voice rings in my head: *If you find in these sessions that there's something that's too hard to say out loud, write it down.*

And then the grating tones of Dennis's moralizing stop, replaced now by my dad's voice for some reason, deep but soft.

I block it out, tucking the papers under the pillow once again, out of sight and out of mind.

WEDNESDAY

Eleven

In the morning, I slide right into the routine as if I've been here for weeks.

Wake up with back pain.

Ryan out on a run, Booker sleeping in. Lou ahead of me by a few minutes.

Make awkward small talk.

Shower in the spidery bathroom. She has laid eggs. Aw, good for her.

Hear the air horn.

Trade shower sandals for tennis shoes. Throw on shorts. Apply ludicrous amounts of sunscreen.

Meet Avery for breakfast.

It's amazing how quickly places like this become your whole world. I have no concept of what's happening outside of our little bubble, and I don't really care. I don't miss my phone at all. I do miss

Evelyn, and I'm sure she misses us. But luxuriating in the empty house is a rare opportunity for her.

At home for some reason there's just always . . . *noise*. Avery blasting music during homework, me banging on something with a hammer or running the power drill, both of us pestering Evelyn about where to find things or what might be for dinner. I know how much she loves taking care of her family, but I can also tell when it's beginning to grate on her. She recently started taking classes at a new Pilates studio a lot farther away than her old one, supposedly because a bunch of the other moms go there, but I'm convinced it's because she likes the extra quiet time in the car. That was a good sign that it was time to make ourselves scarce, so, yeah. I'm fairly certain she's surviving at home without us.

Halfway through breakfast, which seems to be getting better every day—seriously, it's positively OK today!—Dennis ambles into the dining hall and collects all the girls. He ushers them outside, leaving all the dads to finish eating. None of us know the first activity for the day yet. The schedule only said "girls choice," and I put two and two together and figure they're out there taking some kind of vote.

The whole gang is here, and without our girls to act as a buffer, we're forced to interact. We all give one another terse nods as we sip coffee. Without our phones to scroll through or even an old newspaper to peruse, this is torture. I consider apologizing to Booker as we lock eyes but think better of it. Luckily, the girls flood back in after just a few moments, and we're all saved.

"So what's it gonna be today?" I ask Avery.

"Ugh," she says. There's that word again, though, this time, it doesn't seem to be my fault.

• • •

After breakfast, followed by rise and shine, which causes one dad to barf his breakfast up in the lawn, we're all ushered over to the general-purpose building, where we had men's group yesterday. I've come to understand it's called the Triumph Lodge.

Instead of a chair circle there are now a few long, portable plastic tables at the center of the room with chairs lining each on both sides, like we're about to sit down to breakfast all over again.

We take our seats, dads on one side of the table and daughters on the other, as instructed by Dennis. He paces up and down the length of the tables as we settle in. We have no sense of what's coming, no visible supplies or games anywhere, not a single clue in sight. Only the girls know, and they're not saying. Only stifling laughs and, in Avery's case, frequent eye rolls.

"I want to start our day with a simple question," Dennis begins. "Girls, by a show of hands, who here has ever felt let down or left out by your dad?"

Ah, all right, so we're here to do some emotional work. Great. Awesome.

"Who here feels like Dad always seems to be busy, or tired, or he's got some other excuse why he can't do the things you want to do? Maybe you want to play in the backyard, but 'Oh, it's too hot,' he says. Maybe you want a piggyback ride, but 'Not now,' he says, *he's too tired.*"

A few hesitant hands go up, slowly at first, then a few more join in.

I watch Avery closely to see what she'll do, but I'm not worried.

If there's one thing I've always been good at, it's saying yes. Can we climb this tree? Yes! Can you pretend to be a robber so I can take you to jail? Absolutely! Can I stand on your chest and jump up and down and laugh at the funny noises you make as your ribs buckle beneath my weight? Why not?!

Avery's hand doesn't go up, but she does seem to be listening intently.

"I think it's time for your dads to meet you where you're at, don't you?" Dennis says. "Why should he always be the one who gets to decide what you do and don't do together?"

A few nods from around the table.

"In any good relationship, there's a give-and-take," he continues. "Compromises on both sides. If they want to be great dads, they're going to have to get used to doing things they don't want to do. Things they know will make *you* happy."

He's saying this like it's supposed to be news to us, like being a parent isn't getting smashed in the face with a bucketful of compromises the instant your first child is born.

"And that's the whole point of this girls' choice session today. Sorry, dads, *none* of the choices were ever meant to be fun for you. But I have to say that I, for one, am pretty excited by what the girls chose."

Avery leans over toward me and says, "For the record, I voted to play field hockey."

Megan and a few other counselors suddenly enter the room through a backdoor, all holding brown paper grocery bags.

"Today," Dennis continues, "we're transforming the Triumph Lodge into our own personal . . . nail salon!"

Groans ring out from a bunch of the dads, while the girls look to one another with excitement. The counselors walk the table, placing nail brushes and vials of colorful, sparkly nail polish and those sandpapery tongue depressor things in front of each pair.

"That's right. You'll be giving each other manicures. And, hey, let's try to do it without the attitude, huh?" Dennis adds.

It's all a little anticlimactic, if you ask me. All that buildup for . . . manicures? Is this supposed to be intimidating?

And then, almost as if on cue . . .

"Oh, this is absurd," Ryan cries out from the end of the table.

Jessie, across from him, tries to calm him in a low voice. "Dad . . ."

"No, no, I've had enough." He stands and addresses Dennis directly. "What the hell kind of camp is this? All we've done is sit around and talk about our feelings, and now manicures? We should be out there chopping wood or learning to build a fire, not this sissy crap."

He takes a few powerful strides toward the door and says, "Jessie, come on."

But she doesn't. She looks around, catching the eyes of some of the others around the table and searching for help. None comes.

"Jessie," Ryan commands in a booming voice.

She stands. "No."

"No?"

"No! We're supposed to do what I want to do, that's the whole point. We're supposed to laugh and play games and eat too much sugar. This isn't a boot camp, Dad! It's supposed to be fun!"

"If you don't get over here in the next three seconds . . ."

"God, you're impossible! See this, *this* is exactly why Mom left!"

"Jessie—"

"And you don't even care that she's gone, do you?! Tell me I'm wrong."

Jessie waits for an answer, but Ryan says nothing. She knocks her chair over and storms out, whooshing right past a stunned Ryan in the process. Holy shit. *She left him.* Initially, I feel angry. Duped. *What a hypocrite*, I think. But then I begin to imagine the pain he must be hiding, and poor Jessie, and what would it be like if Evelyn and I— No, I have to cut the thought off. It's not somewhere I want to go.

There's a thick silence in the room, everyone staring at Ryan, waiting to see what he'll do or say. He scans our faces and then quickly ducks out of the building himself.

"Megan, can you?" Dennis says.

Megan nods and goes out after them, presumably to check on Jessie. "The rest of you can get started. Go on, nothing to see here."

There's a long pause as the awkwardness dissipates, then a slow murmur begins to form as everyone gets to work.

"All right, what do you want?" I say, shaking the moment off, and I begin reading off the absurdly cutesy color names on the nail polish vials. "Peachy Keen? Pink Me Up Before You Go Go? Better Off Red?" I'm infusing my voice with as much cheer as possible, because—while I'm not concerned about a little nail polish threatening my masculinity, I know Avery's going to hate every second of this. And, well, that would be a major setback. It's her I'm worried about.

"I guess I like this blue one, if I have to pick."

"Azure Shootin', sounds good."

I unscrew the top of the vial, and Avery plops her hands awkwardly on the table in front of me.

"Oh, just so you know," Dennis says, pausing by us while walking past, "The premium colors are a five-dollar upcharge. We'll just add it to your account and bill you at the end of the week."

"Premium colors? Well, which ones are free?" I say.

"Clear. Oh, and Rainy Day."

Rainy Day? I scan the table and find it. It's a sickly gray, the color of once-white carpet that's accumulated years of grime.

"Clear and gray?"

Dennis shrugs and walks off. Just when I think I'm coming around to this place, it hits a new low.

"All right, clear or gray, then?" I ask Avery with a sigh.

"Oh, get gray!" Erica calls out from a few seats down. "We'll all get gray and we'll match!"

"OK," Avery says with a smile. "I guess it's gray."

Is she . . . actually enjoying this? It's taking me a bit by surprise that she's even willing to participate in something so traditionally, well, girly. She's never been into stuff like this, and when all the other girls her age were going through the princess phase, and the unicorn phase, and the Disney channel teenybopper phase, Avery was much more into things like rocks and bugs—before she discovered competitive sports, anyway.

"It's nice to see you getting along," I say. "Making friends."

"You sound surprised."

"Not at all," I backpedal. "Who wouldn't want to be your friend?"

"I'm just trying. Like you said."

I can't help but smile that she actually listened to me for once.

"So what were the other choices today?"

"This, baking, and hair braiding."

"Wow. A little . . . stereotypical, don't you think?"

"I thought so, too. But I dunno . . . This isn't so bad."

She takes a peek around at the other dads and daughters, the men fumbling hopelessly with the supplies. I follow her gaze, and I spot the incredible display of ineptitude all around the table, dads spilling polish, slopping it on. Just a total mess. At the far end of the table, Lou applies Rainy Day to Tam's nails with care but can't seem to stay inside the lines.

"Daaaad," Tam whines. "You messed it up."

"Sorry, I'm trying!"

"You never make mistakes like this at home. We've only done this like a *million* times."

Heads turn toward Lou and Tam. He lets out a nervous chuckle. "Kiddo, let's try to use our inside voice."

A few of the guys at the table chuckle, and Lou turns bright red. I feel bad that he's embarrassed, but personally? I'm fascinated by this image of him, in his tattooed form, sitting at home with his daughter, giving her regular manicures. Suddenly, I find myself liking him just a little bit more.

I grab the little nail sander from the table. "Do you want me to do . . . whatever this thing is?"

"Do you know how to do it?"

"Not a clue."

"Then no."

I slosh a heaping portion of Rainy Day gray on Avery's left pointer finger nail, realize it's way too much, and try to transpose some of it to a few of her adjacent fingers. My only relevant experience in this area is painting drywall.

"Wow, you're good at this," she teases.

"Gimme a break, I haven't had a lot of practice."

"It doesn't look that hard to me."

"You know, I used to actually know how to do this pretty well. Before you were born, after your mom and I found out you were a girl, I started reading up on things like braiding hair and painting nails and trying to learn the names of all the big Disney princesses. I may or may not have practiced my manicures on Mom, to her horror."

She giggles.

"But when you never ended up needing any of that stuff, I got rusty." I don't mention that I kept up the practice for a little while longer than she thinks. Just in case we ever had another girl.

"Oh . . . sorry."

"For what?"

"I don't know. Sounds like you were excited to have a girly girl to do all that dad-daughter stuff with."

"Psh. You think I'd change a single thing about who you turned out to be?"

"I think I would," she says casually, but I'm stopped in my tracks.

"Like what?"

"I dunno," she blurts, getting a little red in the face. "Just like little things. My toes are weird, for example."

"Well, now I'm insulted, because you have *my* toes."

She laughs.

"What else?"

"I can't think when you put me on the spot."

"So just the toes, then?"

"They're freaky! They curl up and it hurts when I wear cleats, which is pretty much all the time."

I shrug. "Well, I like you. Freaky toes and all."

She beams, but after a moment she adds, "I'm just not perfect. That's all."

"Respectfully disagree," I say.

Avery gets quiet, and I keep on painting—some of the technique is coming back to me, but the overall polish job still looks pretty awful. And it suddenly dawns on me that the two of us are genuinely having a good time, bonding with each other and connecting in a way that we haven't for months. Maybe more.

And right on cue, Dennis cuts in.

"Are we having fun?" he interrupts from the front of the room.

A vaguely positive murmur from the group.

"Well, then, it's time to turn up the heat," he says. "Remember, I told you we'd have fun, but I also told you we weren't going to let you off the hook this week."

Why? Why now, when things were going so well?

"Girls, I want you to take a minute to think about a time that your dad really let you down. Find the image in your mind, take yourself back to that place. Feel the *disappointment* . . ." His voice sinks, and Dennis trails off for just a moment. Quickly, he collects himself. "And then, I want you to look him in the eye and tell him about it."

No one speaks, and there's a palpable silence in the air.

"Don't be shy, girls, he's the one who should be worried. Because now's your chance to tell him how it feels when he puts himself first, or when he doesn't make time for you, or when he hurts you with his selfishness."

Jesus Christ, Dennis. I get that we're all here to do some work on our relationships, and maybe for some of these girls and their dads it means healing some past wounds. But is it really worth taking a blowtorch to a paper cut? Here Avery and I are finally on the same page and getting along, and now she's about to rip into me for dragging her here more or less against her will, just when she had finally let it go.

"I, um . . . ," Avery stammers, looking at me.

Dennis walks the length of the table, eavesdropping as he goes, listening in to these strained confessions.

The girl next to Avery tells her dad in a squeaky voice, "Sometimes you say I can't have a juice and then you have a beer. That's not fair." She's got a point.

Dennis stands behind Avery and pauses, our turn to impress him with our honesty. "I don't, um . . ."

"Here, I'll start you off," Dennis says, leaning down next to her. "Dad, it really hurt my feelings when . . ."

"Dad," she echoes, "it really hurt my feelings when . . ."

"Go on. Tell him."

Here it comes, *Dad, it really hurt my feelings when you selfishly stole my last week of summer to drag me here so we could make s'mores and yell at each other.* I white-knuckle the edge of the table and brace myself for impact.

"Dad, it really hurt my feelings when," she says, starting over, "when you . . . when you . . . when you farted at my birthday party . . . in front of all of my friends."

I stifle a laugh—if I had a drink in my mouth, I would have spat it all over the room.

"You embarrassed me with your huge fart. And it smelled. It smelled so bad."

Dennis just sighs, clearly not fooled by the ruse.

"You're right," I say, eager to play along. "I never did apologize for farting at your birthday party in front of all of your friends."

"And stinking up the whole laser tag arena."

"And stinking up the laser tag arena," I say.

"Good work, Avery," Dennis says, monotone, patting her on the shoulder without breaking eye contact with me. He reaches out and turns the small vial of polish on the table toward him.

"What a pretty color," he says, *still* looking at me, as he knocks it over, quite clearly on purpose, spilling it into a small puddle. "Oops. Avery, would you mind grabbing me some paper towels?"

He gestures to the front of the room, where there's a small bathroom just to the left.

"Uh, sure," she says before scooting her chair out and scurrying off.

"Three days," Dennis says as soon as she's out of earshot.

"I'm sorry?"

"There are three days left of this camp. And I gotta tell you, John, I don't think you're making the most of this opportunity. You don't get many like this."

"I don't know what you're talking about. Avery and I just had a serious moment, didn't you notice?"

"A fart joke? Really?"

"This just in: eleven-year-olds love fart jokes."

He purses his lips and nods.

"OK. I won't force you out of the nest yet if you're not ready. But I might have to if you don't start flapping those wings soon."

"Am I a baby bird in this scenario?"

"Just, don't . . . ," he begins, his voice suddenly turning deeply sincere. "Just don't leave anything unsaid, OK?"

"Dennis, I am extremely *annoyed* at the way you keep badgering me, and I am becoming more and more *frustrated* with this entire experience. How's that?"

He chuckles. "I know you're making fun of me, but that's actually a good start. Keep practicing!"

Avery reappears with a giant wad of toilet paper. "This was all I could find."

Dennis pats me on the shoulder and moves on to the next group.

"That was good, right?" Avery says, grinning as she sits back down. "Hit me down low."

We sneak a low five under the table. But my heart's not in it, because I'm busy replaying what Dennis just said.

"You know," I say. "If there was something, a time when I let you down, you could tell me about it."

"I know," she says.

"I can handle it, really. You know that, right?"

"Of course." But she won't meet my eyes, and that makes my heart sink.

I feel the weight of A Moment upon me. As obnoxious as springing this exercise on us out of nowhere is, we *are* here to work, and I *do* want to walk out of here better than we arrived. We should start over, and we should talk about the soccer tryouts, and I should tell her the truth. And I should offer to take her home early, because there's still time.

But I don't. Maybe Dennis is right—I'm not ready to leave the nest.

I grab the toilet paper and begin sopping up the mess, and after that I get back to work on her nails, and we talk and we laugh and we make jokes. It's exactly what I wanted. But I can't stop thinking about what I would say to her if I was brave enough to be really honest and what she might not be ready to say to me.

Twelve

"Great parenting back there, jackass."

I think Lou's talking to me, and my heart skips a beat, but I turn to see him standing in the doorway of our cabin and he's addressing Ryan instead, who's brooding on the edge of his bed.

We're back at the cabin for a little downtime before the afternoon's activities.

"The hell did you say?" Ryan responds.

Yep. Nothing like a little R & R.

"I mean that was just a top-notch hissy fit. Bravo," Lou says, clapping sarcastically.

Ryan stands and meets him eye-to-eye. They're about the same height, well-suited for a showdown like this.

I shuffle a little closer to them, doubting they'll actually come to blows, but figuring I should be ready to pry them apart anyways. I'm the only neutral party here if things go sidewise.

Lucky me.

"Take it easy, guys," I say, placing a hand on Ryan's chest, my pink fingernails sparkling under a sunbeam.

Avery convinced me to splurge for the upgrade, and in this moment, it's worth every penny.

"Don't worry, I'm not about to get my feathers ruffled by a guy who bakes cookies and plays dollhouse all day long," Ryan snaps.

Huh? I have no idea what he's talking about, but Lou's face sinks, and he backs down just a tad.

"Yeah, yeah, I got you figured out, bud. You're a *stay-at-home dad*." Ryan says this with such disdain, like it's the worst possible thing a man could be.

"OK, you got me. I admit it. At least I'm man enough to tell the truth. How about you?"

"If you want to have a conversation about being a man, I'm gonna need to call your wife and talk to her. She is the man of the house, right?"

"Hey, if you need to talk to mine because yours won't answer your calls anymore, be my guest." Lou shrugs, playing aloof but not sounding fully convincing.

"Keep going." Ryan laughs, taking a menacing step forward. "I'm literally dying for a reason."

"Daddy?" Tam cries out. She's standing in the doorway.

Lou glares at Ryan, then kneels down to his daughter. "What's up, kiddo?"

Ryan backs up and plops himself on his bed, kicking his feet up casually.

Tam looks back and forth between the two men, sensing the hostility. "Are you fighting?"

"No, of course not, baby. Just talking, that's all."

Tam's not completely buying it, eyeballing Ryan like he's an intruder. She wraps her arms around Lou for protection. "He seems mean," she whispers.

Lou squeezes her tight; Tam buries her head in his shoulder.

Something about the tender scene breaks something in Ryan, who watches them closely, not angry but something else. After a moment, he pops up and storms off, front door slamming behind him.

"Don't worry about him. What do you need?" Lou asks his daughter.

"My braid came out. Can you redo it for me?"

I watch Lou operate on it, his fingers moving gracefully but his gaze landing vacantly somewhere on the wall behind Tam.

I could never claim to fully understand what it's like to be in his shoes. But I might understand more than most. Evelyn outearns me by a laughable amount, and I spend more time washing dishes and driving Avery to dentist appointments than she does. It works for us, but it's not usually something either of us is keen to highlight in conversation because, well, because of people like Ryan. I feel horrible that Lou had to endure that, especially here, among what should be his people.

"There," Lou says, stepping away.

Tam, with no mirror in sight, pats her head gently on all sides, gauging her fixed-up do.

"It doesn't feel even."

"It's even."

"I can feel it." She frowns. "It's not right."

"Tam," Lou groans, growing exasperated. "It's even enough."

"Make it *even*!"

"I'm not a professional hairdresser, am I?!" Lou finally snaps.

"You're old enough to do it yourself now, or you can ask one of the other girls if you don't like the way I do it."

Tam sinks, eyes welling up just slightly. Without another word, she walks out.

Lou slumps over. "Idiot," he mutters to himself, rubbing his temples. "I should go after her, huh?" he says in my direction—but he doesn't get up.

"You want me to check on her?" I offer.

"No, I'll go. Just . . . I could use a minute."

He looks up at me expectantly, and I realize he wants me to leave him alone. I stand and place a hand on his shoulder, my body suddenly feeling foreign and stiff and uncomfortable. Lou is vulnerable now, hurt, upset, and as much as I want to comfort him, I just don't know him well enough to know what to say.

"Don't let him get to you," I land on.

Good one. That'll fix everything.

"Thanks." Lou throws himself facedown on his bed, and I make my way quietly out of the cabin.

I walk for a while, aimlessly at first but then consciously avoiding the well-trafficked areas of camp—the field, the cabin area, the bathrooms. The last thing I want is to run into Ryan. In my head, I'm counting up to an appropriate amount of time until I can safely go back to the cabin.

Eventually, I stumble upon Booker—absent during the confrontation—standing sort of aimlessly by a boating shed on the edge of the lake.

"You're not going to believe what just happened," I say, but he doesn't respond. He's facing away from me, staring at the water.

"Booker?"

"Yeah, yeah, I hear you," he says, but I realize he's not talking to me. He's got little white earbuds poking out the side of his head and his cell phone held down by his waist.

"The thing is I'm supposed to be off this week, I put in for it months ago, and I've been helping out as much as I can . . ." He trails off, listening to whoever's on the other end.

I should probably let him have his privacy, I think without budging.

"Uh-huh. Uh-huh . . . ," he goes on. "Well, I sent over my edits last night despite having no Wi-Fi and a half a bar of cell service, and I got a hold of that angry contractor this morning. Got my ass reamed out for it, and . . . Yes, yes I understand . . . No it doesn't sound like something a team player would say."

From behind, I can see his body slump dramatically, and he lets out a huge sigh.

"I'll get it to you as soon as I can . . . Tonight? Well . . . OK. I'll get it to you tonight."

I shuffle away and make myself scarce before he hangs up and turns around. I don't know him that well. I hardly know him at all, in fact. And besides, he'd probably just think I was eavesdropping, which I wasn't. I just happened to be standing near him during a private conversation, minding my own business.

I decide I've been gone long enough and I begin to head back to the cabin. As I round the corner of the trail taking me back, I hear him behind me—he lets out a primal, furious yell that echoes across the lake.

LOU

Babe,

Greetings from camp! I'm lying in my bunk right now—we've got a little downtime—and since I can't call or text you, I thought I would write and tell you a little about how the week is going. So old-school, right?

I guess the short version is, it's going great! The camp is beautiful, and it's been so refreshing to be around other dads. They're all great. Just awesome. We're getting along fabulously.

But enough about me.

Tam is taking it slow, of course. She hasn't fully let loose yet, but I think she's getting there. She likes the other girls in her cabin—they're all a few years older than she is, but they're really sweet with her. So that's good.

Still. We miss you. I'm used to missing you, but it never seems to get any easier.

You've been working too hard. Don't think we don't notice, me and the girls. Especially Tam. Of course she does—she tells me all the time, whines for you, doesn't understand why you have to be gone so much. And I don't tell you that to tug on your heart strings or guilt you in any way, I know how agonizing it is to video call us from the plane and see Tam's little tears and be stuck so far away, knowing you're the only one

who can make them stop and still be unable to. I know that sucks.
Believe me. But I also know how proud you are of being a female pilot
among the gaggles of men who can barely hide their disdain for your
presence, the little girls who beam at you during cockpit tours when
they realize their captain is a woman. Still, it's a sacrifice to be gone so
much, missing so many things, and I just want to tell you that the girls
are so lucky to have a mom like you. They are, really! They won't want
for anything, and they'll grow up with the most badass role model of a
mom ever, and they'll get older and they'll believe that anything is
possible for them, because you showed them it was. And they'll thank
you one day. I'm thanking you now.

Now that I've buttered you up, and I have all these blank pages to
fill, there's something I wanted to talk to you about:

The job.

The restaurant doesn't open for another two months, but they
actually want me to start next week, once Tam is settled in school. I've
already put in a lot of work, developing the menu, interviewing staff.
Very fancy, very high-end. Everything is in place. It's a done deal.

The only problem is I'm pretty sure I don't want to do it.

OK, so there's the minor issue of our budget. We've already
factored the money in, and we're counting on it now. But it doesn't feel
right to me. I've had a pit in my stomach since the day I accepted the
offer. I can't sleep, can't shake this feeling that something is wrong.
I just haven't been able to tell you, because I didn't know exactly what
it was that was bothering me, how to put into words that make sense.
Until now.

The nannies we've interviewed are great, I'm sure the girls would love
them. But the thought of being away from the kids so much—missing
weekends, evenings, needing to catch up on sleep during the day when

they're home, both of us gone all the time and leaving our kids with strangers, spending all of our extra money on childcare—it's sending me into a panic. I don't think I can do it.

I don't think I want to.

I've been saying for years that this is what I wanted, to be able to go back to work and do a job that I'm proud of. But that's just not who I am anymore. I haven't been that person for a while.

The girls, being their dad—that's what I'm most proud of. I admit, sometimes it bothers me, the way people judge me everywhere I go. I can't seem to get away from it. But it bothers me more when I think that soon, I'll be just like everyone else, all the other working dads. Like I'd be caving in or something. Letting the bullies win. Conforming.

I'm a realist, though. The girls don't need me sitting at home twiddling my thumbs and folding laundry all day waiting around to pick them up from the bus stop. I need to do something with myself, something more for our family.

And it's got me thinking.

I could finally open a place of my own, like we used to talk about years ago. Remember that? A little lunch place for the business crowd—small plates, upscale sandwiches, maybe cocktails if I can get the license—nothing that would keep me too late into the evenings. Something I could do on my own terms, my own schedule, and still have time to be Dad first and foremost. Maybe I could even find a space not too far from school. Tam could walk there after dismissal and settle into one of the booths. She could do her homework there at the table and snack on whatever she wanted from the menu, I could make funny-face quesadillas, burgers with extra cheese, whatever she wants. When she's done, she can help me behind the counter for a while—earn a few bucks from her old man while I teach her how a restaurant works, how to operate the register, how to clean up after yourself (she'll need a lot of help there). She'll like that, right? I can dream, anyway. And hey, I was thinking, maybe I'll get a milkshake machine and when she's done and I'm closing up so we can head home for dinner, she can make herself a milkshake sometimes. Not every day! But sometimes, as a special treat, and that'll be something she remembers fondly about all the hours spent there at the restaurant. With me.

Maybe it'll do well, really well. I think it could anyway. And you won't have to fly so much. Of course if you want to, we would support you, but maybe you'll have more down days at home where you can settle into that booth with Tam and check over her math (you know I'm no help with math). You don't have to come behind the counter and help out, you can sit and read a novel, I'll bring you blended smoothies, plates of truffle fries, anything you could possibly want. It'll be my turn to take care of you.

In the evenings, we'll all be together. I get so excited just thinking about it. I'd have more time to make us wonderful family dinners, assuming Tam grows out of her mac-and-cheese-only diet one of these days, and we can play board games together or read books until the girls fall asleep. And then it'll be just you and me again, glasses of wine by the fire, complaining half seriously about the pile of dishes, maybe doing some . . . other things. You can use your imagination, too, you know.

You think I'm nuts, don't you? It sounds impossible, writing it out like this. Believe me, I know the risks. Restaurants have a way of swallowing all of your time, and all of your money, becoming a never-ending series of disasters. Clogged drains and floods, broken equipment, bad reviews. There's no limit to the number of things that can and will go wrong.

But I think I have to try. I just have to. I want the girls to see me fly, like you.

We'll talk more when I get back. We'll figure it out together, like always.

I can't wait to get home to you.

Love,

Lou

Thirteen

As bad as I feel about Booker, there's not a whole lot of time to think about what he's going through, or Ryan and Lou, or anything else. We're due at the Triumph Lodge for men's group, volume two. To say I'm dreading it would be a massive understatement.

We all gather outside the building, first me and Ryan—shockingly, we don't have much to say to each other—then Lou comes straggling in. There's, yet again, no sign of Booker.

Dennis is the last to arrive, a few minutes past the scheduled start time.

"Sorry, sorry," he huffs. "Was just finishing up with another group. Now . . . who's excited for today's session?!"

None of us offer a reaction. A real live crowd we've got here today, great vibes.

"As we discussed last time, you'll all be taking turns this week leading a session. Ryan was brave enough to handle the first one, thank you, Ryan, and today I was feeling *spontaneous* and decided to just pick someone . . ."

Oh please God, not me, not me, not me.

"But then Lou here volunteered. And, good sport that he is, he prepared something really special for you. Thank you, Lou."

"I just couldn't sit through another session of Man Cards," says an agitated Lou, clearly pissed at his past self for agreeing to this.

Instead of walking us into the lodge, Lou leads us to the dining hall, through the cafeteria, and back into the kitchen. There are a handful of stations set up with ingredients, aprons, and tools for each of us. Well, four in total, even though only three of us are here.

"This is where I leave you, gentlemen," Dennis says. "You're in excellent hands, and I hope you can all learn something—hey, aren't we missing someone? Where's Booker?"

Ryan and Lou shrug. I'd answer, but I truly don't know where he went since I saw him at the lake.

"No one knows?" Dennis sighs. "He seems to be missing in action a lot this week." Then, changing his voice to an annoyed grumble, he adds, "I've got half a mind to kick him right out of here if he's not going to bother putting in the work."

"I think he's got a stomach bug," I find myself piping up with.

"Oh?" Dennis raises an eyebrow.

"Yeah, bad one. Been bothering him all week."

"What on earth could have given him a stomach bug?"

"It could be food poisoning," I say, looking around the kitchen.

Dennis swallows hard and clears his throat.

"I think he's working his way through it," I add. "He'll be back on his feet in no time, I'm sure."

"Hmm. Well, let him know I hope he feels better next time you see him," Dennis says with obvious suspicion.

Then he walks out, leaving the three of us standing awkwardly in the cramped kitchen, unsure where to put our bodies. Feeling crowded, I shuffle my way over to one of the stations and start fiddling with a wooden spoon.

"So as you can probably guess, we're going to cook," Lou announces. "I may not be a *professional* chef anymore, as some of you have so kindly pointed out . . ."

Ryan turns a little red but meets Lou's gaze.

"Still, I like to practice my skills at home when I can, to stay sharp. The only problem is, this kitchen doesn't have, well, anything. So I pulled together what I could find, and what Dennis would let us use. And it looks like we're going to learn how to make homemade pasta."

I look down at the stainless steel counter in front of me. I see flour, eggs, olive oil, salt, and nothing else. Ryan lets out an audible groan.

"Hey, if you'd rather sit around and *share our feelings* more, as you put it, you can be my guest. Otherwise how about we all shut up and mix up some dough so we don't have to talk to each other?"

"Fine by me," Ryan grunts.

Lou then walks us through making a simple pasta dough. We measure flour out onto the counter, make a little well in the middle of it, pour in a few eggs with olive oil and salt, whisk the wets together, and start mixing everything with our hands. It's messy, and, frankly, I don't really see the point. I could have boiled Barilla and been done with this fifteen minutes ago. This is the kind of thing I might consider doing in a class setting, with Evelyn and a few glasses of wine. In fact, I think she actually booked us something like this a year or two ago, but we never got around to using it after rescheduling twice. Eventually, the class credit expired.

"So do your kids really eat these noodles?" I ask.

"Oh, heck no," Lou says. "Tam and her big sisters all prefer out of the box."

"So why go through the trouble?"

He gives me this look, like he can't believe how big an idiot I am. I'm not sure what I'm missing.

"I don't do it for them, I do it for me. Something about the kneading, working with my hands, having something at the end I can be proud of. I don't know. When you spend all day with the kids like I do"—he shoots Ryan a look—"you need something like this at the end of the day sometimes."

I still don't really get it. We're just squeezing gooey flour. Yay, I guess? I can think of a lot of different ways I could spend the time. Hey, I'm sure the noodles will taste great, but personally I'd rather spend less time making dinner and more time enjoying it with my family.

"Argh," Ryan growls. "This isn't working. It's all just a slimy mess. You must have gotten the recipe wrong."

"I used to run the entire kitchen at a Michelin-star restaurant, but you're right, a basic pasta dough is *technically* above my pay grade."

"Well, something's fucked up, that's all I know."

"Be patient, you have to knead it for a while. If we had a mixer, that would help, but . . ." He gestures around the dilapidated kitchen.

"What a waste of time," Ryan says, flicking wet dough off his hands.

Lou ignores him and continues working his own dough, looking somehow forlorn. Tired. Ryan watches him for a moment and softens, opens his mouth to speak, but nothing comes out. Lou looks up just as Ryan looks away, and I can't help but chuckle at the silly little dance the two of them are doing.

Finally, I catch Ryan's eye and nod my head, encouraging him to mend the fence. Ryan shakes me off with a furrowed brow and gets back to kneading. Too stubborn.

I peel a bit of dough off my hands and roll it into a perfect ball. Then I toss it at Ryan. It plunks him square in the forehead, getting his attention. I nod my head toward Lou again. *JUST DO IT, ASS-HOLE*, I scream with my eyes. Ryan gives me the finger, and then a smirk, and then—believe it or not—an honest-to-God smile.

And then we're both laughing.

"What did I miss?" Lou says, looking up.

"Could you, maybe, uh"—Ryan grunts—"give me a hand?"

Lou blinks.

"Sure," he finally says. "Here . . . Take a break." He walks over to Ryan's station and puts his hand in the gooey dough pile.

Then he begins to knead the loose ball of dough expertly, hands weaving up and down and folding and pinching. Ryan and I just watch him work for a minute, transfixed. And in what seems like no time at all, the dough ball has taken shape, formed a drier and more manageable consistency, and started to look . . . tasty.

"All yours," Lou says, yielding the station back to Ryan.

"Thanks, Lou."

"Thank me at the end when you taste it."

We keep going, kneading and folding away. None of us says much to the others.

Eventually, when the dough balls are ready, we cut them into pieces, roll them out thin, fold them over like an accordion, and slice them into long ribbons. Once unfolded, they become noodles.

Thick, misshapen noodles, at least in my case, but noodles nonetheless.

"They have to dry for a while before we can cook them," Lou says. "But hey. We did it."

There's something welling up inside of me as I stare at these stringy shoelaces of dough. Pride? Maybe a little.

But more than that, it's been a long while since I thought of food as an experience like this, something that can bring joy beyond the way it tastes, beyond the way it fills your stomach. Since I've thought of it as more than just another chore to fit into the evening routine, a battle over how many vegetables you can harangue your child to eat. My thoughts go back to Evelyn and the pasta class we never took, and back even further to our earliest dates. The fun and chaos of rotating sushi bars, drinking too much sake, colorful plates whizzing past us as we laughed and fumbled to grab whatever we could. Homemade fondue, us flirting over the top of the steaming pot while cheap cuts of meat cooked slowly in bubbling broth. My first attempt to impress her in the kitchen, a soggy, collapsing soufflé that took nearly all day to make—and her pretending she liked it even though she could barely choke down more than a couple of bites. That was it, the moment I knew she liked me as much as I liked her. At some point all of that gave way to a different culinary experience, what could be cooked quickly, what made sense for the meal plan, what would give Avery the nutrients she needed without her hurling it across the room. I guess it just feels nice to be reminded of the way it was before.

After we clean up, the three of us head outside. Dennis is already waiting for us, like an excited mom anxious to hear how a play-date went.

"So . . . ?" he pries.

"Dinner is served," Lou says.

Just then, Booker jogs up, breathless.

"Sorry . . . sorry I'm late," he pants.

"Feeling any better?" Dennis says.

Booker gives a quizzical look, but I jump in as quickly as I can to add, "You know, from the stomach bug. I know you've been stuck in the bathroom most of the week."

He meets my eye, gives a thankful smile, and says, "Yeah, the stomach bug. I'm feeling a little bit better, thanks. So . . . what did I miss?"

Thirteen and a Half

Avery is six and a half years old, and she's a Tasmanian devil of excitement, spinning in circles and sprinting a loop around the house.

The house, which is a mess. It's early evening, and our floor is covered in Avery's clothes, which she's kicked off and thrown haphazardly so she could change into shorts and a tank top.

Her shoes are sitting in the middle of the hallway, ready to trip an unsuspecting parent or two. There's a water bottle rolling around on its side in the corner, a gym bag half zipped and about to fall off the table, and an assortment of snack choices scattered on every surface in eyesight.

It's Avery's first soccer practice tonight. The first one ever. Her first time playing organized sports at all, and she's bursting out of her skin in anticipation.

She finishes slipping on her second cleat and runs up to me in the kitchen, giving me a huge squeeze.

"Daddy, why can't you come?"

Evelyn, scooping up the bottle of water and placing it in the bag, answers for me. "Because Daddy has his magic group tonight, you know that. It's every Thursday."

Every Thursday like clockwork, for, at the time, something like six straight months. We meet up—me and a buddy Jason, who lives a few neighborhoods over, we met through the PTA when Avery started kindergarten, plus a few other guys I met on Reddit, and yes I know how that sounds—at this deserted shithole of a bar near my house. It's quiet, and no one will be there to judge us for being absolute, irredeemable nerds as we pass around a deck of cards, working up a buzz while we try to fool one another like we're on that Penn and Teller show.

Avery taps me on the shoulder to make sure I'm watching, then slowly contorts her face into the saddest puppy-dog pout you've ever seen.

"Hey, knock that off," Evelyn says, playfully bopping Avery on the head with a shin guard. "Mommy and Daddy both need a little time for themselves every now and then, that's all."

"Besides, I'll be at the first game on Saturday. I wouldn't miss that for anything," I say. "Not even if I slipped on a banana peel and broke my leg, or got trapped under a boulder."

"Even if you died?"

"I will be there, even if I'm dead."

"Even if you turn into a zombie?"

"I will be there, and I'll turn the other team into zombies like me, so they'll run slower."

"Ew, stop it, you two," Evelyn scolds. Our dark and goofy sense of humor isn't always her thing.

"But I really want you to come to the first onnnnnnnne," Avery insists.

I bite my lip, thinking it over. She's got a point. The first sports practice *ever*? It's a pretty big deal. I love meeting up with the guys, but I do that every week. I'm no good when it comes to magic anyway, not really—there's no point to it, no end goal. I'm not trying to book any children's birthday parties or make it big in Vegas, not interested in the dark-eyeliner-and-leather-pants look. Though, I tease Evelyn all the time that she'd be a lovely assistant. It's all just a way to blow off steam, that's all. And it's fun being able to pluck quarters out of Avery's ears or make her laugh by pulling an endless scarf out of my mouth. What I'm about to miss could be a once-in-a-lifetime event. Evelyn catches my eye, and she knows what I'm thinking. Her laser-focused pupils seem to be speaking to me: *Don't give in.* I ignore them.

"All right, I'll come."

"Yay!"

Evelyn sighs, but we're already running late, so we scramble around, grabbing everything we need and then we're out the door. In the car, I tell Evelyn that I texted the guys and they said it was cool to meet later that night. They're night owls anyway.

Even though Avery's a total newbie, not just to soccer but all sports, she's completely dominant in her very first outing. Sure, it takes her a few minutes to warm up, but then it's like something clicks in her mind; I can almost see it happen, like she's seeing the code of The Matrix. And by the time we reach the short scrimmage session at the end of practice, she's weaving through her teammates with ease, blowing past other girls with her speed. Her shots are wild

Evan S. Porter

and all over the place, but she has an unmistakable knack for finding the ball. This bizarre sensation comes over me for the first time, and it's one I'd get more and more familiar with over the years, watching my child, a person literally constructed of pieces of me, do something that I could never do. I am and always have been a terrible athlete, and I'm a casual sports watcher at best, but watching her unleashes something in me, and it's all I can do not to rip my shirt off and paint *AVERY* on my chest with Evelyn's lipstick.

Afterward, it's late and dark, and we rush home and throw together some grilled cheese sandwiches with microwave vegetables. Everyone scarfs their dinner so we can get Avery to bed, but she's completely filthy from practice. So bath time it is. We finally get her to bed, and I hustle downstairs to grab my keys and head out to the bar. By this point, I'm exhausted and I barely want to go. My eyes sting with the effort of keeping them open, and I swear I can hear our bed whispering its siren's call.

But I feel too bad about letting the group down to bail.

Before I can make my exit, I can't help but take note of the massive pile of dishes climbing out of the sink, as if it's coming to life. How could there be so many dishes? All we did was make grilled cheese! I put it out of my mind and walk toward the door, stepping over everything we didn't pick up before we had to leave for Avery's practice, which is a lot. In the living room, Evelyn sits cross-legged on the floor in front of a mountain of laundry.

"Have fun," she says, blowing me an air-smooch.

God. I can't leave like this. The house is a wreck. I wouldn't feel right abandoning Evelyn to tackle it all by herself. And it's not because I'll be in "trouble" later if I go—Evelyn has never been that type. She legitimately wants me to go. But I legitimately don't think I should.

I pull out my phone and send a text on the group thread:

SORRY GUYS. CAN'T MAKE IT TONIGHT AFTER ALL.

And then I sit down next to my wife, and I grab a pair of Avery's pants from the stack and I fold them, poorly, and place them in the folded pile.

"What are you doing? Aren't you late?"

"Some of the other guys couldn't make it, so we called it off."

I reach into the pile again, and this time my hand comes away with an extremely tiny pink shirt, maybe something shrunken from the dryer? Checking the tag, I realize the size is twelve–eighteen months.

"What's this doing in here?"

"Oh, I was packing some things away, it must have fallen in," she says. "Gosh, I can't believe she was ever that little."

"Should we put it aside to give away, or . . ."

"Keep it?"

"What do you think?"

"What do *you* think?"

The truth is I don't have to think about it at all.

"It's still in pretty good shape," I say. "Only three or four major stains on it. Seems like it'd be a bit of a waste to just get rid of it."

I smirk at her, and she smiles back, knowing exactly what I mean.

"Sorry again about your club tonight," she says as we continue working.

She's bummed for me, I can tell. But I don't bother telling her that I'm the one who canceled. She'd just give me a speech about how I deserve a night off, and how it's good to take a break every now and then, even if you have to let a few things slip.

But the truth is I'm exactly where I want to be.

Fourteen

We're huddled behind a massive tree in the middle of the forest lining the camp, panting and speaking in hushed tones. There's a raging game of capture the flag swirling around us—this afternoon's main event. It's eerily reminiscent of a Civil War battle. Think bayonetted men running through dense tree cover, bullets whizzing past in a cloud of musket smoke, lots of yelling and cries of "Medic!" and nearby explosions.

It's like that just with, you know, less weaponry and fewer muttonchops.

"OK," Avery huffs, sporting a new hairdo I don't recall seeing from her before, a messy bun, reminiscent of the way her counselor Megan wears it. "I need your help."

She needs my help because she's getting her ass kicked. All the girls are. Hey, it was their idea to play kids versus adults. The handful of dads who are actually in decent shape (I consider myself on the outer fringe of this group) are dominating the game, and we're currently up four captures to two. One more capture for the grown-ups wins the game.

"You must be desperate to come to me," I whisper, laying it on thick.

A panting, beer-bellied dad comes plodding past. Avery and I duck down low and wait for him to pass, twigs and leaves crunching beneath his feet, getting softer and softer until he's gone.

"I'm the only one on the girls' team who's any good," she says, and I hate to admit it, but she's right. Apparently she's back to playing at full speed again, so she's scored her squad's only two captures. Meanwhile three-quarters of the girls' team has been tagged on our side of the field, landing them in "jail" deep within Dad Territory.

Unfortunately, this has led to a bit of a stalemate. The few remaining girls have hunkered down to play defense, and since all the dads are winded and looking ahead to dinner, no one's been able to get close enough to score the final capture.

"We can't win unless you help me," she pleads.

"Are you asking me to sabotage my own team?"

"I just need you to create a division."

"You mean a diversion."

"So I can break the others out of jail."

"If you're so good, what do you need them for?"

"Once they're out, *they* can make a division—"

"Diversion."

"—for me, and I can get a capture."

It's a decent plan, but the dad in me has to pause and think for a second. Last time I was over by our base, I caught a few of the jailed girls talking—and I'm not sure how keen they're going to be on this plan. They're in no hurry to get out. In fact, I think they were happily playing some kind of game with sticks. One of them said, "She's gonna beat us all to the flag again anyway, so we might as well stay here." It didn't take a genius to figure out who they were talking about. Avery's been playing possessed today.

"All right, if I'm gonna stick my neck out for you," I say, "you gotta do something for me."

"OK, what?"

"Work together with the other girls. I'll distract the dads guarding the flag, and you guys can come up with some kind of maneuver to steal it. Just . . . try to involve your teammates a little."

The group of girls seemed to start off on an OK-enough foot, so it bums me out to see that they might be souring on Avery a bit. As much as I want her all to myself, no parent enjoys seeing their kid get left out.

"But it'll be easier if I do it alone."

"Probably. But I think it would be a nice gesture."

"So I should, like, let one of them get the flag instead of me?"

"Maybe, yeah," I say.

"You know Megan says I shouldn't ever have to hold back for anyone, I should give a hundred percent and if people can't hang with me, then that's their problem."

Megan's influence. Of course.

"She said that?"

"Yep."

"Well, she's right—I mean, kind of. But you don't want to be a show-off, either. Teamwork is important, too."

"You think I'm a show-off?"

Some more footsteps crinkle leaves. A stick snaps. We have to hurry this along. I'd love to explore the nuance of this situation more with her, but we're out of time and I'm just going to end up looking like the bad guy who doesn't understand her as well as *Megan* does.

Suddenly, out of nowhere, a pang of guilt hits me as I remember that today is the day of the rescheduled soccer tryouts, and we're not there. If winning this stupid game is what Avery wants, that's the least I can give her.

"All right, fine, I'll help you."

• • •

Jessie, Tam, Erica, and a few other girls sit in a circle near a thick tree in the jail area of the dads' base. Three dads mill around about fifteen feet away or so—you're not allowed to guard jail or the flag too closely, otherwise the game would never end.

"Guys!" I sprint up to them, hands on knees and panting. "The girls' base is unguarded, I think they all went to the bathroom or something."

"Why didn't you get the flag, then?" offers Bob, the dude who criticized my burgers.

That's two rude interactions with him now, so any trace of remorse I have for sending him on a wild-goose chase disappears.

"Figured we should send a full squadron, just in case they're laying a trap. I'll stay here and guard the jail, you three go."

Jeff, Mark, and Bob—the three survivors—look at one another, shrugging.

Mark sighs. "I should probably go rescue Steve, anyway, or I'll never hear the end of it."

Bob grumbles, "Let's just wrap this up already, I'm starving."

Once my teammates are out of sight, Avery creeps carefully out from behind a small, gnarled deadfall.

"Clear?" she asks.

"Clear."

The imprisoned girls look around.

Jessie speaks first. "What . . . is going on?"

"I'm breaking you out," Avery says as she tags each of them one by one. "Now you distract any other dads that show up while I grab the flag!"

"We're gonna finish our game first," Erica says. There's no malice in her voice, she's just saying what she'd rather do, even if she is being rather blunt about it. Honestly, I respect it and wish I was half that good at speaking up for myself. The girls all get back to whatever they were doing, pretending their sticks are a family of people or something like that. Avery sinks, stung by being ignored, and I'm about to go comfort her when Jessie taps me on the shoulder, staring at her own feet.

"Mr. John?"

"Yeah?"

"Have you seen my dad?"

I haven't seen Ryan since our little Taste of Italy earlier. I'm sure he's off being a dickhead somewhere, but I don't tell her that.

"No, sorry Jessie, I haven't."

"I'm just afraid he's still mad at me."

"Why would he be mad at you? He was the one who . . ."

I pause and realize all of the other girls are watching our conversation, listening intently. I kneel down a bit to catch Jessie's eyes.

"It wasn't right of him to yell like that and make a scene. I think even he would admit that. He loves you very much," I say, not really knowing if that's true—I don't know much about the guy, and the little I know isn't great, but I'd wager that Jessie has a tight foothold deep in his heart somewhere, even if he does suck at showing it.

"Hey, YOU!" a voice booms out, interrupting the serenity of the moment. What now?

I whirl around and there's Booker stomping toward me like a raging bull. He must have known I was listening in on his conversation earlier. Maybe he caught sight of me as he followed the trail back to the cabins from the lake and pieced it together. But why didn't he say something before, after the pasta-making class?

"I can't find my laptop," he says expectantly.

"That's a . . . bummer?"

"It was there when I went to take a shower, and then suddenly it was gone. There are only three people who could have taken it, and my money's on you."

Oh shit. I panic as I remember his work assignment that's due tonight (that I'm not supposed to know about). He must be absolutely freaking out. Still, I'm not going to sit here and be accused.

"What, why me?"

"I don't know, you're clearly bothered by me, and you haven't been afraid of showing it. So maybe you decided to take your insecurities out on me and—"

"*What?!* Whoa, whoa, whoa. I covered for you, man! Weren't you there for that? They were gonna throw you out of here."

"Oh, well then by all means, *thank you*. You know what—"

"It's in the box," Erica squeaks, looking up from her stick game. Booker stops and turns to his daughter. "What?"

"It's in the sad-face box."

"Why . . . How did it get in the sad-face box?"

She picks at the dirt with a stick nervously.

"I put it there."

Booker's flabbergasted, his brain struggling to choose between anger and understanding. After a few breaths, his more tender side wins out, and he kneels down next to Erica.

"Sweetie, why would you do that?"

"You're not supposed to have a phone or a computer," she says, standing now. "Mr. Dennis said so. And all the other dads are following the rules. It's not fair." Face-to-face with her dad, her breath speeds up, her voice growing a little louder with every word.

The color drains from Booker's face in an instant, and you can almost see his heart dropping down into his stomach. "Erica, it's just that my work—"

"No!" she says, with anger now. "This is supposed to be *our* time, you promised! And this whole week—" In an instant, Erica's breathing catches. "You . . . you . . . y—" Loud wheezes pry their way out of her heaving chest. She drops down to a knee.

"Erica!" Booker cries out as he grabs her and sits her on his bent knee. He strokes her hair furiously, as if it will magically heal her, panicking. But just as quickly, he regains his focus.

"Here, here, use this." From his fanny pack—and it's the first time I've noticed that he has a fanny pack on, and now that I think about it, he always does—he pulls a blue inhaler similar to the one I saw Erica use before, and though he fumbles with it, he's able to help her take a labored puff. While he scrambles to help her, two other inhalers and a bottle of pills fall out of his pack and land on the ground.

"It's OK, just relax."

Then another puff. Her breathing eases in an instant, and her body relaxes.

"You can't get yourself worked up like that," Booker says.

I'm about to run and get help, but Booker must notice my body language, and he gives me a gentle *We're fine* motion with his hand.

"Erica . . . are you OK?" Avery asks sweetly, genuinely, and Erica nods. Avery looks to me, cogs in her brain spinning, and I know what she's thinking.

"So we should finish the game, then?" and I notice she's now holding our yellow flag.

Erica may be OK, but she's still catching her breath. Jessie's slouching against a tree, looking like the epitome of sadness. And the other girls are still shell-shocked from the flurry of everything that just happened.

"Maybe let's just take a break," I tell Avery.

"So, what, the dads win?"

"No one wins."

"That's not fair."

"Avery . . ."

"Megan says—"

"Avery!" I shout finally, having heard enough about Megan for one lifetime. The *scholarship water polo player.* We get it. She's tall and athletic. Good for her!

My tone takes Avery by surprise, and she retreats a step or two, so I soften my voice. "There are more important things than the game, OK?"

"I'm going to score, unless someone wants to try to tag me," she says, defiant once again, looking back and forth between Jessie and

Erica, giving a sort of half-hearted attempt to nonverbally comfort them, and then she takes off sprinting toward the girls' side of the course. No one moves to give chase.

There's a hideous energy in the air. I look around, and for the first time I consider the fact that maybe this camp, for all its faults, really does need to exist. These men desperately need it.

For the first time, I think that maybe I do, too.

Ryan's so obsessed with being the family alpha male that he can't take one tiny little baby step out of his masculine bubble to actually connect with his daughter, and now he's off throwing a tantrum about it. Lou, wherever he is, is so ashamed of who he is that he's taking it out on Tam, of all people—I've lost count of how many times he's snapped at her because he's too embarrassed to do "mom stuff" in front of the other dads. And Booker, well, I understand the pressure he's under, but I feel a little less sorry for him watching how his lack of affection is absolutely destroying his daughter.

And then there's me. Despite my best efforts, I have absolutely no idea what's going on with Avery. One minute, she's a sports star and a straight-A student. The next, she's blowing off homework, dropping extracurriculars, and slipping on the field. And now, in a new swing of the pendulum, she's unleashed the full fury of her competitiveness again, but with a selfishness I've never seen from her before. One minute, the girls are getting along great. The next, Avery seems to be almost purposefully alienating herself. I don't get it. And I can't get through to her. Can't get her to talk to me. The only person who seems to have any sway over her now is Megan, who has known her a grand total of three days.

I can't help but feel like I've completely failed her.

Up ahead, I can still see Avery running, though she's realized no one is chasing her and has adopted more of a light jog, and I think, *It might not be too late for me.*

I run after her.

I'm no runner, but these old legs of mine still have enough juice in them to get the job done when needed. You ever hear of a 105-pound mom lifting a school bus off her child with pure adrenaline? I've got a bit of that going on, except instead of lifting a 25,000-pound vehicle, it's attempting to outrun an eleven-year-old girl in a short sprint.

I take off with everything I've got, stray branches whipping at my face and torso as I go, loud footsteps announcing my progress.

Avery hears and turns around and sees me barreling down on her like a freight train. She doesn't stop to ask questions but rather turns on the jets and hits her own top speed, but I've got the momentum, and I'm gaining on her fast.

We're about twenty feet from the girls' base, and seconds away from a capture, when I tackle her to the ground, gently breaking her fall at the last second.

"*Dad!* What are you doing?!" she shrieks.

"I changed my mind," I pant, lungs burning already.

There's the difference between us. Even though I caught up to her, I'll be out of breath for several minutes and probably sore for numerous days after this.

"We had a deal!" she says, beginning to scrape herself off the ground.

"I got a deal for you," I say, and I pull her back to the ground and start tickling her.

It sounds childish, but it's a calculated maneuver on my part—she's bound to be pissed at me for betraying her, but if I can make her laugh, I can teach her the lesson *and* still walk away from this situation as friends. Win-win.

She laughs and snorts, squirming to get away from my wriggling fingers, "DAD!!! OH MY GOD, DAD!!!!" she yells, breathless, letting out loud barreling laughs alternating with high-pitched squeals as I focus in on her ribs and armpits.

"OK, STOP, STOP!" she finally yells. And I always stop when she says stop.

But I guess it's too late, because she just kind of sits there on the ground for a minute, frozen. And then I see it.

A wet stain appears on the crotch of her shorts, growing and spreading fast.

"Oh God, sorry," I say, laughing. "Here, let me help you up."

I can't remember the last time I tickled her past the breaking point like this. At some point I figured I was losing my touch, but apparently I still have it.

"I'll walk you back to the cabin for a change of clothes," I chuckle.

I offer her a hand, but she smacks it away—literally smacks it with some serious force.

"Avery!"

She climbs to her feet and looks around—everyone's there, staring, all the girls and all the dads. Booker and Erica have walked over. There's Jessie and Tam and even asshole Bob sitting in girl jail after a failed capture attempt. No one says anything, and no one laughs.

Then Avery looks at me, and I can see it in her face, a look I will never forget as long as I live. I took it way too far, and she's beyond humiliated. Deeply wounded. Destroyed. In front of an audience no less. And all at the hands of someone she thought she could trust to never hurt her—me. Tears accumulate in her eyes, and she's so mortified and upset I can feel my soul ache.

"Avery, I—"

But she runs off before I can get out the word *sorry*, and she's running full speed now, no use in even trying to catch her.

I just wanted to make her laugh. That's all I've ever tried to do. I didn't mean for any of this to happen.

After that, the game just sort of . . . ends. Everyone floats quietly back to their cabins, and I'm left alone there in the woods.

All I can think is that now, it's official: I am the world's worst dad.

BOOKER

Mom,

You read the name on the envelope right. It's me, Book. No really, it is.

I know, I know, you don't believe it. All I've sent you the past few years are hastily jotted emails with hurried grammar, "Sent from my iPhone" italicized at the bottom like a smarmy reminder of how busy I am. So now one day out of the blue you open up your mailbox and see an honest-to-God letter from me, I don't know how long yet, but maybe several pages. You're probably worried that I've run off to South America somewhere to flee from the FBI, who's after me for some kind of money-laundering Ponzi scheme. I don't know how many times I have to tell you I don't work for that kind of company.

Don't worry, I'm OK.

Or, I guess I am, at least. I don't know. I'm at the camp with Erica, the one I told you about. Not that I really <u>told</u> you anything, but I think I sent you the website link and the dates, as if you'd slot them into a digital calendar somewhere so you knew not to book me for any meetings.

Anyway, we're here together and I'm meant to be having the time of my life, forming forever memories with my daughter, but somehow every day that I'm here I just end up feeling worse and worse. Like a total failure.

You're shaking your head right now, I can see you, and saying what a great dad I am. I know you are, and that you've always thought that. But you're wrong. Because here it's like I've been thrown into the deep end, sink or swim, and I am absolutely drowning. Completely exposed.

Erica had an asthma attack today. Nothing really bad, but it could have been if I hadn't been there. I swooped in like some attentive caregiver, whipped her inhaler out of nowhere, and saved the day. It was a great performance, really. You'd never know that I was completely paralyzed in fear just moments before, and that I had to mentally flip through the little pocket-size notebook Jasmine sent me off with, like an instruction manual, to recall what to do (wheezing and clutching the chest, turn to page 7).

How pathetic is that? I admit it. I don't really know what her medicines are or what they do. There's the blue one, for emergencies, and then the red one, which is for everyday use. And then there's the pills twice a day. I study the manual constantly, Jasmine's extremely thorough instructions for every scenario, and I can barely get my head around it. There's just no space left in my mind, no available storage. It all keeps getting pushed out by plans and deadlines and meetings I'm tracking in my brain. I just feel so behind. I know enough now that I know she needs the blue one when she starts having trouble breathing, but I don't know why she needs it. I wasn't there when it was prescribed, I wasn't there when the doctor explained the need for this specific inhaler versus another, what it does to her body when it's in crisis. I haven't been able to ask questions about it, read up on side effects. I just know <u>blue make breathe good,</u> like some useless caveman.

But if there's one good thing coming out of this camp, out of what happened today, it's that I'm determined to make a change. I don't have a clue yet how to do it. But something has to give. There has to be a way to find better balance. This just can't be all there is. Can it?

And I'm dumping all of this on you now, and I realize how awful it must sound. After all, there's you, with your own doctors' appointments, your own little cube organizers full of medicines. And the best that I could do was outsource all of that to someone else and offer to pay for it.

It's all I ever seem to be good for.

At least I'm trying to keep up with Erica, but with you, I am so hopelessly behind that I think I've given up trying. Don't shake your head, you know it's true. We don't talk, not really. A few chirpy texts about nothing of substance here and there, and the aforementioned emails I spit out between meetings at the office. One or two visits per month where I play the role of attentive son, bringing baked goods and a check, like it's the best I can do.

But what can I do? I don't have enough time for my wife and daughter as it is. If I scratch and claw and make some big, big changes, I might be able to fix it. Might. If it's not too late. But there will be nothing left for you. It's not fair. You're not supposed to have to choose like this. Is this your fate as a parent? Is it going to happen to me, too?

I did have one idea. It's kind of crazy, so bear with me. And I haven't had a chance to talk it through with Jasmine just yet. But what if . . . you came and lived with us? It's very in vogue in a lot of places around the globe, this multigenerational-living thing. And more people are doing it here, too. You might say it's trendy. Hip! You won't miss your bingo nights there at the retirement home too badly, will you? I'm kidding. I know you've made friends there, made a life there, and it wasn't easy to do that with Dad gone. You wouldn't want to "burden" me. Secretly, whether you'll admit it or not, you don't think I'd be able to handle it. Maybe you're right. But we could try. Me and Jas could get you to your appointments, between the two of us. We've got the spare room gathering dust anyway. And Erica would love to see you more. Maybe we could put in one of those little stair elevator things you see on TV! Erica would love riding it up and down endlessly with you. And, well, it would save a lot of money. Give me a little more wiggle room to figure out the next step, how we make this all work. More than anything, it would be nice to have you around more. If it feels like I'm asking you for a favor, it's probably because it is. The truth is, I still need my mom.

Now that I've thoroughly shocked you, it's time for me to go. I'm running out of paper. Probably a good thing. I could fill volumes with all of my failings as a husband, father, and now a son. But give it some thought, will you?

Love,

Booker

Sent from my iPhone
(Just kidding)

Fifteen

The best thing I can do right now would be to go back in time to this morning and take Avery home early, in time for the soccer tryouts.

The second best thing would be to at least stop myself from accidentally humiliating her in front of everyone.

The third best thing, and unfortunately my only realistic option, is to give Avery a little time to cool off.

One of the worst mistakes you can possibly make as a parent is trying to fix a fuckup too soon. You don't cook a stove dinner and immediately start scrubbing the pot—you'd scorch your fingerprints clean off.

Come to think of it, it's not so different in a marriage. But it's even harder to find that space, sometimes. There's a household to run, after all, and the two of you are comanagers. It's like being forced to put the hot kitchen dish right back into use for the next meal, no time to cool, no time to clean, over and over again, with bits of the previous meal hardening into a permanent crust over time. Evelyn and I don't fight—not knockdown, drag-outs, anyway—but there are plenty of petty squabbles. Domestic disagreements. I forget to pay a bill on time. She forgets to add an appointment to the calendar and it gets missed. No one dies in either case, but we get a little snippy, anyway, too tired and claustrophobic to just fucking let it go sometimes and give each other a break.

Admittedly, sometimes it's just easier to let the crust build up than to get in there and really scrub.

I did apologize to Avery, standing outside her cabin, speaking genuine words of regret through the door while she refused to come out (or let me in). Despite my best effort to set a world record for number of times using the word *sorry* in five minutes, I knew it wasn't likely to get me anywhere, and it didn't.

She needs her space.

And I need a distraction.

"Beers?" I say now, standing in the doorway of our cabin, holding a case of bottles in each arm and invoking the ancient spell to initiate an epic guys' night.

The response is tepid at first. The gang is, pathetically and predictably, tucked in and ready for bed at this point. I can't blame them, though. Out here in the woods, all the lights out and no real point of reference for what time it is, 9:00 p.m. feels like the dead of night. Plus, we're all fighting through a sleepy haze brought on by a carb-heavy dinner, an impromptu spaghetti night. Our noodles were fantastic, but none of us were able to enjoy them properly.

Ryan's whittling a stick into what I hope is not a weapon of some sort to kill the next person who ticks him off. Lou's reading with the help of a bendy, battery-operated light. And Booker's lying in bed, staring at the slats of the top bunk, a vacant look on his face. I don't really know what to say; I'm still not sure who's mad at whom, so I had figured "Beers?" would be a safe choice.

Ryan speaks first. "Where did you get those?"

"The beer fairy. What does it matter? You want one or not?"

I stole them from the kitchen, of course, but that's not important. Neither is the fact that I've never heard of this brand before and they very well could taste awful.

Booker swings his legs around, and his feet onto the floor. He's in. Ryan and Lou look intrigued but then catch each other's eyes across the cabin and both pout and harrumph. Still prickly, I see, despite our hour of pasta making.

"I'll sit in the middle as a buffer. What do you say?"

I jiggle the beers, which tinkle magically as they bump together, like beautiful music. Ryan and Lou both offer reluctant grunts of agreement.

We all trek down to the lake's edge, sitting in the deep shadows of the boat shed. The water is dark and placid, with twinkling stars reflecting off its surface. Hidden insects around us create a symphony, fading easily into the background of our conversation. But when you actually stop and listen to them, it's absolutely deafening.

"So you dragged us all out here," Ryan grumbles, pausing to take a swig of his beer. "Now what?"

"Now we get drunk," Booker says vacantly. "That's it."

I nod. He gets it.

"And talk about what? I don't have shit to say to any of you."

Tiny waves lap against the shore of the lake. Beer is audibly gulped. Every once in a while, someone takes a sip and lets out an obnoxious *Ahhh*.

"So . . . ," I say, grasping for an inoffensive discussion topic.

Luckily, I know a good one that never fails. "Anyone watch anything good lately?"

And like magic, the conversation cracks open. Ryan asks if we've seen this new cop thriller on Netflix, and when no one has, he aggressively insists it be the next thing we watch, securing uncomfortable promises from each of us that it will be. Lou is a big movie guy, apparently, up to date on all the new releases . . . for kids.

"Disney/Pixar is slumping a bit right now, but they brought in this new chief creative officer who I really think can get them back to their glory days."

We all stare at him blankly.

"What?"

Booker steers the conversation to podcasts, a staple of his long daily commutes. "I listen to a lot of industry-specific pods. *Archi-TALK*, *Blueprint*, *Design Debate Club* . . ." Then, realizing he's lost us: "Plus I mix it up with shows about whatever sport is in season. That kind of thing."

I talk about Evelyn and my favorite comfort shows and movies, the twenty-year-old comedies we put on before bed to help us wind down and drift off to sleep.

And while the conversation flows, in a certain sense, it quickly becomes clear that we have very little in common, and the shallow well of TV, movies, and media dries up just as quickly as it sprouted.

My main plan, however, seems to be working. The alcohol does its thing, and after only a few more minutes of squirm-inducing silence, the mysterious brew has everyone loosening up. Although it has yet to produce the numbing effect I'm after, blunting the deep self-loathing I feel, wiping Avery's humiliated face from my mind, at least temporarily. But it's coming. I open another beer.

Suddenly, Lou and Ryan, both about three beers in, are leaning across me, hands on the other's shoulders, staring almost lovingly into each other's bleary eyes.

"I shouldn't have criticized your parenting earlier, man. That was messed up. It wasn't my place to judge you," Lou says.

And Ryan, instead of having his hackles up and baring his fangs, accepts the olive branch. "You caught me in a bad moment, Lou. What I said to you was extremely uncool. I'm gonna make it up to you. I have to make it up to you." He looks around. "Here, I'll smash my head into this tree as punishment."

He stands and walks toward a towering oak near where we're seated, fully intent on bashing his face directly into the trunk. Quickly, Lou and I grab him and sit him back down.

"You're forgiven; you're forgiven," Lou says. "I didn't know what you were *going* through." He clutches at his own heart like he can physically feel Ryan's pain. "Why didn't you tell us that she was the one who left?"

"And say what about it?"

"How about the truth?"

"The truth? You want the truth?" Ryan spits, swaying back and forth ever so slightly as he talks. "I was taught that you needed certain things to be a badass, OK? A job that makes a lot of money. A full beard. Some goddamn muscles, for crying out loud. You didn't have any of those things, and you, you are the fucking *man*. It sounds ridiculous, but it completely turned me upside down."

I'm not feeling the buzz just yet, not like these guys are. But it's on its way. I'm sure of it.

"Hey, I have muscles," Lou says, lifting his shirt and revealing a skinny-fat stomach.

We all laugh with him.

"It's what I do," he says. "I can't help myself. I get around other dudes, and I tell myself, I say, *Just be yourself,* but every time, every damn time, I try to take charge and show everyone what a big, tough guy I am. I think, I dunno, I think maybe it'll soften the blow when they find out the truth about me."

"You're ashamed of being a stay-at-home dad?" I ask, still shockingly sober.

"*Fuck* no," Lou says. "I love that shit. I love it. That's right, I'll say it right here and right now, I love braiding hair. I love cooking. I love being silly. I love nurturing my kids, being there for them. Hell, I wish I could do more—I wish I could have birthed them. I wish I could have breastfed them. I would have breastfed the fuck out of my kids, man. And I don't apologize for it! But I don't want people knowing because I don't wanna hear what they have to say about it. It's not because I care. It's because I'm exhausted. I'm tired of the looks I get from moms on the playground like, *Who's this fucker, is he a creep or something?*" He hiccups, then continues. "The shit I get from other dads is worse. I don't need it."

He takes another swig and looks down at his shoes.

"You know, I was a really good chef. Once upon a time. But then kids come along and . . . You can't be at a restaurant all weekend, smoking and drinking with the kitchen staff all hours of the night, coming home at three a.m. I had to give it all up. And you know what? It was the best thing I ever did. I'm tired of pretending it wasn't."

There's a long silence as Lou's words wash over us. Nothing but a few crickets chirping in the grass inches away. I'm expecting the ground to wobble, my vision to spin in dizzying circles, but I'm about as fresh and lucid as ever, despite chugging several potpourri-flavored bottles. What the heck is going on?

"Can I tell you guys something?" says Ryan, whose floodgates seem like they're about to burst open, too. "I would never admit this if I was sober, so if you tell anyone I'll kill you: But I wasn't always like this. Like the way I am now."

"What do you mean?" I ask. I'm expecting my tongue to feel like it's coated in thick Elmer's glue, but it moves freely, and the words come out crystal clear.

"If you can believe it, I was a shy and scrawny kid. Then, I was a shy and scrawny adult. But my wife, my ex," he says, his voice softening. "God bless her, she fell in love with me anyway."

It's so hard to imagine Ryan as anything but, well, Ryan.

"But one day I realized scrawny had turned into tubby and shy had turned into afraid. And I wasn't happy with who I was, where I was going in life. And I decided I wanted to be better. For my boys, mostly. Be a role model and all that. And it started out OK. I got into shape, started dressing better. I got more confident. It was a good thing. For a while."

At this point, I look down at my bottle. And in the corner, in tiny, almost imperceptible, handwritten black text, are the letters NA.

NA?

"But then there are, like, all these rules that come with this stuff. That come with being a quote-unquote *alpha male*, or whatever. And I mean 'rules' literally. I actually googled this shit. *How to be more alpha*."

NA, NA, NA.

And then it hits me. The beer is nonalcoholic. And nobody here is actually drunk at all.

"You can't lean your body in certain directions, you ever hear that? It's too *needy*, too *beta*. You can't ask your wife for permission, for anything. Makes you a *cuck*. There's a whole fucking glossary of terms like that you gotta learn. And, for damn sure, you can't show any emotion around her, or anyone else. You're either happy or angry. Those are your options."

And here's Ryan, and Lou before him, absolutely gushing their inner truths. It occurs to me that they're probably not actually feeling it, either, that maybe they were just looking for any old reason to finally let it out, playing along like an audience member pulled onstage by a hypnotist.

Would it be shittier to tell them now? Or not tell them at all?

"Grace, that's my ex-wife, we stopped spending any time together because I was always so busy working on myself, or trying too hard to show her I didn't need her. And the same with the kids. I was always off with the boys, at martial arts classes and going backpacking with them and teaching them these manly things, but Jessie? Well, she became my wife's responsibility. So I ignored her, too. Who wants to guess how that turned out?"

"You're being too hard on yourself," says Lou.

"Men are supposed to be hard on themselves, right? Do you know I get up at five every morning, fucking *five*, and I run three miles. Then I read and meditate, and then the kids are up and I get them off to school. Then work, where I bust my ass all day long—driving all over the city visiting work sites, meeting contractors. Lift weights at lunch, every single day. When I get home, it's paying bills and fixing shit around the house until midnight most nights, or doing shit like checking my wife's tire pressure, replacing the fire extinguisher—who actually replaces their fire extinguisher? Making sure I . . . always have a plan. Well, I guess it used to be like that. I've had a little more time on my hands lately since I moved out. Not as much to work on. No one to impress. But damn it, I'm still tired! I want someone *else* to drive on road trips so I can look out the window and doze off. I want someone to bring *me* flowers out of the blue. I want to take a *motherfucking bubble bath* sometimes, you know?"

I feel for him, I really do. More than anything, he sounds like someone who's been duped. He put in all this work to become the ultimate manly man and when he reached the mountaintop, he found out it was really a house of cards. No wonder he's so angry.

I also feel a little bad about the circumstances of this confession, the false pretenses, so to speak. And I wish that *I* didn't know that I wasn't actually drunk. It seems so freeing. Because instead of turning down the volume on the pain I'm feeling right now, sitting here listening to the guys has only made me *more* pensive, made me dig even deeper, forced me to unearth memories and feelings I had, not forgotten about but pushed down. Stuff that's itching to get out. This is the right time, the right place. I just can't form the right words just yet.

There's a silence now, a break in the natural rhythm of the conversation. Someone else's turn to go, but I'm not quite ready for it to be me—the only one who knows the truth serum is really a fake.

"It's a wonder anyone has kids at all." I laugh sadly. "It sure fucking hurts sometimes."

"You can love and hate something at the same time," Ryan says.

"And yes, I said hate. It can be the hardest and most unforgiving thing a person ever does, and it can and will take everything from you. Everything."

"But it's impossible to even measure what it gives back," I finish for him.

He nods, like I read his mind.

"I'd start it all over again in an instant," he adds. "You?"

"Of course," Booker says.

A "Definitely" from Lou.

"In a heartbeat," I say without even a thought, and suddenly it all crystallizes for me. Suddenly, the only thing I can see is the little stained, pink onesie I had imagined another little girl—or boy!— wearing. How they never did. How I was OK with that, until I wasn't. How I never regretted our choice, until I did.

But I'm still not ready to speak this out loud. At least, not here. I never used to have trouble opening up in front of other guys—I can still remember sleepovers with my best friends in school, dawn creeping in with all of us sprawled in sleeping bags across my living room floor, whispering about anything and everything (mostly girls), no bit of information too private or sensitive to share. I don't know exactly when that started to feel forced, like swimming upstream, eventually stopping altogether. All I know is that the boys from magic club and I never got particularly deep. I'd come home from an hours-long meetup and Evelyn would ask, "How are the families/wives/kids doing?" and I'd literally have no idea, which always baffled her.

I'd tell her guys just don't share like that with each other unless they're really, really drunk.

Apparently, *thinking* you're drunk can have a similar effect.

"Guys . . . ," I say, ready to clear the air about the beers, because they deserve to know. It feels wrong to keep something like that from them, string them along with a placebo they never signed up for. But the last thing I would want is to embarrass anyone, make them feel humiliated about opening up like they did. I know how hard it is for guys to do that, even under the best of circumstances. Which . . . is why, maybe I definitely shouldn't tell them.

"Booker hasn't had a chance to talk yet," I stammer.

"That's because he's not really here. His mind's been somewhere else all week," Lou says. "It's obvious."

"At least the rest of us are trying, man," Ryan adds, then, "Sorry, fuck. I'm being a judgmental asshole again."

"Nah, I deserve it," Booker finally says. "We're halfway through this camp, and I don't have a single good memory with Erica to show for it."

"Just put the phone away," Ryan says. "It's not that hard. That's what I do. If work doesn't like it, they can eat shit."

"Your job is pretty flexible, then?"

"Yeah."

"That's great. But mine's not."

"So quit. Find another one, man. You only get to enjoy your kids while they're little for so long," Lou says. "That's what I did."

"Quit." Booker laughs. "Just like that?"

The men nod and say *mm-hmm* and take swigs. But not me. I think back to the conversation I overheard not far from where we're sitting now, Booker getting completely chewed out by a swamp monster of a boss. The resignation in his voice, you could feel it. It was like he was trapped and he knew it.

"Let me tell you something . . . ," he begins, like he's gearing up for a spooky campfire story. "Erica has always needed a lot. You've probably seen her running around with her inhaler, a couple of different ones actually. She has asthma, has since she was a baby. She's fine, one of the happiest kids you'll ever meet. But when we're not here it's a treadmill. Nonstop doctors' appointments, and she's got four different inhalers that need refilling constantly. Allergy testing and treatment every month so one day maybe her immune system will be strong enough to come off the medicine. Regular breathing treatments with a specialist. The whole shebang. Of course, I'm not the one who's there for all that stuff." He pauses. "And then there's my mom, all of her care. Do you know how much that all costs? My job might not be flexible, but the benefits are the best around. So . . . I'm stuck."

"Can't you cut your hours back or something? There's gotta be a way," I say.

"Can you walk into *your* boss's office and tell him you want to work half the hours for the same pay?" He sighs. "Sorry, don't mean to snap. But I've heard all the advice before."

"Shit," I say.

"Fuck," Ryan adds.

"Goddamn," Lou chimes in.

"*Shit fuck goddamn* is right. But I guess it doesn't matter, since I'm probably getting fired anyway."

"Why?" I ask. "You've been busting your ass all week here, even though you're supposed to be on vacation. They can't fire you after all that."

"I said I'd send my boss my revisions to some plans he sent, just this stupid thing, and I was almost done with it. But now my phone and laptop are gone and it's"—he pauses to check his watch—"almost midnight, which means I'm gonna miss my deadline."

194

"They're back in the lockbox, I'd bet," I say.

Booker laughs. "Yeah, and? What am I gonna do, break in? Erica's already furious with me. If I get us kicked out of camp, she'll never forgive me."

"Only if we get caught," Ryan says.

I stand up first, then Ryan and Lou follow. The others are a little wobbly at first. I offer a hand to Booker and hoist him off the ground.

"Come on. Let's go rob a summer camp," I say, stifling a burp. We all laugh at the sheer absurdity of it all.

And off we go, like the Fellowship of the Ring. A motley crew of dads, venturing into the dark forest of Camp Triumph to save our friend.

I don't want to be alone in my own head right now, and this is exactly the distraction I need.

Sixteen

The four of us slink our way across campus to the main office.

It's dark and empty inside as we approach the raw wooden wrap-around porch.

"The box was over here on the side of the building," I whisper. "I remember it being bolted down, but we might still be able to get in."

"You guys really don't have to do this," Booker says.

Lou responds with a pat on Booker's shoulder. "We may not be brothers, like Dennis said. We may not even be friends. But we're at least drinking buddies now. That counts for something."

We creep around to the side of the building, near the parking lot where Avery and I first arrived, and I look to the spot where the box should be and it's . . . gone.

Completely gone.

"Shit!" I whisper-yell. "It was right here."

"Relax," Ryan says. "They probably moved it inside."

"That's bad, right? That's really bad," Booker says, looking to me. "Taking my own stuff out of a box is one thing, breaking into a building . . . we can't do that. Right? Let's just turn back."

He turns to leave, but I grab his shoulder.

"Lou's right. We've got your back," I say. "Do you know the kinds of things moms do for each other? There's no line they won't cross in the name of friendship." Then, for effect, "We're dads, dammit! Let's go!"

"We've come this far." Ryan shrugs.

"Guys," Lou announces. "There's no one around us for ten miles, easy. I doubt it's even locked."

"Well, let's get moving, then, I don't like standing out here in the open like this," Booker says, eyes darting around like we're robbing a bank and the cops might show up any second.

Without a word, Lou turns the handle, and the door pops open effortlessly. "See? Easy."

It's a relief, for about half a second anyway before *BEEEEEEEEEEEEEEEEEP.*

"Christ, the alarm!" Ryan yells. "Someone find the unit!"

I burst into the office, past a small reception desk with a couple of chairs facing it to form a sort of waiting room, and scan the walls for an alarm keypad. If it's anything like our system at home, we have something like forty-five seconds to turn off the alarm before it actually calls the police.

Shit.

Lou finds the alarm panel first. "Over here!" he yells, and we all huddle around, but of course, our presence is useless because none of us know the code.

We all stare and contemplate it like it's the *Mona Lisa.*

"We need a four-digit number, anything related to the camp," I guess.

"Try one-two-three-four," Lou says.

"It's not gonna be one-two-three-four! What's the address here? Three thousand something?"

"3220 Elk Ridge, try three-two-two-zero," Ryan says.

I type in the numbers frantically, but it doesn't shut off the incessant *BEEEEEEEEEEEEEEEP.*

"Another one, quick. How about . . . uh . . ."

"Guys, I'm starting to think maybe we should get out of here."

"IT'S TOO LATE FOR THAT!" Ryan bellows with the intensity of a Navy SEAL trying to board an escape helicopter out of a hot zone.

"The-the-the . . . the year the camp was founded maybe?" Booker says.

"1952!" Lou blurts immediately, then: "What? It was etched into that huge boulder. Was I the only one paying attention during the scavenger hunt?"

Here goes nothing: one-nine-five-two. I type each number in deliberately and slowly, no room for mistakes.

A quick *BEEP, BEEP, BEEP,* and the alarm shuts down, finally, mercifully. Thanks to Lou.

"That was close," Booker says.

"We still don't even know if the box is in here," I say, and I take a step toward a small office off the main waiting room, and my foot hits something, and I tumble down hard, hands smacking into the carpet, just barely saving my face from annihilation.

I turn and look back to see what I've tripped on: the box. "All right, so it's in here."

The problem is, the thing is still secured with a thick combination lock.

I try three-two-two-zero and one-nine-five-two and neither work. If I'm being honest, we didn't really think through this part of the plan. The idea was to find the box and then figure out everything else. At least the first part of the plan was a success? But this might be the end of the road. It's not like any of us has a pair of bolt cutters on us.

"What now?" I ask the group.

Ryan picks up the box off the floor, as if inspecting it for vulnerabilities. He gives it a little shake, like a kid trying to figure out what's inside a still-wrapped Christmas present. Then he places it gently down, lifts one of his boots, and stomps clean through the lid, snapping his foot back the instant the wood breaks so as not to damage the goods inside.

"Dude!" I say.

"Holy shit," Booker says.

"Awesome!" Lou adds.

No, not awesome. Not awesome at all.

Ryan kneels down and rips off what's left of the lid, revealing a treasure trove of devices within.

"Problem solved," Ryan says, a smug grin plastered to his face.

"*Guys!*" I shout. "Don't you think Dennis might notice the giant hole in the box?"

Based on their faces, none of the other three had considered this.

"We make it look like some crooks broke in," Lou says. "Trash the place so it looks like a robbery."

"It *is* a robbery!" I say.

Ryan rubs his beard. "Won't work. We're already on those security cameras." He points out two cameras in opposite corners of the office building.

"You knew about those the whole time?!" Booker shrieks. "Why didn't you say something?"

Ryan shrugs. "What can I say, I'm drunk."

I hadn't even thought to look. We're not exactly Clooney and the gang in *Ocean's Eleven*. No, we're idiots. And we're screwed.

"OK, OK . . . I'm pretty tech savvy, I could get into the video storage database and try to erase the footage," Booker offers.

It's a solid idea, in theory, but I'd bet my liver this place stores their security footage on VHS. We could steal the tape?

"This is getting way too complicated, besides, someone might have already heard the alarm anyway," I say, exasperated. "Here's what we do . . . we take everything. We take the box, take all the electronics, clean up the wood fragments, and hope no one realizes it's gone until the end of the week."

The other dads murmur among themselves and consider the plan, then nod their approval. For the record, it's crap, and we all know it. But it's all we've got. Booker reaches into the pile of debris and pulls out his cell phone and laptop, tucks them under his arm, and addresses the group.

"I better hurry and finish up my report," he says. "Can't thank you guys enough."

"Go, get outta here," Ryan says as he picks splinters out of the carpet. I lean down and help him, pinning some of the bigger chunks under my arm. God, there are so many pieces, we are never going to get away with this. Amid the rubble, I find the lock, clinging to one C-shaped piece of wood. I pocket it. I don't know why, it just seems weird to throw it away. Lou finds a spare trash bag in a supply closet and tosses all the phones and tablets into it while Ryan and I go over the carpet with a fine-tooth comb.

"Hey," I say to Lou as we finally walk out, the floor looking pretty much spotless, somehow. "Let me see that real quick."

He hands it over, and I reach in and fish around for my own cell phone. I find it just as Ryan closes the door behind us and locks it up again. The office is dark, and it's like we were never there—if you don't count the giant missing box of expensive electronics.

We walk back toward our cabin, and once we're a good distance from the office, Ryan chucks the wood scraps into some dense brush. Lou jogs ahead with the bag, and by the time we reach the cabin, he meets us empty-handed.

"They can mysteriously show up on the last day, when there's no time for questions."

"Where did you hide them?" I ask.

"Somewhere safe." He winks.

After that, we all head inside and climb into our respective beds. We tuck ourselves in and try to doze off like nothing happened. We don't speak another word about our little heist.

• • •

A little later on, sometime in the middle of the night, I'm lying in my top bunk and I can't sleep. The other guys are passed out from the adventure and the off-brand O'Douls, except for Ryan, who's scribbling away furiously at his letter with help from his phone's flashlight. I'm surprised to see him taking on this assignment with so much zest, but I guess he's still feeling uninhibited. I'm still not quite there, even though there is something on my mind, gnawing at me.

With the adrenaline from earlier long gone, I can't stop thinking about our talk by the lake. The other dads' words echo around in my brain nonstop. The things we've all given up for our kids, suddenly I'm in awe of them, overwhelmed by them. Jessie, Tam, Erica . . . even Avery . . . they'll never know, and it's not their job or responsibility to know, or care. But the sacrifices are immense. Mostly, though, I keep thinking about Ryan asking us if we'd do it again, knowing how hard it is. And how the only answer I could think of in the moment was an Absolute Yes.

My fingers start moving on my phone's keypad, as if on their own, and I send a text to my wife, late as it is.

ME: **Are you up?**

I laugh as I think about what that message would have meant to her when we were younger and dating. A few minutes later she types back:

WIFEY: **Am now. What's wrong, is Avery OK?**

ME: **Everything's fine.**

And then, fueled entirely by the .01 percent alcohol content of the beers but writing with 100 percent sincerity, I text again:

ME: **Do you think we made a mistake?**

I'm about to explain, but I stop myself. She'll know exactly what I'm talking about.

Sixteen and a Half

Avery is eight and a half years old, still an only child, and I am extremely cranky.

Not about that, no. I'm cranky because I haven't had my coffee. In three months.

Plus, it's blisteringly cold outside, and dark. The sun's not even up yet to give us a tease of warmth. My feet send shudders up through my knees as they pound on the pavement. My labored breath turns into thick clouds of steam as soon as it escapes my mouth.

We're running. I hate running.

Evelyn's up ahead of me, bundled in a thick quarter-zip with an ear-warming headband, and I'm struggling to keep pace. She's being really nice about it.

"Keep up!" she shouts. "It's annoying trying to talk with you all the way back there."

"I'm too . . . out of breath . . . to talk . . . anyway," I wheeze.

She just grunts and keeps pushing even faster, leading us down a sidewalk next to an eerily empty residential road.

Yeah—she's cranky, too.

We've given up coffee together. And alcohol. And almost all sugars and other processed junk foods. Basically all the stuff that makes life worth living. And we're waking up to exercise at hours you should only ever see on your clock if you need to catch an early flight.

We're not trying to lose weight or anything. Quite the opposite, actually. We're following a strict fertility protocol, hoping that Evelyn will steadily gain about thirty-five pounds over the next nine months or so.

I dig deep for a little speed and catch back up, going stride for stride next to her now. Up a steep hill.

"I remember this being a lot easier," I say.

"It hasn't gotten any steeper since yesterday."

"Not the hill."

She looks over at me, cheeks red from the cold and the exertion.

"Pining for our twenties isn't going to bring them back."

She's right, but I still can't help pining a little. Avery was easy. A dream, really. We just decided we wanted her, "pulled the goalie" as they say, and voilà! We made a baby.

But trying in our mid-thirties has been different. First it was months and months of agonizing *Yes? No? Maybe so?* moments, almosts, but, ultimately, nothing. And for the last three, we've been trying to optimize our chances as much as we can, tweaking and tracking absolutely everything that's in our control. Diet, exercise, sleep, ovulation cycles, sexual positions. You name it.

I'm even applying an ice pack to some pretty . . . *uncomfortable* areas a couple of times a week to try to maximize sperm production. File that under things I never thought I'd have to do.

Now, on the plus side—we look incredible. We're trim and toned, our skin glowing. I'll just say it—we're the hottest we've ever been. Who knew eating clean and exercising a lot was the key all along? And, though we're exhausted, we're having sex at a nearly inhuman clip.

Yet, neither of us is happy. Because so far, none of this is working. We both know what the next step is, but neither of us wants to be the one to say it and admit we need help.

DING! My phone goes off in my pocket. I reach a hand in, struggling to corral it as it jostles around, and finally pull it out. As I suspect, it's a text from my mom—Avery's with my parents for the weekend because we have our first couple's acupuncture appointment later. It's a bit of a reach, acupuncture, but it can't hurt—a funny thing to say about having dozens of needles jammed into you. Plus we need to get caught up on sleep, workouts, and meal planning—lots of fish and little snack packs of walnuts for me, tons of fruits, veggies, and whole grains for her.

"Put that away. You're going to trip," Evelyn huffs.

I swipe the message open and there's a giant picture of Avery staring back at me, her mouth open in an enormous smile, showing off a brand-new gap where one of her teeth should be. My heart sinks. This tooth has been hanging on by the thread of all threads for days. We've actually had an active betting pool going, between the three of us, over when it would finally fall out. And I absolutely cannot believe we missed it.

Then, of course, I trip. My toes come down on the back of Evelyn's sneaker, flipping it clean off, and we both stumble, barely catching ourselves from a fall.

"What did I just say?!" she yells, picking up her shoe and flinging it at me for effect.

"I'm sorry, I just . . . look." I flip the phone around so Evelyn can see.

She softens in an instant. "Aw," she coos, then "Damn it!" as she turns away from me.

"I know. If it held on one more day, you would have won."

Suddenly, she hunches over. I can tell from tiny, almost imperceptible shivers in her back that she's holding back sobs.

"Hey," I offer, "you were still closest. You did a heck of a lot better than me, I thought that sucker would fall out like a week ago."

The crying doesn't stop.

"Evelyn?"

"I don't want to do this anymore," she chokes, finally turning back around to face me, face puffy and pained, eyes red.

"OK," I say. I jog over to her and place a hand on her lower back, which is drenched in a freezing-cold sweat. "Let's just walk back, then."

"No, not this. *This*," she says, gesturing at, well, everything.

"What do you mean?" But I know what she means.

"We're missing things," she says. "And when we *are* with Avery, it feels like . . . like we're not."

"It's just a baby tooth."

"One of the last ones left," she says, standing there on the curb with one sneaker on. "I don't know about you, but I can't think about anything else. It's like I'm always *somewhere* else."

I don't particularly want to admit it, but I've been feeling the same way. The early wake-ups and the never-ending workouts have been hard, but struggling to be present with Avery has been absolute torture.

"Do you want to make an appointment?" I say.

"Honestly? No."

"No?" I say, tilting my head like I couldn't have possibly heard that right.

"I really don't. Maybe that sounds nuts," she admits. "It might help us, but there might be a lot of pain and heartache down that road."

I swallow hard. I feel like I'm being run over by a tractor trailer, but instead of being thrown violently aside, it's dragging me along the highway, ripping me into pieces. But the last thing I'd want is for her to feel like she's letting me down.

"And bills," I say gently, to let her know I'm on her side. Always. "So many bills."

"So what, then?"

"So nothing. We got the little girl we always wanted, and she is perfect. Maybe that's enough."

She hugs me, burying her face into the crook of my neck. "Are you upset?"

"No," I say. "How could I be? We have Avery, and each other. We're the lucky ones."

It's not a lie, I'm not upset. Disappointed? Maybe. Yeah. OK, yes, I'm disappointed. But how could I not be? I've always wanted a big family, gaggles of kids coming home on holidays when they're grown, stringing along significant others and grandkids and making our house look like one of those overstuffed Hallmark Christmas movies.

I wanted another chance to do the baby thing. Do it right. I'm figuring out this dad gig, ever so slowly, and I think I could do it better this time around. Enjoy it a little more. Suffer through it a little less.

But in my arms, I can feel the tension melting away in Evelyn's body, her shoulders relaxing, her breath softening. And I can feel how much of a weight has been lifted off her. That's all that seems to matter right now.

It's not the way I always pictured it, but it's a perfect moment. Realizing, right here and now, that we've got everything we ever dreamed. We won. We made it to Happily Ever After and now the only thing left to do is actually live it.

If this is it, if our family is complete, I know one thing: I'm going to make every second count.

THURSDAY

Seventeen

I wake up half expecting the usual headache, sandpaper tongue, and skin reeking of alcohol that often follow a night of drinking.

Instead, all I've got is a pit in my stomach. Dread, guilt, and failure, all matted into a thick knot stretching from belly to throat, like some awful hairball in need of being hacked up.

Other than that, I feel great!

Eventually, Evelyn did get back to me last night, saying only **We should talk when you get home,** followed by a **I love you, dummy.**

Probably for the best. In the moment, there was a lot I wanted to say—was it my fault that we stopped trying those years ago? Should I have been stronger for you, pushed us to keep going? Would it be crazy to start trying again with both of us pushing forty? Would we be ready to face the unknowns we might find inside a doctor's office?

We'll talk when we get home. Like she said.

For now, every fiber of my being wants to pull the covers tight over my head and go back to sleep. But I have to get up and be a parent.

It seems like a lifetime ago that in moments like this (where I was actually hungover), I used to chug a water and as many ibuprofen as I could fit into my mouth and sleep for another six hours, or until I felt like getting up and staggering my way to a greasy brunch. Having a baby was a brutal awakening. *Hey, asshole!* tiny Avery would seemingly yell at me from the monitor at 5:00 a.m. *You don't matter anymore! No one cares if you feel like you're going to die! Get your pathetic human form out of bed and wipe shit off my ass and then feed me! And then stay awake all day feeling like hell because fuck you!*

I laugh about it now, but at the time it felt like the hardest thing in the world. Not just being hungover, of course, but the fact that there was never a day off. Not for illness. Not for mental health. Not for nothing.

It's not their fault. Kids need things. When they're babies, they need everything, and they slowly need less and less, but it never really ends. And even now, when my daughter hates my guts and won't speak to me, she needs me.

Not to tickle her into fits of laughter, God no. Not to try cheering her up with excruciatingly corny jokes. No goofy distractions. She needs a dad who understands what she's going through, who can listen and offer advice, who can show her that everything's going to be OK.

Except I've blown my chance at being that guy. Failed miserably at every opportunity.

I feel like a victim of the Peter Principle, where people who are otherwise good at their jobs get promoted over and over again until they reach their level of incompetence. That's me. I was a star employee in the toddler years, exactly what Avery needed in her prime innocent age of five to seven, but now I am wholly unequipped to deal with the mood swings, lashing out, and heavy emotions of the teenager era. Completely out of my depth. Only there's no two-week notice. No layoffs or mercy firings, though I'm sure Avery would love to send me packing.

No, I'm in this for the long haul. I've got to figure it out, one way or another.

I drag myself out of bed and hobble over to the dining hall, figuring that some food will help me decide what to do. At the very least, I'll deliver a bribery platter of waffles and cinnamon rolls to Avery's door, reiterating how sorry I really am and hopefully getting us back onto level ground.

Before I can make it there, I'm intercepted by the counselors, herding everyone toward the big field like a flock of sheep, ignoring pleas from grumpy dads that they be allowed to at least get a cup of coffee first. The rumblings turn into concerned murmurs as a group of us walk.

Something major is going on.

When I arrive at the field, most of the camp is already there, sitting cross-legged in the grass with perplexed expressions. Dennis and the counselors huddle together, discussing something at the front of the group. I take a seat next to the guys.

"What's going on?" I whisper to Lou.

"Not sure. Dennis just said they have some kind of announcement and they're waiting for everyone before they make it."

Oh no. I know what this is about, and suddenly my heart's pounding so hard I worry it might be visible through my shirt.

The phones. The box. They found out, they must have. And now they've canceled the morning's activities so they can sniff out the guilty parties. Shit, shit, shit. I'm not good under this kind of pressure. I'll crack in an instant and we'll all be sent home, with my relationship with Avery in absolute tatters and no chance to fix it. I might as well burn the Adventure Box because there's no way in hell I'll be able to keep the tradition alive now.

A few more stragglers filter in, and it looks like everyone's here. Except Avery. I assume I would have heard if she'd run off in the middle of the night, so I can only imagine she wasn't feeling up to leaving the cabin this morning. Not a good sign.

I gulp as Dennis stands facing everyone, clears his throat, and begins to speak.

"Good morning, everyone. I'm sorry to say that I have a bit of an . . . unfortunate announcement to make."

He looks at me. Is he looking at me? It feels like he's looking at me.

"I got some news yesterday that I want to pass along to you. I'm feeling incredibly guilty and conflicted about it, to be honest. And, well, I'll just be upfront. The news isn't good."

Dennis's voice is surprisingly emotional. Heavy. His face droopy and forlorn. I look over at the other dads, and we all share ominous glances.

"Look, I'm just going to come out and say it. We'll be shutting down this week's father-daughter session one day early, due to extenuating circumstances. We'll have a midmorning activity today—your men's groups and girls' groups, respectively—and then lunch, and after that you'll all be asked to head home."

A murmur ripples through the crowd. Is this our fault? Are they not even going to try to figure out who was responsible for stealing the phone box? Maybe if we give it back, we can clear this whole mess up. Everyone shouldn't have to suffer because of what we did.

"I know, I know," Dennis says, trying to quiet the crowd. "I hate to do this, but believe me, I wouldn't if it weren't absolutely necessary. You'll all receive a prorated refund for the final day of camp, of course."

"What the hell?" Bob cries out.

"What about the dance?" yells another dad.

"Canceled, I'm afraid."

"No!" Steve wails dramatically above the fracas.

"Again, I'm very sorry, and we'll do everything we can to make it up to you. And by that I mean, again, the refund," Dennis says.

A few people start booing, but none of this is adding up to me. If a group of us clearly broke the rules, why would Dennis be so apologetic? Why the refund? There has to be something more going on.

"I'll ask that you head back to your cabins and pack your things," Dennis yells over the crowd noise. "We'll blow the horn when it's time to meet up for group. Thank you for understanding."

And on that, he whizzes off, dodging questions and yells from the men like a beleaguered president being ushered out of a press briefing. If we had access to rotten fruit, we'd surely be throwing it at him right now.

But I can't just let this go. The camp can't be over yet, it just can't. So I hoist myself off the ground and chase after him.

"Dennis! Dennis, wait!"

He doesn't slow up, walking briskly into the camp office. I follow him in and close the door behind me.

"Mr. Collins, I know you're upset, just like everyone else. But I've already apologized, and I have a lot to get ready before tomorrow."

"Wait . . . Get ready for what?"

He's shuffling papers around on his desk, looking for something, then stops and sighs.

"Look," he says, resigned, sounding exhausted. "I got an offer from a big private group that wants to rent out the entire camp for the long weekend. I said no, of course, but then they made an even better offer and . . ." His voice trails off.

"Well, when do they get here?"

"Tonight."

Wow. This is . . . low. And my opinion of this place wasn't very high to begin with. "So you're kicking us out early to make an extra buck?"

I think back to a few bizarre moments over the last couple of days. The parking fee. The "premium nail polish." The way this place has just been bleeding us for extra pennies at every opportunity.

"So I was right from the very beginning. You take guys like me who are desperate to have a better relationship with their kids, and you make them all these promises, and what . . . you just squeeze them for money?"

"You have no idea, Mr. Collins, so just don't."

"Now all those men out there know what you're really about, and they're gonna tell their friends, and they're gonna write bad reviews. How's that gonna work out for you next year?"

"There isn't going to be a next year!" Dennis snaps, voice raging. Quickly, he collects himself again. "I've tried, OK? I've really tried, but we get fewer dads every year. The mother-and-son retreats are a ghost town. Even the regular summer camp is a hard sell these days—everyone wants to send their kid to STEM camp or sign them up for extra sports. Something that will help them 'get ahead,'" he says, adding air quotes. "I've been losing money on this place for years now, and I can't do it anymore. Here's a chance for me to get just enough to pay off some debts, sell this place, and . . . try to move on."

I want to be more surprised—how could summer camp ever go out of style?—but I know he's telling the truth. Evelyn and I never once considered sending Avery to a camp like this just to be a kid and have fun. We're always signing her up for as many sports as possible, and when there are no leagues active, she's in special training camps, or extra after-school academic stuff. The closest thing might have been the survival camp earlier this summer, but Avery made it very clear—she was there to learn the skills, not to goof around. When you have a high achiever like her, you feel like you have to push them endlessly or you'll be failing them. But I guess every parent feels that way these days, and places like Camp Triumph are suffering because of it.

While I feel bad about the camp, it doesn't change the fact that I'll do damn near anything to get what I came to this place for.

"I just wish you'd reconsider," I say. "There's got to be something we can do."

He reaches down, slides open a drawer at the bottom of his desk, and produces two bottles of beer, tilting one my way. I cock an eyebrow at him.

"Relax, it's a *nonny*, as I call it. Nonalcoholic. I wasn't lying when I said this was a dry campus. Sometimes just the taste is enough to soothe me when I'm feeling all . . . caught up in my emotions. You might be surprised to hear that it happens a lot." He chuckles sadly.

"I'm good," I say with as straight a face as I can muster.

"I have reconsidered," he says after taking a swig. "Over and over and over again. But if I'm being honest, for as much as I love this place, I'm not even sure it really makes a difference. A lot of dads only come because *mommy* signed them up, or because they want to get a little Instagram clout. It matters to *me*, and there have been a lot of great moments, but does what we do here really create lasting change? I'm not so sure anymore."

Dennis is so dejected, a deep sadness oozing out of him. I haven't known him long, but I've never seen him like this. The only thing I can think of that might get through to him now . . . is the truth.

"You were right about me, you know," I admit, sitting down across from him and sinking into the chair like I just walked into a therapist's office.

He says nothing, only leaving space for me to go on.

"Avery's been begging to join this team, this travel soccer team back home. And I didn't want her to. So I lied. I said the tryouts were canceled, and I made her come here with me so she'd forget about them. And I think somehow all I've managed to do is make everything worse."

"Then maybe there's a silver lining to all this. Take her home. Take her to the tryouts."

"It's too late." Then, trying to read his mind: "I'm a piece of shit. You can say it."

He takes a breath, opens his mouth, and prepares to unload on me with a barrage of judgment and insults and—

"I get why you did what you did," he says instead, softly, gently. "You just wanted to keep her for yourself a little while longer. There are worse things."

"Yeah," I say, taken aback. "Yeah, that's it. It's like, suddenly I feel so mortal. Like time is slipping away from me and everything I do only makes it go by faster, and then one day . . . I'll just be gone. Poof."

Dennis smiles. "Look who's getting better at describing their feelings."

I guess so. Doesn't feel like much of a victory at the moment, though.

"The best thing you can do is come clean and own up to it. She'll forgive you."

"I will. Eventually. I just keep thinking . . . what if she doesn't?"

Suddenly, he pounds a fist on the table, knocking over a picture frame. It falls toward me, and for a brief moment, I can see two people in the photo. Dennis (judging by the nearly bald head) and someone else. A girl.

Quickly, he sets the frame upright again, facing away, and gathers himself.

"There's no eventually. There's never as much time as you think."

"Then let us stay," I plead. "What you do here, it does matter. It *is* making a difference. Not just in me but all of those guys out there. We deserve a chance to see it through. We need more time."

"I'm sorry," he says. "It's done. I've already taken the money, and there's just not enough room here at the camp for both groups. If we had ever gotten around to renovating those old cabins? Maybe. But we're at half capacity right now, and it just doesn't work."

"Old cabins?"

"Across the field here." He points at a large-scale map of the camp on the wall, indicating a cluster of structures tucked away from the rest of the camp, shrouded by little illustrated trees.

"We just never found the money for repairs in the budget," he sighs. "Not that it matters much anymore. Now, if you'll excuse me."

He gets up, gives me a pat on the back, and says, "From the bottom of my heart, I'm sorry," before disappearing into a back room.

I leave his office feeling completely dejected and lost. A total failure. I've made a complete mess of things with my daughter, and I keep thinking there will be more and more time to fix it. And now there's not.

All that's left is a couple of hours with the other dads, and then Avery and I will have to leave this place forever, whether we're ready or not.

RYAN

Dear Grace,

How've you been? I'm here at the camp with Jessie. Thanks again for letting me have a few extra days with her. We can trade days another time, I'll make it up to you, I promise.

Sorry if I scared you. You probably thought this was a letter from my lawyer or something. It's just a regular letter. Sorry about that.

They put this stack of paper and an envelope on my bed, and I keep shoving it away, and it keeps reappearing somehow. I just keep staring at it. I'm supposed to write to someone and tell them how the week is going. But I've been putting it off this whole time. They're sending us home soon, and I don't want to leave without having done this. You probably don't want to hear from me, but the truth is I have no one else to write to.

The pen is moving now, and I really have no idea what to say, so sorry for rambling. But come to think of it, there is something I've been wanting to tell you, and that's that I've decided I hate the smell of our house.

I know that's weird. Let me explain.

It didn't used to smell like anything, not to me at least. I know I haven't been inside in a long while, but I can smell it every time you open the door, even when I'm standing on the mat just outside. It's the previous night's vanilla cupcake candles mostly, or papaya-something-or-other in the summer. Sometimes fresh-baked bread if I'm bringing the kids by just as you're finishing getting dinner on the table. It kills me not to be coming in and sitting down with a plate. All of us, a family. I never noticed any of it before, which seems unfair, but now it always hits me hard, like the way it does when you walk into a stranger's house and you can just smell a completely different way of life, different coffee grounds, different scented trash bags, different everything. I hate that our home, and I'm sorry to call it that but that's how I'll always think of it, smells like a stranger's house. I absolutely hate it.

It's why I've been fighting so hard for us to sell it. I know you think it's all spite, all my anger, trying to get back at you. It's not that. It's just that I can't keep showing up and not being allowed inside anymore. I know that's selfish of me. I'm sorry.

Are you seeing anyone? You don't have to answer that.

I didn't mean this to get all weepy. How are the boys? I worry about them, you know.

The time with Jessie has been good, though, it really feels like we're getting somewhere. All right, that's a lie. It's been a disaster. She told me off something fierce earlier. Had a lot bottled up, I guess, about you and me (mostly me). A serious tongue-lashing. I deserved all of it. Tell you the truth, I was proud of her, the way she spoke up to me like that. She's strong. Like you.

But I'm really trying, I swear. It'll get better I think. She reminds me of you so much, more and more as she gets older, you know. So this week has been a bit like a dream, having a little version of you around all the time, nothing to do but be with each other and laugh and have fun. I know what I need to do to turn it around, I think. I swear I am going to try.

Before I go I wanted to ask you something. I've been horrible to deal with (that's not the question, I already know I have), but I'd like to do better. Maybe when I'm back, I could come in, past the front mat at least, even just into the entryway. You don't have to let me in any farther than the coat hook if you don't want. But maybe we could stand there by the spot on the wall where the dogs have rubbed the paint off and we could just . . . talk. Not about us, I wouldn't dare (unless you want to?), but about the house. Our home. Sorry, I'll always call it that. I know you and the kids don't want to leave. We'll work it out so you don't have to, I promise. I owe you that much, at least.

So what do you say?

(And, again, I'm so sorry.)

Love always,

Ryan

Eighteen

Back at the cabin, we all pack our bags, slowly, mindlessly. Shell-shocked by what just happened and the realization that today's men's group will be our last activity at the camp.

I've been coming around on these guys, but still—not exactly how I would have chosen to go out.

Ryan doesn't have his usual edge, he's shoving clothes haphazardly into his suitcase with abandon. Lou picks up his book from the bed, and I can finally see what he was reading, *Success-taurant: A Restaurant-preneur's Handbook*, and I'm too morose to even laugh at the over-the-top name. He takes a long look at the cover and then chucks it in his bag.

And Booker is gone, again. It feels like very little has changed since day one, and almost none of it for the better.

We all drag our luggage outside and down the steps without a word.

And then, a sound. An electric hum, tires rolling through dirt.

Now we see him, Booker, speeding across the field toward us in a rusty golf cart, face almost maniacal, coming straight for us, and we all flinch and make to dive out of the way, and he slams the brakes, and the golf cart skids to a stop right in front of us, kicking up a cloud of dust. We all cough and wave it away from our faces.

"Thanks for the heart attack," Lou says.

"Look what I found," Booker says coolly, kicking a foot up onto the dash. "It was covered in ivy, over by the equipment shed. But I cleared it off and plugged it in on a whim, and it still works! Can you believe someone just abandoned it there?"

I look it up and down, dilapidated, sagging, sun-bleached.

"Yes."

"Come on, chin up, guys!" Booker says. "It's my turn to run the group today, and I convinced Dennis to let us do something pretty fun. As a thank-you to the three of you. Now get in."

"I'm not sure I have all the necessary vaccines," Ryan mumbles, eyeballing the deteriorating, jagged metal of the vehicle.

Booker rolls his eyes.

"What's the surprise?" I ask half-heartedly, hardly seeing the point anymore.

"I don't want to ruin it."

"Listen," I say, "I appreciate what you're trying to do, Book. But I think I want to go find Avery. Spend the rest of this time with her."

"Same here," Ryan grumbles, scratching his beard. "Things with Jessie still need a lot of smoothing over."

"Lou?" Booker says.

"Suppose I'd better go start clawing my way out of the doghouse, too," he says.

Booker nods, considering us for a moment.

"Can I tell you guys something?" he starts, then, not waiting for an answer, "I spend a lot of time beating myself up about not spending enough time with Erica. When I'm with her and I'm distracted with whatever's going on at work, or I'm down on myself and feeling like a failure, she can feel it. I'll start to feel like she doesn't even want me around anymore, not when I'm like that. So sometimes, believe it or not, I welcome the office. The work trips. Being away from her is hell but then . . . somehow, she starts to miss me, and when I get home, she's happy to see me again. Like nothing ever happened. And I get a clean slate. You know?"

I get what he's saying. It makes sense, but . . . so what?

"So," he says, reading my mind. "You feeling down?"

"Yeah," the three of us mumble.

"You feeling like shit?" Booker cries, louder now.

"Yeah!" our enthusiasm for our own failures growing steadily.

"Yeah?"

"YEAH!"

"THEN GET IN THE DAMN CART!"

We shrug at each other and climb in. And it's only then that I see a golf bag full of rickety clubs poking out of the back of the cart.

"Oh no," I groan.

"Oh yeah," Booker says, speeding off.

• • •

I don't know why I hate golf, but I do. It's ubiquitous where I live, not just a sport or hobby but a lifestyle. A culture. An entire personality for swaths of men. It's an elite and exclusive club that's not really accessible to anyone who wasn't born into it. It's impossible to even play a round if you can't drive or putt properly, if you haven't spent years mastering the intricacies of the game. It's expensive, too. You're expected to have your own clubs, proper attire, shoes, etc. It's obnoxious, and people won't shut up about the high-end courses they've played or their handicap or how far they can drive. Golf clothes are stupid. It's not a sport. The reasons go on and on. Yes, it's close-minded and judgmental, but frankly, I don't care.

Despite all of that, I think I hate it most because it's an antiquated holdover from a deservedly bygone era. Not the activity, not the act of hitting a ball with a club, but the golf course itself. The country club. A haven where "men can be men," and (if you have the cash) you can jet-set around with your buddies for "golf weekends" or you can get sloshed playing an early tee time on a random Sunday with the bros from the office.

And who's taking care of the kids this whole time? Not Golf Dad, that's for sure.

I guess everyone deserves a little time for themselves. But I decided a long time ago I wasn't going to be Golf Dad. I wasn't going to be the kind of dad who spent every weekend shirking my familial duties at the country club and yukking it up with the fellas.

Now, here I am, riding around in a golf cart with the boys when I'm supposed to be bonding with my daughter.

We drive straight past the usual camp haunts, the office, the dining hall. Past the pool, almost neon green in the sun. Now onto a path I didn't know was here, winding through the forest, going up, up, up. The golf cart, and its ripped seats, chugs along, struggling with the incline.

"Should we get out and push?" Ryan says at one point.

"Almost there," Booker says, hunched over the steering wheel, willing the machine forward.

And then we reach the crest of the hill, where the trees open up and the path spits us out onto a glorious overlook. Ahead of us, a nearly endless valley of forest, a stream, and a completely uninhibited view of the horizon. We all climb out and stare at it in awe.

"Wow," I say, the view quite literally taking my breath away. The ugliness of the camp itself has made me forget where we really are—in the very heart of nature. "It's just so . . . peaceful."

Lou and I walk up to the edge together and take in the view.

WHIZZZZZ. Something flies by my head, and I instinctively duck.

"What the hell was that?!"

I turn and am just able to catch sight of a golf ball soaring through the open air.

"Fore," Booker says with a smirk.

I'm dreading this. It's been years since I've even picked up a club, let alone unleashed my elbowy driving form in front of other humans with functional eyeballs. The obvious move, I decide, is to hang back and see what the other dads do. Predictably, they dive into the equipment greedily, selecting well-worn clubs and giving them pensive test swings to see how they feel.

I pull one out that seems . . . fine. It's roughly a good length for me, based on absolutely nothing, not a single criteria, because I wouldn't be able to tell one way or the other.

Ryan grabs a stained-yellow ball from a bucket Booker has brought along and tees it up first, none of us speaking a word. He lines up his shot and crushes the ball with impeccable form and power, the ball streaking down the center of the valley with a whistle. Of course. Of course he would be good at this.

"Great shot," I expect to hear from the other guys, and maybe something short and definitive like "Nice," or "Beautiful!"

But Booker and Lou don't say those things.

"You call that a drive?" Booker mocks instead, his voice gravelly from last night's shenanigans.

"Hey, eat a dick," Ryan says. For a second I think they're legitimately about to fight each other, and the hostility—seemingly from out of nowhere—confuses me. Did I miss something?

Ryan moves aside, and Booker steps up to the tee, places his ball, and launches it with ease. He's a big corporate guy, makes sense that he would spend a lot of time on the golf course. Plus, he wouldn't have planned this activity for us if he thought he might embarrass himself. Still, the others aren't impressed with his showing.

"Should have left you back at camp with the girls, Book." Ryan laughs.

"Outdrove your sorry ass," Booker snaps back.

"All right, make some room and watch how it's done, suckers," Lou announces.

"You heard the man, make room for Mr. Mom," Ryan says.

And finally, like a light bulb going on in slow motion, I realize that this is all just a big, ball-busting show. They're fucking with one another. Duh.

This is what dudes do, how they bond. Especially if they're feeling remotely vulnerable or uncomfortable, which is pretty much all the time. Hurling insults at one another is a solid and safe fallback for almost any situation. I kick myself that I didn't pick up on it immediately, but in my defense, it's been a pretty long time since I hung out with a group of guys without kids around.

It's starting to come back to me just a little bit.

Lou places his ball on the tee and wiggles his feet into position, but his grip on the club is awkward, and his stance just looks . . . off. Even I can tell.

"This oughta be good," says Booker.

Lou shushes him, winds up, and chops clumsily at the ball, sending it hurtling diagonally toward the tree line; albeit with decent power.

"What's up now?" Lou says to us with playful bravado. We all laugh. And then I realize it's my turn and I'm going to be even worse than Lou.

I approach the tee and get myself set, and immediately the mocking begins behind me.

"Come on, John, let's see what those chicken arms can do."

"If you can't outdrive Lou, we're leaving without you."

"Hey, fuck you," Lou responds.

I ignore the peanut gallery and line up my shot, or, at least, I try to remember as many cues as I possibly can. But what the hell, what do I have to lose? I crank the club back and give it my all with a powerful swing and *WHIIIISHHHH*, I'm lucky not to miss completely and I just barely clip a fraction of a millimeter of the ball, sending it flying backward over my head.

The dads let out a roar of laughter.

"The trick is to hit the ball forward," and "Maybe we should stand down there at the bottom . . . so there's no chance of him hitting us next time," they wheeze.

"Whatever," I say. "Anything you can play in slacks isn't a real sport anyway."

"You don't golf much, do you?" Ryan asks.

"Nah, see, I have a life."

I don't. But they don't have to know that.

"All right, all right, you need to at least learn the basics. It's like a rite of passage or something," Ryan says, then he grabs me and moves me roughly to face the tee again. "Can't have you out here embarrassing me."

He kicks my feet apart until they're, I guess, in roughly the right position.

"Like this," he says, adjusting my hands on the club. "A little bend in this elbow here."

Him standing behind me, it reminds me of the cheesy move of showing your date how to shoot pool or hold a bowling ball, when really it's just an excuse to get close. This would almost be romantic if I couldn't feel his beard scratching the back of my neck, if he didn't reek of old beer and sweat.

The others pick up on this and let out a "Woooooh!"

"Ah, he wishes," Ryan shoots back. "There, now you're ready."

"And don't go for such a big backswing," Booker chimes in. "Learn to make contact before you try to crush the ball."

I take it all into account, the verbal tips and the verbal abuse, the right foot and hand position, and I give it another shot and *POW*—I launch a respectable drive, even if it doesn't quite have the powerful crack and whistle of a more seasoned golfer.

"Congrats," Ryan says. "You're now about as good as I was when I was seven."

"At least I didn't grow up to be an asshole."

This gets a laugh out of him.

"Look who found his trash talk." He chuckles. "Now move out of the way, dickhead. My turn."

"Hope you choke on your club and die an excruciating and violent death," I say. I'm pretty sure I hear a record scratch somewhere, and everyone gets real quiet. "Too much?"

They nod. I'm still a little rusty.

We go on like this for the next hour or so, taking turns off the driving tee, ravaging each other with insults and mocking one another with something like genuine affection.

We don't talk about anything real, not our jobs, not our partners (or exes), our children, our fears, our worries. We just hit balls and call one another names and this hour or so of absolutely nothing is everything I didn't know I needed. It's the best I've felt in a while, and I'm bursting to take this good energy back to Avery. A clean slate. Booker was 100 percent right.

There's just one thing still working against me. Time.

"I really do wish we could have one more day," I say from the back seat of the golf cart, headed back to camp, as we careen down the hill.

"Yeah, me too," Booker replies, the bumpy ride giving his voice a staccato quality.

Back at the cabin before we left for golf, I had filled them in on the gist of my conversation with Dennis. Like me, they were all relieved that the camp closing down early wasn't our fault. But that didn't stop it from closing down early.

"Too bad the camp's not bigger," I say, without much thought. "If they had enough room, who knows, maybe they'd let us stay."

"Wait, Dennis said that?" Ryan asks, turning around from the front to face me.

"Not explicitly. He mentioned some extra cabins that, I guess, have fallen out of repair. If it weren't for that, there might have been enough room."

Ryan reaches back, slugs me in the arm. "And you're just mentioning this now?"

"First of all, ow. Second, I want to stay more than anything, but I'm not sure I'm down with sleeping on some bug-infested slab of rotten wood."

"No," he says. "I mean, we could fix them up."

I blink at him, not following.

"Fix them up and . . ."

"And sleep in them?" he says, willing me to catch up to his train of thought.

"We'd need an architect to draw up some simple plans," Booker says. "Hmm . . . Wonder where we could find one of those?"

"OK," I laugh. "But we're not really talking about this. Are we?"

"Why not?" Lou asks. "There's four of us. That's enough to do some damage."

"Two cabins is all we need, one for us and one for the girls. It's doable," Ryan adds.

"Are you guys serious? Staying here for one more day . . . it really means that much to you?"

"Well, yeah," Booker says. "Doesn't it to you?"

Of course it does. I already botched the soccer tryouts, the one thing that could have made Avery happy. No taking that back now. So if I leave here without getting to that dance with Avery and exchanging Adventure Box presents, the whole week will have been for nothing.

Yeah. One more day could make all the difference in the world.

Eighteen and a Half

Avery is nine and a half now, and she's home with her mom. I'm about four hundred miles away, sitting on a dark balcony, listening to waves crashing down on the South Carolina beach below.

In chairs next to me are my best friends since I don't even know when, Jordan and Wyatt.

"OK, so I have a serious question . . . how do you handle the poopy diapers?" Jordan asks, ocean breeze tickling his long curly hair. He's got a baby on the way, and he's been peppering me with questions for the last half an hour.

"You put them in the freezer, in case you need them later," I say. "What kind of question is that? What do you mean, how do you handle them? You just . . . get in there."

"Doesn't it make you gag?"

"Dude, a regular dirty diaper is like, the least of your problems. Call me when you're trying to clean up bright yellow diarrhea *and* treating a wicked third-degree diaper rash."

"Oh God," Jordan groans.

"And hey, if I find out you become one of these dads who makes his wife change all the BMs—that's what we call bowel movements in the industry—I'm gonna come find you and kick your ass."

"Can we *please* talk about something else? For the love of God," whines Wyatt, straightening the collar on his pressed button-down. Wyatt is single and shows no signs of settling down any time soon. He stands, looking physically restless. "Let's go out. There are a bunch of cool bars right down the street. Bet there are a ton of girls there."

"It's like, nine o'clock," I say. I don't know what's more appalling—that he'd think I have any interest in meeting girls, or that he'd suggest *starting* our evening this late.

"So?"

"I'm game," says Jordan.

I don't know how to tell them I'm wrecked from the flight in without sounding like a total loser. They wouldn't understand, anyway, the way your internal clock shifts permanently after having kids. Jordan'll find out soon enough. But neither of them really gets it yet.

"Can't we just stay in tonight? We've got plenty of beer, an ocean view . . ."

"Don't be such a pussy," Wyatt says.

He's being playful, just busting my balls, but it makes me wince anyway. Getting married and having a daughter changes your perspective, I guess. Certain words get tossed out. And it makes you wonder why you ever found it OK to use a variation of the word *vagina* to accuse someone of being afraid, because the two women I live with are tougher and braver than these idiots can possibly imagine. But again. Wyatt doesn't get that yet.

"Fine, I'll admit it—I'm exhausted from the trip, guys. I'll be good to go tomorrow. And we have the whole week ahead of us."

Wyatt groans like a child denied a cookie after dinner. I really don't remember him being so obnoxious. Has he changed? Or have I?

"Come on," Jordan says softly. "This might be my last hurrah for a while. Let's make the most of it."

I sigh. Now *that* I can get behind. It's taken us years to finally make this guys' trip happen. We'd have it planned, then something would come up with Avery. Or one of the other guys would run out of vacation time at work. So now that we're finally here, it makes sense to maximize the time. It doesn't make me feel any less tired, but I guess I can suck it up for one night.

We all cheers, clinking the bottles we've been nursing.

"To best friends," I say.

They both laugh . . . at me. I guess being a dad has made me more sentimental, too.

Then they disappear inside—Jordan, to change, and Wyatt, to throw on excessive amounts of cologne. I'm about to do my version of that, which is changing from sweatpants into my *good* sweatpants, when my phone rings. It's Evelyn. I answer.

"Don't freak out," she says. "Avery is fine. She's fine, really. So there's no need to rush home."

"Just tell me, what is it?"

"Avery broke her leg."

Naturally, I rush home. This involves booking an outrageously expensive last-minute flight and eating the cost of four more days at the beach condo I had booked with the guys. I walk in our front door at about 2:00 a.m.

Evelyn's already in bed. I told her not to wait up for me if she could get Avery down OK. So I drop my bags in the front hall and creep up the steps, cracking Avery's door open just a tad.

She's asleep, too, half her body sticking out of her covers. And there it is—a thick cast on her right leg. Evelyn said it happened during a softball slide gone wrong. Luckily, it was a clean-enough break and wouldn't put her on the sidelines for too, too long.

I slip into bed with her, trying not to disturb her too much. I want her to know I'm here, but she needs her rest.

"Daddy," she says sleepily.

"Hi, sweetie, I'm here now."

She nuzzles into me.

"Does it hurt?"

"Not anymore."

Watching her slip in and out of sleep, she looks so peaceful. You'd hardly know she was screaming in pain a few hours earlier. What a tough kid.

"You know, I was thinking on the plane," I whisper. "When you get your cast off, we can cut a chunk of it off and put it in our Adventure Box for this summer. What do you think? Wait," I say, realizing. "Does it still count if I wasn't there when it happened?"

She doesn't say anything. And at first I think it's because she's fallen asleep, but then I look down, and I can tell she's been crying. Not hours ago but just now. The skin around her eyes is wet and glistening.

"What's wrong? Is it hurting again?"

"I can't play for six weeks," she chokes out. To her, this is worse than any physical pain.

I sigh and squeeze her tight.

"Tell you what, tomorrow, you and me, we'll go get ice cream. The biggest ice cream they have. And you can keep eating until your stomach hurts worse than your leg. That'll help, I think."

She rolls away from me.

"I'm ready to go to sleep now," she says.

I kiss her good night but stay a little longer.

Maybe I didn't need to, but I'm glad I came back. I didn't feel right being away in the first place, and even less so when I felt so different and disconnected from my best friends. These two guys who were my family . . . before this one.

Should friendship be so hard? Should I be putting in so much effort to stay in touch, when it feels impossible to sustain any longer?

Maybe that effort would be put to better use here. Either way, I promise myself that I'll never not be there for Avery when she needs me, ever, ever again.

Nineteen

"This seems a little too good to be true," I say.

The four of us stand in the muddy, overgrown woods by the abandoned cabins—on the other side of the field from where we've been staying all week. Shady and hidden away without a trace of life, save for something furry skittering about inside one of the structures.

Finally, after four days of catastrophe after catastrophe, a break. We've just tugged at the corner of a mysterious tarp, draped over a lumpy pile, and unearthed a massive treasure trove of relatively fresh lumber. And not only that, but the cabins? They're not as bad off as we thought. A bit damp, sure, but the windows and roofs seem to be in fine shape. All we really need to do is replace a few rotten boards and these suckers will be, at least, mildly habitable.

"Yeah, I don't trust it, either," Ryan says.

"Come on," says Lou. "We were due to catch a break."

"So what now?" asks Booker.

"I'll scrounge up some tools," Ryan says. "There's an equipment shed, hopefully I can find a few hammers and crowbars, at least. Maybe a table saw. That oughta be enough."

"Someone has to distract Dennis," Booker jumps in. "If he sees what we're doing, he's liable to shut the whole thing down before we even start. But if we ask for forgiveness at the end . . ."

"I'm not sure I follow the logic," Lou says.

"No, he's right," I say, scrambling for a metaphor. "If you found some random dudes demolishing your kitchen one day, for example, you'd probably call the cops. But if you walked in and found it completely remodeled overnight? That wouldn't be so bad."

"Uh, I would still have a lot of questions."

"Right, but questions aren't cops."

Lou scratches his chin, not completely following my logic. I'm not sure I am, either, but I'm running on pure adrenaline. Forward momentum. This is going to work, because it has to work.

"I guess the only other thing we could really use," begins Ryan.

"Is a few more sets of hands," I finish for him.

I haven't spoken to Avery since the incident, since my brief apology. I haven't known what to say, haven't known how to make things better. But now I'm out of time. Time to face the music, whether she's done cooling off or not.

• • •

I trudge across the field to find Avery, not feeling overly optimistic.

She used to be game to do anything, no matter how mundane, as long as it was with me. Grocery shopping, visits to the bank, tagging along to the office on Bring a Kid to Work Day (to be fair, she'd be showered with treats and attention all day long from my coworkers, offsetting the inevitable boredom that set in when she realized my job was actually pretty tedious). An invitation into the garage to help me with a project, much smaller versions of what I need her help with now, was unthinkably cool.

Was.

Now if I show the slightest interest in something, it automatically becomes repellent to her. God forbid I have the audacity to like the same song as her, for example. And that's under the best of circumstances.

I'd be hard-pressed to describe this moment, right now, as the best of circumstances. As far as I know, she's still furious with me.

The girls have wrapped up a morning of tie-dyeing shirts—I can see them soaking in colorful Ziploc bags on picnic tables outside the cabins as I walk up. Now they simply loiter, sitting on suitcases or lying in the grass, waiting to leave.

Avery and Megan are standing in front of their cabin, each holding a bulky rolling suitcase—Avery's and one they must have borrowed from another girl. They're crouched low like sprinters, legs primed to explode forward. I notice, again, the similarity in their hairstyles. Now Avery's even got the sleeves on her T-shirt rolled up to match the way Megan's are.

"GO!" Megan shouts, and they both take off in a dead sprint, pulling wheeled suitcases behind them and jostling them over exposed roots. It's not much of a race. Megan's legs are about twice as long as Avery's, and she pulls the suitcase behind her like a tiny toy dog on a leash. Avery struggles with the weight of her luggage, falling behind dramatically in the suitcase race but never giving up. Megan crosses some kind of invisible, predetermined finish line and throws her arms up in the air.

"A NEW CHAMPION!" she cries.

Avery finishes the race a few seconds later, drops her suitcase to the ground, and doubles over to breathe.

"Best of seven," she huffs.

"Oh, come on. You already lost best of three and five. You really wanna go again?"

"I can beat you."

"I love that attitude. You're wrong, but I love it."

Megan ruffles Avery's hair in a, well, in kind of a parental way that makes my heart feel like it's trying to learn to frown. But as jealous as I am, I love seeing Avery with a smile on her face, spunky and competitive again. It comes and goes these days. Right now, I'm just glad to have it back, even if I have to enjoy it from a distance.

"Oh, hey, Dad," Avery says, noticing me, chipper as a hummingbird. Like nothing ever happened.

"Um, hi," I say, taken completely aback.

"What's up?"

"Just came to ask you for a small favor."

"What's going on, are we leaving or what?"

"I . . . I don't know yet. I think we might have found a way to stay."

"Oh," she says, surprised. She chews it over, her expression impossible to read for a minute.

"We might have to switch cabins around because of the other group, but I think we can make it work."

"Would I still be with Megan?"

"If that's what you want, I'm sure we can figure it out."

I still can't tell how she's going to react, but her initial rage at being forced to come here and wanting to leave immediately is still fresh in my mind.

Instead, a smile creeps onto her face, tugging at the corners of her mouth. "Cool."

Cool. I can live with cool.

"I call bottom bunk," Megan teases. "Camp rules."

"No fair!" Avery shouts. "How about, if I can give you a piggy-back ride to that tree"—she points—"I get to pick *both* our bunks."

"You're on."

Megan climbs onto Avery's back, Avery crumbling under the weight. They both giggle hysterically. But before they gallop off, Avery turns back to me once more.

"Weren't you going to ask me for a favor?"

She's happy, flashing an unbridled, toothy grin that reminds me of ice-cream-covered smiles when she was little. I just can't bring myself to pull her away.

"Never mind," I say. "You go have fun."

Avery turns away, and the two girls race off together.

Twenty

On my return to the other side of the field, Ryan and Lou are hard
at work on a cabin each. Tiptoeing around the dilapidated structures
and ripping out the rotten boards with violent force. Trying not
to fall through jagged holes in the floor or impale themselves on
rusty nails. Booker studies a small sketch he's created, deep in analy-
sis mode like we're constructing a massive suspension bridge or
something.

"No luck," I announce. "Looks like I'm on my own."

At least I'm not alone in being alone.

Or, at least, that's what I think at first. Until I see Tam poke her
head up through a gap in the floor of Lou's cabin, extending a tiny
arm clasping a crowbar the size of her entire body.

"You dropped this," she says to her dad.

Lou hoists her up and out of the floor and gives her a smooch.

"Thanks, little helper." He smiles at her, then grabs for the
crowbar.

She doesn't immediately let go.

"Tam, let go. TAM, DROP IT."

"But I like it."

He laughs, and she finally releases her vise grip.

"Jessie!" Ryan yells from the other cabin. "Where are you with that Phillips head?"

And here's Jessie, scurrying over, a bundle of tools in her arms. "I couldn't remember which was which, so I brought them all."

Ryan sighs, playful. "Haven't I taught you anything?"

He grabs a screwdriver from her and ruffles her hair.

"Who's Phillip, anyway?" she asks earnestly.

It's great to see them all together again, Booker's clean-slate strategy clearly having paid off. But it's hard to enjoy. Without Avery, I feel out of place here among the other dads. Like I've just arrived solo for a haircut at a child's barbershop, a bright red firetruck chair straining under my adult weight, everyone staring at me.

And it gets worse.

"Good news," Booker says from behind me.

I spin around and there he is, Erica leaning tight against his leg.

"Dennis is off taking care of something in town. We've got a few hours without supervision."

Booker claps me on the back and leads Erica over to the work area.

"Say, you don't happen to like *breaking stuff*, do you?" he says to her.

She smiles devilishly.

I'm hurting, but I try to think pragmatically. If we can get this done, and if Dennis will let us stay—which is a big if—that'll be all that matters. It'll be worth it. It'll all work out.

Ryan jogs over, leaving Jessie to pick up loose nails and place them in a container for safe disposal. He hoists a power saw up onto a makeshift platform, some plywood laid over sawhorses, and plugs it into an extension cord that runs and disappears in the general direction of the main camp buildings.

"That equipment shed was loaded. Granted, these tools have seen better days, but it's something." Then, off my silence, "Sorry about Avery," he says to me. "I'm sure she'll come around."

"Well, she's not pissed at me anymore, at least. Maybe that's about as 'around' as she's going to come."

He rubs his head and thinks this over. "Hey, it's her loss. She'd be lucky to get this time with you," he says, as if he knows I'm thinking the opposite.

And it's right then that I realize what the difference is between me and the other dads, why all of their girls are here helping them while I'm on my own:

All any of their daughters ever really wanted was to spend more time with their dads. The simple act of being at this camp made that possible.

Avery, on the other hand, mostly wants nothing to do with me, despite my best efforts to be a good father, to always be there for her, to always make the time. If you're absent, or at least emotionally distant, you leave your kids wanting more. Me? It feels like I'm being punished for actually trying.

But if I were a so-called good dad, I wouldn't be here at all, would I? I would have taken Avery home days ago so she could make the tryouts. I'd be ready to let her go.

It hits me with punishing force: I can't blame the strain in our relationship on anyone else, not Megan, not the soccer coach, not Evelyn, not even Avery.

It's me who's driving her away. The less I push against her, the happier she seems to be. Maybe the best thing is for me to just . . . leave her alone.

"Your sons, how old are they?" I ask, changing the subject.

"Nine, seven, four, and two," Ryan rattles off without hesitation.

"I'm sorry, I think I misheard."

He laughs. "I know, it's a lot. I love 'em, though. They're trouble, but I love them."

"Yeah?"

He looks up at me, tilting his head, understanding that I want to hear more.

"Well the nine-year-old is a stick of dynamite. He destroys everything he sees. Loves to blow stuff up, set things on fire. He'll probably be the type to get suspended from school a bunch; I can already tell. And the others take after him. They punch each other and bite each other and . . . man, it's just a lot. I'm doing my best with them, but it's a lot."

"And Jessie?"

"Textbook rule follower." He laughs. "Easy-peasy. Between you and me, sometimes I miss when it was just her."

"When things were simpler."

"Exactly. You just can't be everywhere, can't do everything. Some things are bound to slip. I worry about Jessie, too, though. I do. God, you know how it is. There's a lot to be afraid of, raising a girl and sending her out into the world."

"I have regular nightmares about it, yes."

"I thought if I could raise a couple of good guys, put a few stand-up men out there in the world, that might help make things better for girls like Jessie. Somewhere along the way, I went way off track."

"You two seem OK now. You and her."

He sighs. "I told her I'd patch things up with her mom. I don't think there's much of a chance we get back together, but we can be a lot more civil. *I* can be a lot more civil. Didn't realize how much it was hurting Jessie. It's just so hard to juggle all of it, taking care of five different people, not including myself. Giving everyone what they need. At least you've only got Avery to focus on." He laughs. "You should consider yourself lucky."

Lucky. Yeah.

"You know—" I start.

BZZZZZZZZZZ.

Ryan powers on the saw and slices through a board, the sound ripping through the still air, drowning me out.

"Sorry, what was that?" he asks.

"Nothing," I mutter.

We work for a while longer, Ryan cutting new boards and teaching Jessie proper saw safety, her wearing oversize swim goggles as protective gear. Lou and Booker sending their girls on tool runs and taking breaks to fling water bottles at each other when they get hot. I work mostly in silence.

The whole thing's ridiculous, and I think we all know it. But the two cabins are beginning to take shape, board by board. Even if it's all for nothing, well . . . at least we went down swinging. After a while, each of us beginning to tire in the heat, we step back and take a look at what we've done so far.

"We're getting there," I huff.

"Define *there*," Lou says.

"Come on. They look pretty good."

"Got a few more hours ahead of us," Ryan says. "At least."

"That other group is supposed to show up soon," Lou says. "You think we'll have time?"

"Time for what?" says a voice that I recognize, and here's Bob. And behind him, Steve, Mark, Jeff, and the others, all of their girls trailing behind with suitcases, bags, and pillows held tight to their chests. "I heard the saw and got curious."

Moths to a flame, I think.

We fill them in on the plan, and when we're done, there's a long pause as they all soak it in. I prepare myself for a reality check. Surely, this all seems idiotic to them, and I expect them to say so. But then Bob opens his mouth and says just one thing:

"We want in. How can we help?"

My cabinmates and I look over at the four remaining cabin shells, and Bob gets it immediately.

"On it," he says without another word.

He barks out commands, looking every bit like a construction foreman, routing the other dads into action. They grab hammers, crowbars, screwdrivers, burly sticks—whatever they can find, then attack the four structures at once, ripping them to shreds like a hoard of ants stampeding over someone in a cartoon, leaving only a skeleton behind. All around, dads give lessons in tool identification and, even though it's still light out, the crucial art of flashlight holding. Power drills whir. Hammers bang men's thumbs. Squeals of laughter ring out. Memories and stories to tell years later take shape. Just . . . not for me.

I pull Bob aside.

"All this, it might not work," I tell him. "It's not like I got it in writing from Dennis or anything. I just don't want anyone to get their hopes up."

"What's wrong with getting our hopes up?" he asks genuinely. "Look, when we get home, it'll be back to school and work and normal life. And in my normal life, I'll admit it: I'm not a very good dad. But here . . . there's still a chance. If we have to leave here in five minutes or two hours or two days, well, I want to make that time count."

Our group goes on like this for hours. The sun dips, burns orange and purple, and then sets. Finally, the sky goes dark completely. We work through dinner. At some point Lou brings us plates from the dining hall, and we all scarf down hot dogs and chips and get back to work. And for all our effort, with the last remaining moments of the day dwindling away, everyone slowing down and yawning and cracking backs, we've nearly finished.

"John, want to do the honors?" Bob hands me the final board and a handful of nails. I take it with a grateful nod and line it up. It fits snugly into the last empty space, the final puzzle piece. I'm just about to drive in the first nail when suddenly Avery appears next to me.

"Can I help?" she asks.

It takes me a moment to reply. I'm genuinely surprised to see her, genuinely shocked to hear her say those words.

"Dad?"

"You really don't have to. It's OK."

"Everyone else was pitching in so . . ."

"You missed most of the fun already."

"But not all of it."

She looks away, and I quickly fan my watering eyes to prevent them from overflowing. She looks back, and I hand her the hammer and the first nail, then point out where it should go.

"Have I ever properly taught you how to swing a hammer? I'm sure I have."

Here's where she brushes me off with an eye roll and a smug *I don't need your help.*

"Remind me?" she says instead.

I help her line it up, adjust her grip, and give her all my best fatherly tips. Then I stand back and watch her give it a whack, and then another and another until she drives it in flush with the wood. Without skipping a beat, she holds her hand out for the next nail. I hand it over.

Just a few more swings of the hammer later, we've finished all six cabins.

"You're a natural. No surprise there," I say.

She smirks.

The cabins are beautiful, like a finished product you might see on the back of a truck going down the highway, a "Wide Load" sign chained to the back, ready for delivery. Despite the heaviness I feel, I can't help bursting with pride at what we built—it was just a day or so ago that I couldn't believe I made *noodles.*

The group takes it all in, trading manly, gladiator-style hugs in celebration.

Suddenly we're all caught in the beam of headlights slicing through the middle of camp. A huge charter bus pulls into the comically too-small parking lot, illuminating thousands of moths and gnats in the darkness. Silhouettes of people offload from the bus, carrying bags, and disappear into the half of camp we previously occupied.

The girls group up and move into the new cabins. They roll blankets and sleeping bags out on the floor, like it's all a big sleepover. And they love it. But I can't help but notice that no one, besides Megan, seems to be speaking to Avery.

"I thought I told you," a voice cries out from the darkness, Dennis, ambling out of the shadows. "There's another—" He stops in his tracks. "What . . . what is all this?" he says, inspecting our work.

We all look around at one another, not sure how this is going to go down, no way to predict how Dennis is going to react.

"Ta da?" I offer.

He shoots me a confused look.

"You said if there was enough room, maybe you could handle both groups, right? So we . . . made some room," I explain.

Dennis runs a hand along one of the cabins, as if looking for flaws. Then he turns to look back at us, a rickety work light illuminating all our faces.

"You all . . . did this?"

We nod as a group.

"Together?"

Another nod. It's hard to make out Dennis's face, but from what I can tell, he looks genuinely moved. Confirming my suspicions, he clears a lump from his throat.

"It's a good effort. But it's just not possible."

He says this without much conviction, like the gears in his brain are turning, trying to figure out how to make it all work. I throw my arm around Avery and pull her close, pointing her pouting face at him like a weapon. The other dads follow suit, a small army of girls now begging Dennis with their eyes to have a heart.

"Fine." He sighs. "Fine. OK."

"We can . . . stay?" I stammer.

"You can stay."

A round of cheers erupts.

"How about all the activities tomorrow, everything that was planned?"

"We'll just have to work around the other group when they're in the dining hall and the lodge. Other than that, they're mostly here for the trails and lake. So I *suppose* . . . it's possible."

We pump fists and cheer, and the girls roll their eyes at us.

"I have to say," he says, taking one more look at the renovated cabins. "Bravo."

He walks past me as the rest of the dads celebrate, leaning in slightly to ask, "Have you talked to her yet?"

I shake my head. He pats me on the shoulder and walks off, sending my feelings of pride and accomplishment crashing down on top of me.

• • •

As per usual, once the sun goes down here, I have no idea what time it is. But I know it's late. The others are asleep in sleeping bags and blankets on the floor of our freshly minted cabin. But I can't sleep. There's just one thing still gnawing at my brain.

What exactly is my plan for tomorrow?

I sit up and grab my suitcase, open it quietly, and pull out a small bag. A bag of things I've been saving from this week, things that I thought might end up being special or significant in some way. A bag that's not as full as I had hoped.

There's an arrow I managed to snag from the archery course, well, the tip I broke off of it, at least. Then there's an emery board from manicures, and hey, it's kind of fun that I learned what an emery board is, right? Does that count as adventurous? There's one of the flags from capture the flag, though I'm almost certain it's not going to be a finalist for the Adventure Box. Not exactly attached to the warmest of memories, that one. I also saved the lock from when we broke into the camp office and smashed the phone box to pieces, but that was more about hiding evidence than anything else.

Whatever I give Avery tomorrow, it has to be perfect. It has to say, *I'm here whenever you need me. But also, it's OK if you don't need me.*

And, *Please forgive me for not being the perfect dad.*

And, *Remember how nice this moment was when I tell you that I lied to you.*

It's asking a lot from an inanimate object.

FRIDAY

Twenty-One

Tomorrow is here. And already, I hate it.

I feel squeezed. Rushed. Claustrophobic.

As usual, I roll out of bed and visit the bathroom, only now it's completely jam-packed, filled with another dozen men I've never met before and an equal number of roughly ten-year-old boys yelling and rat-tailing one another with filthy towels. Our new guests. It's incredibly loud and cramped in here, so I splash my face, brush my teeth, and get out of there as fast as possible.

Then it's off to the dining hall. I'm in early enough, before the rush, and before any of the girls. I grab a couple of plates and load up heaping portions for myself and Avery. A skyscraper of waffles with extra syrup, her favorite, ought to get us off on the right foot.

I grab a spot at the usual table as people filter in. My cabinmates arrive and stretch and groan as they sit down with hot coffees. Other dads from our group do the same. Then the other group filters in, now washed and dressed, and I can finally see who they are: a Boy

Scout troop, dressed in full uniform, all of them. Apparently, a well-funded Boy Scout troop that could afford to rent the camp out for the weekend at the very last minute.

Now the girls trickle in, Avery lagging a moment or two behind the others. Erica, Jessie, and Tam sit together at an empty table across from us. Avery and Megan sit next to me. I slide a tray Avery's way with the plate I've made for her sitting right in the middle, waffles piled so high they might topple at any moment.

"Who loves you?"

"Yum," Avery says, smiling half-heartedly. If I didn't know better, I'd say it looks like she's been crying.

"I got here early, stole you the very best of the bunch."

She digs in.

"How come you're not sitting with the other girls?"

I had forgotten about the little problem of Avery making herself persona non grata with her cabinmates. I guess that's one thing that hasn't magically fixed itself with a hands-off approach.

Avery, suddenly with her shoulders drooping, looks over to Megan, as if for guidance. Megan places a comforting hand on Avery's arm.

"We're working on that. Making things right, from the other day."

Megan shoots me a wink, a wink that's meant to say *I've got your back*, but instead it sends a stabbing pain through me. I know she's only trying to help, but I can't help but feel like she's stealing a big-time dad moment away from me. I don't have many of those left.

But I'm trying to play it cool today. Trying not to suffocate. Trying not to overwhelm. It's a strategy that's working, so far.

Though it's taking every ounce of willpower that I have to stick with it.

"You know," I say, holding back as much as possible, treading as lightly as I can. "I just want you to know I'm here for you, too, Avery. If there's anything going on at all that you want to talk about, my ears are wide open."

"Good to know," she says through a mouthful of breakfast.

"What?" I say, cupping a hand to my ear like I'm straining to hear her. "Just kidding," I laugh sheepishly. Another stupid joke. Get back on track. "I really am a good listener. I can be, anyway. I promise. Try me."

"Why are you being awkward?"

"I'm not. We're just two normal people, eating breakfast. If there *was* something you wanted to talk to me about, it would be totally . . . chill."

"Are you and Mom getting a divorce or something?"

"What?" I nearly spit my coffee. "Why would you ask that?"

"I don't know. Some of the kids at school say their parents got really weird and creepy and kept checking in on how they were *feeling* right before they split up." She gestures toward me, Exhibit A.

"OK, so asking how you're doing is creepy now. Noted. But no, your mom and I love each other, you know that." I take another sip to appear casual, but I can't quite let this go. "Why . . . did Mom say something?"

"No," she says, and I breathe a sigh of relief. "But I think she gets lonely sometimes."

"Why do you think that?"

"Because you're always with me." She drops this casually, as if it's not an atomic bomb of an observation, as if it doesn't send a crack along the length of my heart.

"I am not."

"Oh yeah? Where are you now?"

I look around, realizing. "With you."

"And where's Mom?"

"Home. Alone."

She hums a smug *mm-hmm*.

I can see Megan's eyes go wide, her face holding back a monumental cringe. "Avery, wanna go see how our tie-dyes turned out?"

Avery chases her last bite of waffle with a huge chug of water. "Yeah, let's go."

"See you in a little bit, right?" I yell.

Avery throws up a limp hand in acknowledgment, and, once again, I'm left alone.

• • •

"I need help," I tell Evelyn, who answers just a split second before voice mail kicks in.

I'm back at the cabin now with a few minutes to kill before the next activity. I was meant to be spending these minutes with Avery, but letting her go with her friend isn't going to kill me. Not going to make me collapse into a puddle. Still, it's left me with some free time on my hands and a lot on my mind.

"Mm-hmm," Evelyn hums knowingly, almost as if she's been sitting by the phone, waiting for this exact call. "So, how's it *gooooing*?"

"You know. It's two steps forward, three steps back. Did I tell you I made her pee herself?"

"You what?"

"In front of everyone. I tickled her and she just . . . It was mortifying. I don't know what I was thinking."

"Oh, John," she sighs.

"I think she's forgiven me, but she won't talk to me. Not really. She had a falling-out with the other girls, and she's acting like it's no big deal, but I can tell she's upset about it. She's just a brick wall. She's not actively staring daggers at me now, which is nice, and I was going to back off. Just leave her alone, let her come to me when she needs me. But she needs me and she's not coming, she's just shutting down, retreating."

"OK, OK, take a breath."

"I know she's becoming a preteen, and they don't want to talk to their parents ever, unless it's life-and-death, and sometimes not even then. But she's not herself, I know she's not. And she's hiding stuff from us. Have you seen that drawer in her room?"

"The one with the birthday invitations?"

What? Evelyn already . . . knows?

"That says 'keep out' on the front?" I ask.

"That's the one."

She reads my stunned silence and fills in the gaps.

"It's got a bunch of old birthday invites in there. Some from neighborhood kids. A few from school friends. Most of them are from years ago."

So it's not drugs, but I honestly don't feel that relieved. I try to think back in my mental archives, and I'm having trouble coming up with a single birthday party we've attended in the past couple of years.

"I don't get it. Why is she hiding . . . birthday invitations?"

"Why don't you ask her?"

Evelyn already knows, which means Avery has talked to her about it. And neither of them feel like spelling it out for me. This is Chronicles of Narnia all over again.

"She won't talk to me, that's the problem. That's the entire problem."

"Maybe she thinks you won't listen."

"I will! I want to! But I can't listen if she won't talk!"

I bang my head against the fresh wooden walls of the cabin in frustration. I'm losing my mind; I feel like I should be strapped into a straitjacket and locked away somewhere. Meanwhile, Evelyn breathes out heavily, the way she does when she's thinking something over or solving a problem. Then she clears her throat, her trademark indication that she's come up with an idea.

"Have you tried doing the talking? Maybe if you take the first step, she'll meet you part of the way."

"I talk to her constantly. She probably thinks I never shut up."

"She doesn't think that."

"She's told me so. In those exact words."

"Have you talked to her about the travel team yet? About why you don't want her to join? A coach came by the house looking for her the other day. I didn't know what to say."

"I've tried," I say. It's not a lie, but it's definitely not the truth. When she was furious and wouldn't speak to me, that seemed like a bad time. Now that we're at least cordial again, it seems like an even worse time.

"You're gonna have to put yourself out there with her, that's the only way."

"I can't start with soccer. It'll devastate her."

"Then start smaller."

I sink. This is going to hurt. No Easy-button solution here.

"When she was little, she needed you to be her superhero, her comedian, her teacher," Evelyn says. "Now what she needs is to know that you're human. That it's OK to not be perfect. Trust me."

"Is that what you do? How you get her to open up to you?"

"Sometimes. I have other tricks, too. It doesn't always work, by the way. She's not easy right now for me, either."

"I guess that's comforting," I say, letting out a long, slightly melo-dramatic exhale.

"John . . . are you OK? First, your text the other night. Now . . ."

I can feel myself moping, making this all about me, making Ev-elyn feel invisible. Alone. Just like Avery said. Maybe what Evelyn needs isn't space and distance from me because I'm driving her nuts. Maybe what she needs is to feel . . . needed. Wanted. I think about her dressing in athleisure, hiking out to the middle of nowhere for Pilates classes, grasping for anything she might have in common with the other moms from school. Not for peace and quiet, but for companionship. Belonging.

I wish I could see her. I honestly want nothing more in the en-tire world.

"Can you turn your video on? What are you doing right now?"

"I'm . . . in the bath."

"Then definitely turn your video on," I tease.

"I don't know . . ."

"Just for a second. Nothing pervy, I swear. I just want to see your face."

"OK, OK," she sighs.

We switch to a video call, and when she pops up on my screen she is most definitely not naked, not in the bath, and not anywhere remotely close to luxuriating. She's standing in the kitchen in her oldest shorts and sweatshirt, the ones with tattered edges she's been wearing since college, so dingy they've been demoted over the years from loungewear to workout-wear to doing-chores-around-the-house-wear. Behind her I can see our Swiffer angled up against the fridge, a pair of yellow cleaning gloves, and various spray bottles on the counter.

She's not relaxing, she's cleaning!

"Hi," she says, busted.

"Liar!" I say. "This is you taking time for yourself?"

"I did! The first day or two."

"And then?"

"And then I had things to do."

"How often do you get the house to yourself?" I say.

"Exactly! I never get a chance to deep clean like this."

"You're wasting a prime opportunity!" I moan, rubbing my temples.

She laughs. "You're cute, but you're way wrong. Just because you two are gone doesn't mean I don't have things to do."

"Name one."

"Well, the house still needs to be taken care of, the laundry needs to be done. All the while, I'm catching up on work in the evenings, obviously. I have to sort through Avery's clothes and make sure she has enough for school, shop for new outfits for the year, and pack up all the old stuff she's outgrown. I have to pick up school supplies, and I can't find the right brand of markers anywhere, so I have to text the other moms and see if anyone knows where to find them or if I can buy a different brand, I have to—"

"OK, I get it, I get it," I say. "But it's still important to take time for yourself, you deserve that. If I had an empty house for a week, I'd . . . I'd—"

"You'd what?"

That sentence had an ending, I'm sure of it. But suddenly I can't think of it. "Well, I would . . ."

"See, you don't even know! You're no better than me, Mr. *I'm going to mow the lawn even though it's not that long.* Mr. *I'm going to organize the Tupperware on a Friday night because I can't think of anything better to do.*"

"OK, OK . . ."

"Mr. *My daughter doesn't want to play with me anymore so I have no idea what to do with myself.*"

"I miss you," I blurt out suddenly, not remotely smooth.

"Oh," she says, taken off guard. "Yeah, I miss you, too."

I wish I was there with her. Wish I could sweep her away to a fancy dinner or an exotic resort. It's a nice feeling, my appreciation for her somehow managing to outweigh my disappointment in myself. Maybe that's what love looks like when you've been married for a decade and a half.

"I shouldn't be going on and on like this. Dumping on you. I'm sorry."

"John," she says firmly. "It's OK to lean on me. To ask for help. We're a team, right?"

I nod.

"This is nice," I say. "We haven't talked on the phone this long since we were dating. Remember how you'd fall asleep because it was so late and I'd mash the buttons to make the phone beep and wake you up?"

"I remember." She smiles. "You're right. This is nice." Then she puts the phone down on the counter, propping me up against something so I can see more of the room and more of her.

"I guess I always just thought my silliness was my parenting superpower. I could make Avery laugh at the drop of a hat. We could make up a game on the spot without even talking about it, we'd just share a look and we would start playing. Without that I just feel lost. Big conversations and big emotions have never been my strong suit."

"You'll get there. I know you will. And in the meantime, it's OK that she needs you a little less. You can fill your life with other things that make you happy. Hobbies. Friends. And you just make sure she knows you're there whenever she needs you."

"Friends and hobbies? What are those?" I joke.

"You could take your wife on a date for once," she says with a wink.

She's teasing, but not really. It has been a little while. OK, a long while. Mostly because I was so busy worrying about how hard it was to find a good babysitter for Avery that I completely missed the fact that she's almost old enough to babysit other kids herself.

"I'd like that," I say.

"I know it's hard to remember, but there is more to life than just being Super Dad all the time. Which you are, by the way."

For some reason, that reminds me and I check the clock on my phone. It's almost time for the next activity, and after that, to start getting ready for dinner and the dance. And I've got a lot to process before I get there.

"I'd be lost without you, you know that," I tell her. "I can't wait to get home."

She smiles. "Go. Have a fun last night. And don't put too much pressure on everything to go perfectly, OK?"

Twenty-Two

I hang up with Evelyn and discover that, during breakfast, a hastily revised schedule of camp activities has materialized on the doorstep of our cabin. It's frighteningly brief:

Canoeing.

Dinner.

Dance and farewells.

And then it's all over. Avery and I will drive home first thing tomorrow morning, one way or another.

I throw on sneakers, slather on some sunscreen, and rush out to meet the group. We're quickly ushered through the woods, winding our way through cabins and trees and finally arriving at the lake—the small, placid, algae-covered body of water probably better described as a large pond. At one point, I had been hoping for waterskiing, but I figured out a few days ago that those photos on the website must have been stock.

The only waterskiing this tiny lake could handle would be if a frog held on to the back of a little battery-powered boat.

Initially, we were supposed to do some kind of trust-building exercise on the ropes course today—which could have been a cool consolation prize—but it seems the Boy Scouts have it booked.

When we arrive, four boats and a messy pile of life jackets line the shore. The dads grab child-size floaties and secure them around their girls, who arrive just shortly after we do, then struggle to buckle their own straps around beer bellies. I scour the small crowd for Avery. I find her, as usual, clinging to Megan as Megan organizes a bundle of oars near the shed.

Avery turns to me, her head sandwiched between the bulky shoulder pads of the bright orange life vest.

"I wanted to ask you a favor," she says.

"OK, shoot."

"Can I canoe with Megan today?"

I'm not the least bit surprised, but that doesn't stop my heart from sinking. It's a good thing we're on dry land, otherwise I'd lose it at the bottom of the lake forever. Avery can read my face and scrambles to explain:

"It's just that, well, it's our last day and Megan"—she looks down—"she's my best friend here." She says this in a hushed tone, as if it would be catastrophically uncool if Megan overhead us. "You and me can do stuff together when we get home, right? This might be my last chance to hang out with her."

A part of me wants to say no, but I can't help but feel like I've already taken enough from Avery, and Megan seems to really mean a lot to her. What kind of dad would I really be if I denied her this one small request?

"OK, kiddo. Sure," I say with as much enthusiasm as I can muster. "But do me a favor. Save a ride for me?" She gives a thumbs-up as she walks away.

I find a dry log to sit on and make myself comfortable as Dennis stands on the small pier jutting into the lake and rattles off names. Apparently there aren't enough boats for everyone, so we have to take turns. No matter. I can wait.

And wait, and wait, and wait. I watch as every other dad comes and goes, having taken their turn, and I watch Megan and Avery do lap after lap around the tiny lake, laughing and splashing each other. I'm waiting an eternity, it feels like. In my mind, my beard grows to my toes like Rip Van Winkle, moss climbs the sides of my shoes, and birds perch on my shoulders, having mistaken me for part of the landscape. All the while, I think hard about Evelyn's advice, about what I'm going to say to Avery, and though I don't know the answer quite yet, I do know that I would wait right here on this log for her as long as it takes.

Finally, they're back, dragging their canoe ashore.

"You ready?" I say, picking up an oar out of the mud.

"Oh right . . . Dad," Avery mumbles, "I'm kinda beat. Plus there's not much to see out there."

"Come out with me, just for one lap around." Then off her look of protest: "You agreed, remember? Come on, make an old man happy."

She rolls her eyes playfully and agrees. "Fine."

• • •

"My arms are dead," she says no more than two minutes into our trip, studying the lake, both of us swatting at gnats and mosquitoes.

"Mine, too." I'm absolutely drenched in sweat, having done all the work getting us out here in the middle of the water. "Wanna just float for a minute?"

"Sure," she says, turning around in her seat and laying her oar down.

So we float, the two of us face-to-face in the cramped quarters of a tiny canoe, nowhere to run or hide. Though I don't feel nervous exactly, my heart's pounding out of my chest. I think a part of me knows I'm running out of mulligans, out of wrong moves. Whatever I decide to say and do today, I have to get it right.

"Can we play a game or something?" Avery asks.

"You . . . want to?"

"Yeah. Know any?"

"Let me think," I say, channeling a few of my own summer camp memories.

They're dusty and probably mostly fictional by now, my mind having filled in the gaps with a haphazard guess at what actually happened, but I've got a nugget of something in there I can use.

"Oh, I know one. It's called gunwale bobbing, I think. I used to play as a kid."

Avery's face lights up immediately, her competitive fire burning visibly behind her eyes. "How does it work?"

"Just do what I do," I say.

I stand in the boat, carefully, nearly falling over several times just trying to get on my feet. Avery follows suit, far more gracefully and quickly. Then, I put one foot up on the side of the canoe, crouch low to steady myself with my hands, and hop the other foot up on the other side. With some effort, I manage to stand (precariously), barely balanced at the very end of the canoe. Or, the gunwale.

Avery loves this, I can tell, and in a flash she matches me at the other end of the canoe. Both of us standing on opposite ends, toes clenched tight to keep our balance, facing each other.

"Now what?" she says.

"Now we try to knock each other off."

"Into this disgusting water?!"

"What, are you chicken?"

She grins. *Definitely not.*

I do a quick squat, hips all the way down and then back up, and Avery's end of the canoe bobs in the air. She wobbles a bit but doesn't fall, and she lets out a laugh. The first time I've made her laugh in I don't know how long. Not counting her laughing *at* me, of course. There's been plenty of that.

She copies me, sending my end of the boat a foot or two into the sky, but I manage to hang on as it descends. I try to shake her loose again, this time giving a little wiggle that shakes the canoe down to Avery's end and nearly sends her into the water. She squeals with delight.

"OK, this is fun," she admits.

"You sound surprised."

She gives me a smirk and tries to throw me off, but I've found my center, and my balance holds. I feign a yawn—*Is that all you got?* The canoe, though, is drifting toward the bank of the lake, and I'm going to get smacked in the face by a gnarly, low-hanging tree branch pretty soon.

"Hey, I wanted to ask you something. Can we pause for a second?" I say. Something's telling me that this is it. This is the right time.

"Uh-oh."

"No, it's not bad. I swear."

My heart's still thudding loudly, desperate to escape its rib cage prison and jump in the lake and swim away from me. It reminds me of how I felt asking Evelyn to marry me, her knowing it was coming the whole time and how that somehow only made me more nervous. I don't know why I'm so anxious, it's not like I really expect Avery to say, *No, I won't go to the dance with you.* But then again, she does a lot of things lately that I don't expect.

"The big dance tonight," I say. "It's the last event of the camp. I'm supposed to ask if you want to go."

She says nothing.

"I know it hasn't been the easiest week, but I was hoping you'd do me the honor of being my date tonight."

"Do we have to?" she whines. "Dresses and dances . . . they're not really my thing."

"It would mean a lot to me."

She thinks, then a devilish little grin spreads across her face. "If you knock me in first, I'll go."

"And if you win?"

"No promises."

A simple yes would have made me feel better, but I can deal with it. She's just being playful, that's all. That's what we do best. And besides, I'm pretty sure I can knock her in anytime I—

THWUNK! Avery launches my side of the canoe into the air and the top of my head smacks against that damn tree branch, which I had completely forgotten about. I'm momentarily disoriented, and I fall straight forward, my chest and belly hitting the rim of the canoe, and the rest of my body sliding overboard into the water like a wet noodle.

Underwater, I can hear Avery's screaming laughter. I'm able to stand since we're close enough to shore, and rub the gritty water out of my eyes. Mud slurps into my shoes, weighing me down like cement boots.

"No fair," I say, spitting out a tongue-full of foul lake sand. "That doesn't count." She's still laughing, but she catches her breath just long enough to speak.

"Hey, you agreed to the deal."

I throw a waterlogged leg over the side of the canoe and climb back in. But there's something in my shoe, digging into my heel. I slip it off and dump it upside down, then out comes a penny, clattering against the bottom of the boat.

"What's that?" Avery says as I pick it up, inspecting it's extremely weathered appearance.

"Wow. It's from 1943, that's like . . . sixty years ago."

"Isn't it more like eighty years ago?"

Crap. She's right. When did I get so old?

"Well either way. It's a lucky find," I say.

"You should keep it." She smiles. "Something to remember our trip by. And, you know, how I kicked your butt and knocked you in the dirty lake."

I store the penny safely in my pocket and rack my brain. I love that I'm making her laugh again, that we're having fun together again, but I'm going to have to push a little further. I've been getting nowhere trying to get her to talk to me. Time to take the first step, like Evelyn said.

"Hey, do you remember last year when your teachers were thinking of moving you up a grade?"

"Yeah . . . why?"

"I was just thinking. You know, when I was a little older than you, my teachers came to my parents and me and asked the same thing. Wanted to know what I thought about skipping a grade."

"You?" She cocks an eyebrow at me.

"Is that so hard to believe?"

"You were smart?"

I reach down and playfully splash a little water toward her.

"I still am smart, thank you very much. But I think it was just a timing thing. Who was that kid at your school who was like six feet tall in third grade? You know who I'm talking about."

She nods.

"He probably won't grow up to be a giant or anything; he just sprouted early. I was like that, but with math and reading. I'm not a genius, in case you didn't notice, but I picked it up quickly for some reason. And anyway, at one point they thought maybe I would do better if I was around older kids, taking harder classes."

"And did you?"

"I didn't want to do it. Teachers wanted me to, parents wanted me to, but I fought like hell to stay put."

Her body language is closed off, like it's been a lot lately, walls up, not wanting to engage further. A little fun is one thing. Heart-to-hearts are another. But she's intrigued and can't help herself. "Why?"

"At the time I thought it was because I wanted to stay with my friends. And honestly I liked everything being easy for me."

Avery chuckles at that.

"But when I think back now, I think I was scared. We had a couple of kids in our grade who had skipped ahead, and I remember them getting teased and bullied relentlessly. They were smaller than everyone else and really bookish, and I saw how hard it was for them to fit in. I was terrified that that would happen to me."

I can see the dread creep across her face, the way her brain is spinning about her own future.

"But . . . they were really smart kids, and they all went on to do amazing things. One of them works for NASA I think. Another does analytics or sabermetrics or whatever you call it for the Yankees."

"As in, the New York Yankees?"

I nod.

"Whoa, that's cool," she concedes.

"Super cool."

"So what happened, did you ever skip?" she asks.

"No. I didn't."

She looks at me expectantly. I don't speak, I only paddle slowly, in no hurry to get back to the group, even though I'm covered in muddy water like a swamp monster.

"So is that the lesson, then? You wish you had not been so scared of what people might think? Or are you happy that you stayed put?"

I laugh.

"There's no lesson. I just wanted you to know that I went through something like that, too, and I had a lot of complicated feelings about it. Fear. Regret. All those big scary things."

"But now you know how everything turned out, so you should know what the right choice would have been," she prods, as if trapping me with logic.

"Who says the way I feel now is more important than the way I felt about it then? Being miserable at thirteen . . . being a little regretful in your mid-thirties." I pop my palms in the air as if weighing two imaginary objects against each other.

"Late thirties."

I shush her. "My point is, who's to say which one matters more? Your feelings are always valid, no matter how old you are. At my age, I still don't have the right answers. I often don't."

She considers this; I can tell she's hearing me, really taking it in, but she's still waiting for the punchline.

"So no lesson?"

"No lesson."

She finally accepts that I'm not pulling a fast one on her, and she begins paddling again. I stay silent.

"Even though it's a clear violation of the terms of our deal," she announces, "we can go to the stupid dance. It might be fun, I guess."

"Whatever you want," I say, trying and failing to play it cool as I break into a wide smile.

Twenty-Three

I'm trying really hard not to look at the set of balls directly to my right.

We're all crowded into the camp bathroom, and after a week of being overrun by a bunch of dudes, it's in rough shape. Every surface is soaking wet, puddles creep over the edge of the sink countertop and drip intermittently on the floor. Moisture from the showers has taken over the entire facility, coating the walls. Hairs (head, beard, and . . . *other*) stick to every nook and cranny.

And every single one of the dads is in here, trying to make themselves look presentable ahead of tonight's farewell dinner and dance. Plus the Boy Scout troop leaders, who make an already cramped space feel positively claustrophobic.

Most of the men in here are young(ish), like me, wrapped mostly in towels or with hastily thrown on boxers after a quick shower. A few, though, are on the older side, and one of them in particular—from the Boy Scout group—takes an unnecessarily long amount of time, nude, leg up on a changing bench, to blow-dry his nether regions. I'm looking directly into the mirror in front of me, so I can't quite tell, but I think he's trying to make eye contact with me while he does it. He's old enough that I doubt he cares, but all I can think about is how that kind of heat exposure can wreak absolute hell on your sperm counts.

I do my best to ignore him and go on lathering my face in shaving cream. I want to look my best for tonight.

Booker snags the sink and mirror next to me and plops down his toiletry bag. "Big night, huh?"

"Can't believe it's almost over. Bet the office is dying to get you back on Monday."

"Pfffft," he raspberries. "Get me *back*. Like I haven't been working my ass off all week during my 'vacation.'"

I drag my razor through the suds on my face, revealing a trail of smooth skin, praying I don't nick myself and bleed all over the place. I'd hate to show up to what feels like one of the most important evenings of my life with my face dotted with bloody scabs.

"I haven't seen you working as much. Thought maybe you got the boss off your back."

"He never gets off my back. I've just been saving most of my work for late at night, when I'm not with Erica."

I look over at him, and I hadn't noticed until now, but he looks exhausted, puffy bags under his eyes and a bit of a slump in his posture. His voice, too—it doesn't have the vigor it had earlier in the week. He clocks my concern and waves me off.

"Don't worry about me," he says. "Not something to bother anyone with, especially Erica. All she knows is that I've been a lot less distracted, and that's the way it should be."

Well, that's good. I guess. And suddenly I think about Ryan, absolutely glowing earlier about the progress he'd made with Jessie. And then there's Lou, who's actually the only dad not in the bathroom building right now—he was sitting outside with Tam as I walked over here, layering her hair into an absolutely unbelievable fancy braid.

"Sounds like everyone's ending the week on a high note," I say. "Just like we hoped."

Even I'm getting close. Just have to stick the landing.

"High note is a stretch," he says. "I survived. I didn't completely blow it. So I guess I'll take that."

Booker combs his hair with precision, getting the part just right. This is how I imagine he looks in those dark early mornings, quietly getting ready for the office while the rest of the house sleeps.

"Well, there's still time, man. Maybe if you talked to Erica, if you were really honest with her about everything you're trying to juggle . . ."

"And lay all of that at her feet? No way. It's not her problem to solve."

"But if you talk to her, you know, more like an adult, maybe the two of you will understand each other better. Get to that next level in your relationship. This shell game of hiding your work from her and trying to juggle both of them separately, it's going to catch up with you eventually. Let's face it, it already is."

Booker sighs. He knows I'm right. But he still has that pained look on his face. Like a man who knows he's trapped.

"You sayin' I look like shit?"

"Only your face."

He laughs.

"I've got some ideas about how to make it better, or I might. We'll see. One day, I'll tell her how hard it all was. When she's old enough to understand."

I'm about to let it go, not push any further. But then I don't.

"Nah. It's gotta be now. Tonight. You don't want to leave this place without getting what you came here for. You've got to talk to her tonight."

As I say this, I'm looking in the mirror, and the irony isn't lost on me that I'm quite literally saying it to myself. Avery and I are getting along as well as ever, but there's still something I haven't told her. And if I don't come clean, this will all have been for nothing.

I came here to learn how to be a better dad. And better dads don't keep secrets from their daughters.

I turn to leave, just barely catching a glimpse of Old Scout Man, who has switched legs and is now blasting the underside of his other thigh with the blow-dryer on its highest setting. Surely, the area must be dry by now. I hurry out with my eyes down to avoid losing my appetite this close to dinner.

On the short walk back to the cabin, I take my time, plodding along in shower sandals and a clean undershirt, a towel wrapped around my waist. With the sun setting through the tree line, I want to soak up as much of this as I can before we have to leave. And before I have to gamble all the goodwill I've worked so hard to build with Avery, potentially squandering it and sending us back to square one, or further. Even though I know it's the right thing to do.

I finish dressing, slipping carefully into a dress shirt and tie, straightening the knot over and over in a faint window reflection. I haul on a pair of slacks, which has somehow remained relatively wrinkle-free. Then I walk the path to the candlelit dinner by the lake, hoping Avery will keep her word and meet me, and wishing that Evelyn were here to help me with this conversation.

As I get closer, I can start to make out the dinner setup. It's amazing what Dennis and his small crew have done here, how they've transformed the space. Small, circular tables dot the shore, each with a white tablecloth and an old-fashioned lantern-style candle in the middle. String lights connect the trees on either side of the water, dipping low and nearly skimming the surface, reflecting brilliantly and creating a magical, starry effect. Fireflies blink slowly, as if flirting with the string lights.

Dennis plays maître d', outfitted in a full tuxedo and standing in front of what looks like a cheap music stand stolen from a high school band room.

"Good evening, sir," he cheekily greets a dad in front of me. "How many in your party this evening?"

But when he sees me coming, his expression shifts from playful to serious. He scoots out from behind his makeshift host stand and stops me in my tracks, a firm hand on my chest, his voice low and stern:

"John, good, you're here. I need to talk to you. In private."

In his free hand, he's holding an object. Something black and rectangular. It's my phone.

That can't be good.

Dennis pulls me roughly off the main trail, well out of earshot of the rest of the "guests."

But he hasn't said a word.

"What's going on? Where did you get that? Is everything OK with Avery? Also, ow," I say, grasping at some sort of explanation for his serious demeanor and his bear claw grip on my arm.

"Care to explain this?" Dennis says, with a tone that uncannily matches that of a disappointed dad. Wagging my phone in the air like a principal who just discovered a booby magazine in someone's locker.

"Explain what? That's not even mine," I insist.

He taps on the touch screen, which lights up, revealing a giant photo of Avery as the screensaver.

"That could be anyone."

"Oh, give it up, John. I noticed the box was missing right away, though it took a little longer to do a proper search of the cabins. Why don't you just come clean?"

Normally, I wouldn't tolerate this kind of interrogation. I mean, for crying out loud, I paid a *lot* of money to be here—and that was before I decided I had to have the pink nail polish. It's like getting busted sneaking your own snacks into the movie theater. What are they going to do, put you in popcorn jail? That's how I feel about Dennis and his little summer camp power trip, but there's just one problem—I really don't want to get sent home early. Not now. Not so close to the end.

"Just please don't kick me out." I sigh, throwing myself at his mercy.

"Why would I want to do that? I'm not the bad guy here. I just need to know where the rest are."

The problem is, I don't know where Lou hid the bag. And I'm not about to drag him into this, which puts me in quite a pickle.

"I can't remember where I put them."

"You . . . don't remember?" He checks his watch. "It was only a few days ago."

"I just . . . can't recall."

"What were you, drunk?"

I say nothing, only holding back a cartoony *Nothing to see here* whistle.

"Oh my God! You were drunk!" Dennis moans, then reading my face, he gasps. "My nonnies! It was you!"

"I can find them, everyone's phones," I blurt, bringing us back to the point at hand. "Just give me some time."

"This is . . . ," he stutters, struggling to process the situation, "just . . . so bizarre. I don't even know what to say. You took everyone's phones and laptops and . . . hid them somewhere? But kept yours? Why?"

And now it's Booker I don't want to implicate, just in case. So I decide to tell him the truth . . . a version of it, at least.

"You were right, about Avery, about everything. I couldn't run from it any longer. I was going to text the coach back and tell her we weren't going to make it to the soccer tryouts, but . . . I couldn't bring myself to do it. They were Wednesday, anyhow. We missed them. It's over."

Dennis's face sinks.

"I know how it sounds. But I'm going to fix it. I'm going to tell her tonight."

But then I realize that his expression isn't one of disappointment, and it's not being leveled at me. It's something closer to horror, and I follow his gaze over my shoulder.

And there's Avery.

Turns out, she didn't remember to bring a dress even though I gave her the packing list to study before we left. Instead, she's wearing an overly long white T-shirt, tie-dyed into a dreamy explosion of color, with the sleeves trimmed neatly off. And you know what? It almost passes as an actual dress, it really does.

She looks beautiful, obviously, but more important, she looks older. Probably the oldest I've ever seen her look. In a flash I see her at things like eighth-grade dances and proms and graduations and being picked up for a date in a brand-new Jeep by some slick shithead whose parents bought it for him and Holy Shit, someone make it stop.

But this is a problem for another time. Because, based on the look on her face, she's just heard everything.

"Coach texted you?" Avery says, betrayal already welling up in her eyes. "The season . . . was never canceled, was it?"

"It just . . . I'm sorry. . . ." I can't find the words. "Avery, I was going to tell you—"

But she doesn't stick around to hear any more. She sprints off somewhere into the trees, into the darkness, her tie-dye shirt fading fast from view. Running at full speed now, no holding back, leaving me absolutely no chance of catching her.

Twenty-Four

I'm staring at the front door of Avery's cabin, and I know she's in there somewhere, upset, maybe crying. Hating my guts. I've had a lot of time to think on the slow walk over here, and I wonder how many times a man can relive the same horrible moment before it breaks him completely.

At least one more time, I decide.

I knock on the door, but no one answers, so I let myself in. It's dark inside, so dark that I can't see anything at first but shapes and dim silhouettes of blankets, sleeping bags, and duffels. There's crap all over the floor—underwear and T-shirts and sunscreen and food wrappers. God, girls are messy. But as my eyes begin to adjust to the darkness I realize there's no one in here.

"Avery?" I say, just to make sure, but I already know no one's going to respond.

I assumed she'd run right back here. The cabin has been her safe space, her base camp, this entire week. I must have really pissed her off for her to seek shelter elsewhere.

I poke my head inside my own cabin, too, but this whole section of camp is empty, with all the other dads at the lakeside dinner with their girls. A quick peek inside the rest of the structures confirms it.

My heart rate starts to pick up a tad, though I'm not in a state of full-blown panic yet. This is a huge camp in the middle of nowhere, surrounded by endless woods. It's massive and overwhelming, with countless places to hide, if one were so inclined. But at the same time, there's really nowhere to go. If she's not at her own cabin, and not here, where else could she really be?

I poke my head in the girls' bathroom and give a quick "Hello?" to make sure it's empty.

It's as damp and awful as the men's facility. No one shrieks, so I go in, dodging puddles and clumps of long hair on the floor, and I peek into all of the shower and bathroom stalls. No sign of Avery here.

And I'm officially worried. I stop walking and start jogging. In moments I'm back at the lake, where the dinner has resumed following our little commotion.

Dennis is seating another "couple" when I arrive.

"John—" he starts, but I cut him off.

"Avery's gone."

I explain what's going on, where I've looked, and he springs into action, leading me to the path, the one I just came from moments ago.

"If she was upset and in a hurry, she could have taken the wrong fork here," he explains as we walk together. Sure enough, the path branches off subtly away from the cabins and into the woods. I never noticed it before, but it's clear as day now. If your brain were on autopilot, or perhaps in a fog of rage, it'd be easy to go the wrong way. And I definitely saw her take the trail.

"What's back there?"

"More paths," he says ominously. "A whole network of them, miles long, meant for hiking."

"Where do they all lead? Back here?"

"Well . . . they used to. But most of them are overgrown and haven't been cleared in a while. You know, budget and everything . . ."

"What are you saying?"

"I'm saying it would be easy for someone to get lost back there."

"Dennis!"

"We have a protocol for this, it's all going to be OK," he says. "But for what it's worth, I'm sorry for upsetting her. It wasn't my intention."

I want to lash out at him. But even with all the fear and adrenaline pumping through my veins, I know who's really to blame.

"It's not your fault," I say with a sigh. "It's nobody's but mine."

"Never mind that now. You go on and start looking for her. I'll call the sheriff; he's a friend. I'm sure he can send out a deputy or two to help. I'll have everyone else search the camp. I'm sure she's fine, I'm sure of it. But just as a precaution."

"Thanks," I say, and I sprint down the path into the pitch-black night.

"John?" he says, and I stop. "You'll get lost, too, if you don't take a flashlight. And you should probably bring some backup."

He's right. And I know immediately who I want with me.

• • •

Lou, Booker, Ryan, and I walk the path together, each shining a powerful flashlight into the trees and brush on either side of us.

"Avery!" we take turns calling out, but there's no response.

The quiet out here is unnerving and has me thinking the worst.

"She's all right. I'm sure she's out here somewhere," Lou says, a comforting attempt to fill the empty air space.

"Good news is this area isn't really known for any dangerous animals like bears or coyotes," adds Ryan.

"Oh my god," I say. "There could be bears out here?!"

"I said there *weren't* bears. Probably. That's a good thing!"

"AVERY!!!" I yell louder.

Suddenly, the path seems to narrow and close in on us. Now as we walk, our arms brush against tree branches and overgrown weeds. The light dirt path starts to disappear entirely, losing ground to moss and ivies and grass and fallen leaves.

"How did this happen?" I ask no one in particular. "We don't fight, not like this. No, how it works is I try to get through to her, and she gets irritated and ignores me. That's how it's supposed to work now. But nooooo," I whine, swatting a thorny branch out of my way. "That wasn't good enough for me. I had to push it, didn't I? God, I'd give anything to have her right in front of me, rolling her eyes, and sucking her teeth, and completely ignoring every word out of my mouth. Whatever abuse I'd have to take to get her back, I'd take it."

"Kids run sometimes, they hide from things," Lou says. "One time I told Tam she couldn't have mac and cheese for the fourth night in a row, so she stayed in her room for an entire Saturday. I just let her stay there, and eventually she fell asleep. Next day she completely forgot she was even mad at me."

"Jessie runs off a lot, too," Ryan adds. "Hides in her room. In the tree house. Sometimes on the roof. Her altitude of choice depends on how mad she is at me."

"Bet you've never lost her in the forest," I say.

"No. But I will say, she always comes back sooner or later."

I cock an eyebrow at him. "What's that supposed to mean?"

"I'm just saying, she might not be ready to be found. That's all."

"She can't be out here alone. Not at night. Not with bears and coyotes on the prowl."

"I said there *weren't* bears or coyotes. *Weren't.*"

"She's just a little kid," I say. And she needs me.

But is she? Does she?

We soldier on, and now the brush begins to suffocate us. The path is almost completely gone, just a rumor of slightly broken-in dirt buried under mounds of forest. I wonder aloud if Avery could have even realistically gone this way.

"Kid her size could have easily gone under or through," Booker says. "I mean, it depends on how motivated she was to get away from you."

"Let's assume *very*," I say.

We keep going. But first, Ryan stops, kneels, and pulls something from the side of his backpack. It's long and reflective, causing a slice of my flashlight beam to bounce back and nearly blind me.

"What is that?" Lou says.

"Behold," Ryan says, holding the object up for us to illuminate with our lights. It's a massive machete.

"You brought a giant knife to a dads-and-daughters camp?" Booker gasps.

"A camp in the *woods*, Booker." As if only an idiot would leave their machete at home from summer camp.

He walks to the front of our little conga line and begins hacking away at the brush, clearing it easily. Huge branches and thick vines fall limp and lifeless to the ground as Ryan carves a new path for us. The three of us stay back a few paces as he pushes forward faster and faster. We're making great time until—

"AHHH!" Ryan yells, and he tumbles awkwardly to the ground, landing with a thud.

"You OK?" Booker calls out, and we all rush forward.

"Oh, God . . . Oh, no . . . ," I yell, preparing myself mentally for a bloody scene.

"I stepped on a root or something, *fuck*." Ryan winces. "Rolled the hell out of my ankle."

"Oh," I say, the relief in my voice almost reminiscent of a laugh. There's just something a little funny about the camp tough guy being taken down by something so . . . mundane.

"Whadya mean, *Oh*? It fucking hurts!"

"Let me take a look," Lou says, kneeling down and shining his flashlight on Ryan's exposed leg.

"I'm fine, someone just help me up," and he tries to stand but lets out another pained yelp and collapses again.

"Stop being such a macho douchebag and let me see your damn ankle," Lou snaps.

Ryan reluctantly relaxes and allows Lou to handle the damaged limb. "Before Tam was born I took a ton of different classes. First aid, CPR. I'm good at this stuff."

I feel like this, among plenty of other things, is my fault. Ryan should never have been out here, running full speed into thick weeds while swinging a machete. In the dark. He should be sitting enjoying dinner with his daughter. We're lucky he didn't hack his arm off.

Still, we need to keep moving. Or I do, at least.

"Well?" Ryan says.

"Good news is nothing feels broken, but I'm not a doctor. It is starting to swell, though, so we need to get some ice on it."

"Are you . . . are you massaging it?"

"Elevation and circulation are key. Why, does it hurt?"

"No, it feels . . . good. I mean—" Ryan clears his throat loud, manly-like, dispelling any hint of softness or vulnerability. "It feels fine."

Once again I'm amazed by Lou and how his softer, nurturing side makes him stand out in a moment like this, a man among men.

"You two go on," Booker says, eyeing me and Lou. "I can help him back."

"Are you sure? Lou, you can head back, too, if you want. I don't want anyone else getting hurt or lost or mangled by a bear," I say.

"For cryin' out loud . . . ," Ryan sighs.

"Nah," Lou says. "I'm coming with you."

• • •

"It's a good thing you were here, you know, for Ryan," I tell Lou after we've walked for a while and unleashed a few fruitless calls of *Avery!*

"Just too bad I was out of *Paw Patrol* Band-Aids." He laughs. "I guess treating boo-boos is my superpower."

"One of many, apparently," I say, picking up on the fact that he's making fun of himself. "And just take the damn compliment."

He chuckles a little and nods. But we're not lucky *just* because he was able to offer Ryan a little relief after the fall. I feel like I've learned a lot from him. About bravery, mostly . . . and a little about pasta. But there's something that's still not adding up.

"What are you looking for, Lou? What brought you here?"

"To the middle of the woods?"

"To the camp."

"Yeah, I know, I know . . ." He hesitates. "You're not the only one who's scared of what might come next."

"But Tam's only, what, six? You've got tons of time."

"It won't be the same. She's been home with me her whole life, so it's all either of us know. But she's starting school now. I might even go back to work. Maybe open up my own place, who knows," he says, swallowing away a shakiness in his voice.

"Your own restaurant? That's amazing, man."

"It's expensive is what it is. I like to dream about it, but pulling the trigger terrifies me. The loans, the risk. It could crush us financially if things go south."

"They won't."

He laughs. "You don't know that."

"I wouldn't bet against you, that's for sure."

"Thanks. It's just a big change, that's all. It's scary."

We walk on.

"If you wanted time with Tam, you could have taken her anywhere in the world," I say. "And you chose . . . this?"

He laughs.

"She's gotta learn how to be around other kids, so I thought about sending her off to summer camp, but she would never go without me. So I found this place. Seemed like a safe way for her to test the waters."

"And what about you, then?"

"I just thought . . . I wanted to not feel like I was the only dad at the playdate, for once, like I do at home, you know? I wanted to feel like I belonged somewhere. And after the first few days, where I frankly hated all of your guts," he says, and I laugh, "I finally feel like I do."

I stop in my tracks suddenly. Not due to any sound or discovery. But there's a nugget of a thought forming in my head, and I need to concentrate to unearth it. Lou's got me thinking about just that. Home. I've put all this pressure on the last night at camp like it could magically fix everything. But he's right. I've got to figure out a way to take what I've learned here and bring those lessons home with me.

"Everything OK?" Lou asks.

"This is ridiculous, isn't it?"

"What is?"

"All of this! She's not out here. We've got this knife to hack away the brush and we're still barely getting anywhere. There's no way she came this way and, what, army crawled under the thorns?"

"Definitely not."

"You already figured it out, didn't you?"

"Uh-huh."

"Why didn't you tell me I was being an idiot?"

"I know how it feels when you think you're doing the right thing for your family and people won't stop telling you you're wrong. Figured you could use someone in your corner."

"I'm just sorry for wasting your time, taking you away from Tam on your last night."

"It's all right, really."

"I mean, if Avery is out here somewhere . . . it would be the stupidest, most reckless, most childish thing she's ever . . ."

I stop again, shutting my mouth and listening to the night. Though we're deep in the woods now, it's anything but quiet. The air has an orchestral quality to it, like we're in a Louisiana bayou and all sorts of bugs are screeching and chirping at one another.

The rhythmic buzzing gives me a chance to think for a second, and Lou doesn't break my concentration. Just waits as I turn it over in my mind, what Ryan said, *Maybe she's not ready to be found*, and what I just said, *It would be the stupidest, most reckless, most childish . . .*

Avery is none of those things. Not stupid. Not reckless. And, as much as it pains me to admit it, not childish.

I've got this image of her, barely older than a toddler, lost and scared and alone in the woods. Waiting for me to come rescue her. But that's not who she is. She's capable. She's smart. She's, quite literally, trained in wilderness survival.

Though it kills me to admit it, she's a stone's throw away from being one of the fiercest, most independent creatures on the planet: a teenager.

"We should head back," I say, finally.

"All right, then, whatever you think." Lou nods, and he turns without a word and starts the trek back.

It sounds weird, I know, like I'm giving up or something, just letting her go without even a fight. But I think that might be the only way I'm going to find her.

Twenty-Four and a Half

Avery is twenty hours old and swaddled up in one of those coarse, blue-and-white-striped hospital blankets. The ones they send you home with by the dozen. She's red-faced and fast asleep and being rocked back and forth by my mom, who, along with my dad, have popped in to officially meet their first granddaughter.

Evelyn, in the hospital bed, has dozed off. Deservedly. We speak in whispers in the low light of the recovery room so she can rest.

"She is absolutely precious," Mom says. "She's going to have you wrapped around your finger when she's older."

"Too late." I smile back.

My dad, a long man with a short beard, stands off by himself in the corner. Not in a grumpy way. He just likes to be able to stand back and see everything, is all. Keep an eye on things.

"Dad, you wanna hold her?"

He ignores me and instead nods over to the little makeshift bed toward the side of the room, with the wafer-thin blanket and limp pillow I've been using to sneak tiny bits of sleep here and there.

"Is that where you're sleeping?" he grumbles. "They should give you a better blanket. And a real pillow."

"It's fine, Dad."

"I'm sure it's no trouble. I'll talk to the nurse. And, Evelyn, poor thing, she needs heavier blankets. She looks cold."

"Don't bug the nurses. We don't need anything, I swear. I packed extra blankets if Evelyn needs them. And a pillow, too. She said it was all making her hot, so she didn't want it anymore."

"All right, all right," he relents.

I walk over to my bag and pull out a small cardboard box, then take it over to Dad, hiding it close to my body, almost conspiratorially. He looks down at it, puzzled, and I open it slowly, like some relic out of an Indiana Jones movie. I'm making the moment last on purpose. I've been waiting to do this with my dad for a long time.

Inside the box are two thick cigars.

"What do you say we fire up a proper celebration?"

"You can't do that in here."

"I know, I know. We'll go outside."

"I've never really liked cigars, you know that."

"Neither do I, they're disgusting, obviously. But it's a tradition. Have one puff?"

"You enjoy. This is your moment. I'll go see about those extra pillows."

I stop him from leaving with a hand on his arm. "Hey. I'm gonna be OK, right?" I ask in a hushed tone. "I'm gonna figure this out?"

I've never taken care of anyone before. Never been responsible for another life. And, though I don't want to advertise it, I'm kind of freaking out. Against my will, my eyes begin to well up.

"Of course you will," he commands, less comforting than I'd like. "Now pull it together."

He gives me a pat on the back, like a coach sending an injured player back out onto the football field, and slinks out the door. I wipe at my eyes and sidle up to my mom, whose gaze hasn't left Avery's puffy little face for a second.

"Same old Dad," I huff.

"And you were expecting . . ."

"I don't know. I just don't get why it's impossible for him to let his guard down for two seconds. It's always arm's length with him."

She gives a shrug, still fawning all over the new baby.

"I'm not going to be like that," I declare dramatically, more to myself than anyone else. "I'm not. Avery is going to know me. Really know me. I'm going to be vulnerable and real with her, no matter what."

Mom laughs.

"What?" I ask.

"Your father said the same thing when you were born," she says. "Almost verbatim." Well, that's just a lie. And if it isn't, he went horribly wrong somewhere along the way.

Look, he's a fantastic dad, and I'm truly an ungrateful bastard for complaining about him. I've never wanted for anything my entire life. He's been supportive. Strong. Present. All the things you could ever really ask for.

But there was always this separate side of him that he never let me see. I could never come to the ballpark on those muggy summer nights and catch a game with him, those were always just for him and his buddies. He never let me stay up late to watch a show or a movie with him, one I really shouldn't be watching. He taught me how to throw a ball, the mechanics of it, but would never just run around, the two of us making up our own game with it. Things like that.

There's a time when you're young that you want your parents to be your best friend. Eventually, you're supposed to grow out of it. But since that bond never happened for me and him, I guess I never grew out of wanting it.

"He and I must have very different definitions of what that means, then," I say.

"You were too young to remember, but the two of you were inseparable. BFFs before the phrase even existed."

"And what happened?"

"Being a parent is hard. And not just because you're tired and you have to change diapers all the time. But because there's no handbook that tells you what to do. He tried so hard to be your best friend and to discipline you when you needed it—and boy, you needed it sometimes—and give you space at just the right times. You can't be too hard on him for not getting it exactly right. After all. You turned out OK."

She's still looking at Avery as she says this, and somehow that makes it more meaningful. But . . .

"I still don't understand." I sigh.

"You will," she says.

Twenty-Five

Still no sign of Avery, and by now I've stopped looking, and I'm just waiting. For what, exactly, I'm not sure.

For a second, I think I feel a light spit of rain, and it triggers a memory in me. On dreary days, when she was little, Avery and I used to play hide-and-seek in the house. In the beginning, it took her some time to get the hang of it. But it was fun. Our games would devolve into fits of giggling when she'd hide under a table, 90 percent of her body still visible, or throw a blanket over herself on the couch with half a leg sticking out. I'd pretend I couldn't see her, wondering aloud where in the world she could be, maybe "accidentally" sitting or stepping on her in the process. And we would both laugh.

Over time, she got a little bit better, mostly by learning from me. Copying my favorite hiding spots. She'd give up trying to find me when I had sandwiched myself between an open door and the wall, and then the very next turn, I'd find her in the same space.

Eventually, she became the master. Her creativity and skill grew and grew, and soon enough she was wiggling her small body into spots I'd never even considered before. I could still usually find her—after all, our house isn't very big—but I'll never forget the first time I couldn't.

I spent about thirty minutes looking, no joke, and finally I wandered back into the living room, exasperated, and begged her to come out. I thought maybe she legitimately went outside in the pouring rain and was watching me, sopping wet, through a window somewhere. Her voice yelled from the other room, "Close your eyes first!" and I did, and when I opened them, she was there in front of me without a sound. She refused to tell me the hiding spot, in case she wanted to use it again (her words, not mine). I could vaguely tell what direction her voice was coming from when she called out, but I never could pinpoint it any further than that.

Now, instead of our living room, I'm sitting on the front stoop of Avery's cabin, the aroma of fresh-cut lumber still just barely there. And instead of me shouting, begging for Avery to come out, I sit in silence. Waiting and trusting that she'll come out on her own sooner or later.

The county sheriff, a bored-looking toothpick of a man, walked past my perch with Dennis and offered to bring out a few deputies to help with the search. He offered to arrange for a bigger crew and maybe even some dogs to come out, if I wanted, but he didn't seem alarmed. I wanted to shake him and scream in his face like I was in a Liam Neeson action flick, "THAT'S MY DAUGHTER, DAMMIT"—but in reality, I thought he was probably right not to overreact.

After sitting here for half an hour without a sign of her, I start to second-guess my approach. If she is out there in the woods, maybe lost, we're losing precious time. I don't know. I just don't know what the right thing is anymore. Maybe this is just how parents are supposed to feel every second of every day. It's how my dad must have felt at times. But I don't like it.

I'm so used to trying to get her to trust me, earning it from scratch over and over every day, that I never considered what it would feel like to trust *her*. Fully, truly trust her—no peeking through the blinds to make sure she's safe playing outside alone, no standing right next to her as she walks along a high wall, ready to catch her just in case.

Finally, after what feels like an eternity, I see a figure walking toward me out of the shadowy tree line. Avery. And though I'm not surprised to see her, I let out a powerful exhale of relief.

"God, I'm so glad you're safe," I say.

"You're not out looking for me?" she says, as she climbs up and sits next to me.

"I figured you would come out when you were ready."

"How did you know I wasn't lost?"

"I guess I just trusted you."

She says nothing for a moment, just dangles her legs and swings them in the way kids do whenever their feet can't reach the ground, then:

"That was pretty stupid of you."

"I know."

"I could have been eaten by a bear."

"I know, I know!"

She laughs. A little.

"Where did you go?" I ask.

"I did hide at first. For a while. I was just so angry . . . And I still am."

I nod.

"But then I thought about what Mr. Dennis said, and I went looking for the phones. I couldn't find them, but I ran into some of your dad friends, and I asked them."

She must have caught Ryan and Booker coming back from our disastrous search and rescue effort.

"They said they hadn't seen them either but they helped me look, and eventually we found them under your old cabin, buried beneath some leaves. I gave them back to Mr. Dennis."

"So he knows you're OK? When did you see him?"

"Just now."

Another sigh of relief. I'm so, so, unbelievably glad that Avery's all right. But I'm also happy that a brigade of search dogs isn't about to burst out of a van in the parking lot, a whirring chopper hovering overhead and blasting a spotlight into the forest surrounding camp.

"What did you do all that for?" I ask.

"I didn't want you to get in trouble."

"You don't need to worry about me. It's my job to worry."

She looks down at her feet.

"What's going on with you, kiddo?" I say.

"Nothing."

"C'mon. Talk to me."

"I'm just not in the mood to be bought off with ice cream, or, like, tickled until I forget that I'm sad. That's what you always do."

This stings, but I press on. I've got to meet her halfway, at least.

"I'm so sorry I messed up the soccer team for you. I really am," I say.

She hangs her head. "Why did you lie? Why didn't you want me on the team?"

I think for a minute about where to start, how to put this all in terms she can understand.

"You might not remember, but for the longest time, the thing you wanted most in the entire world was—"

"A little sister?"

She remembers. Of course she does.

"Well, me and your mom wanted you to have one, too. We really, really did."

"So what happened?"

"It's not always easy. You don't just snap your fingers and get a baby." Come to think of it, I don't think we've ever had *the talk* with Avery, and so I ask her, "Do you know where babies come from yet?"

"I know they don't come from storks."

I smile.

"Aren't there, like, doctors who can help with that stuff?" she asks, surprising me. This kid is so damn smart.

"Yep. But your mom and I decided that we just wanted to focus on being there for you, and that would be enough to make us happy."

She blushes a bit, a kid who's never really realized that she's the love of someone's life before.

"But what does that have to do with anything?"

"Well. I guess I lied because . . . I was afraid of losing you. Being your coach is one of the best parts of being your dad, and being your dad is the best part of my entire life. Once you grow up, I won't ever get to do it again. That's a scary thought."

"You could have just told me that."

"I know," I say. "I'm telling you now."

I nudge her with my elbow. "All right. Your turn."

She shrugs.

"How come you never told me about the drawer in your room?"

Avery's face flashes red with embarrassment.

"Mom told you?"

"It wasn't exactly inconspicuous." I laugh, then: "Hey. I'm listening now." I reach out and gently tilt her chin toward me.

"I just feel . . ." she begins, face tightening to keep tears from welling up in her eyes, "different from everyone else, you know? Like I don't fit in anywhere."

That's not true, you're amazing! Everyone loves you, and you're so great at school and at sports and—I have to silence these first-reaction thoughts before they come pouring out of me. Instead, I give her space to keep going.

"Most of those invitations are from years ago," she admits, sinking a little lower. "I never went to any of them anyway."

"Why not?"

"I always had a game, or at least a practice, or a test to study extra for. And if I wasn't busy with that stuff I was probably . . ."

"Hanging out with me," I add, realizing. Fishing trips and carnivals and long hikes flashing in front of me. Our adventures.

She nods, and I wince as one of the worst pains I've ever felt slices through me. Realizing that my insistence on spending all of my time with Avery might have actually made her more lonely. It's more than I can take right now. She notices.

"But I loved doing stuff with you! Or I *love*. I don't know," she grunts, grasping for a way to synthesize a complicated stew of preteen emotions. "You're not supposed to like hanging out with your dad. No one else my age does. But I never wanted to give that up. And I didn't want to give up anything *else* because I thought you and Mom would be disappointed. Anyway, eventually I just stopped getting invited to things. I guess I kept those cards because . . . I miss getting invited."

She allows a few tears to fall.

"The girls you're always texting, though. They're your friends, right?" I say, clearing a lump in my throat, trying to rally.

She doesn't answer but reaches into her pocket and pulls something out. It's her own cell phone. "I went looking for this, too," she says, handing it over to me. Understanding that she wants me to look, I pull up her messages, and my heart breaks into pieces. Her texts are a ghost town, nothing there but months and months of one-way conversations.

To Kayla: **Are you going to the pool today? Lmk!**

No reply.

To April: **Are you trying out for soccer?**

No reply.

Then: **I won't have my phone for a week, ugh. Text you when I can!**

Again, no reply.

"Kiddo . . . ," I say, feeling even more like shit.

"When we came here I thought I could try being someone else, someone who fits in. But I couldn't keep it up, it's like the real me was just bursting to get out. And then I got *too* competitive during capture the flag, and now no one likes me. No matter what I do, I just can't seem to get it right."

All I can think is whether there's a joke I can come up with that might make her laugh. Maybe a game I can make up, like I spy or, I don't know, who can hit the skinny tree with a pine cone first. But I manage to suppress this urge, too.

"And you thought that if maybe you got on a team with older girls, girls who were as good or better than you . . ."

"That we might be friends."

I've known Avery was different for a long, long time. Good different. But it's been too long since I was a kid, I forgot that all you want at that age is to be like everyone else. This whole time, I thought she needed me more than anything. What she really needed was friends like Megan who actually understood her. What she needed was the soccer team, a place where she could belong without compromising. Without holding back. Where being the fastest was a *good* thing.

"I wish I had an easy answer," I say.

"It's OK." She sniffs. "I'm just relieved you know now."

Then, she rests her head on my shoulder, my heart skipping a beat, and we stare out into the blackness, though there's nothing to see.

"I'm sorry about the baby stuff. That must have been hard," she adds.

"Don't be. I have everything I need." I kiss the top of her head. "I did come look for you, you know. But I couldn't find you. Where were you hiding all that time?"

She smiles. "You know I'll never tell."

I chuckle.

"Can I say one annoying fatherly thing? And then I'll shut up."

"OK. Just one."

"Fitting in is overrated. At some point you realize you need to stop trying to be more like everyone else and start trying to be the best version of you. And the cool thing is that you get to decide what the best version of Avery is. Not me, not Mom. Not the kids at school. The best version of Avery doesn't have to *be* the best, you know, at everything. She can do less and still be enough. I will never, *ever*, be disappointed in you, you understand?"

She nods.

"I know that doesn't help much right now, and that it doesn't mean that much coming from your dad, but it's the best advice I've got."

"It helps," she says softly.

But lest she let me off too easy . . .

"I'm still mad at you," she blurts. "And don't think I forgot about you making me pee myself in front of everyone. That was seriously uncool."

"What if I make it up to you?"

"Oh! You could let me dye my hair. Or get a nose ring. I think the best version of Avery would have a nose ring."

I roll my eyes.

"What?" she protests. "You said fitting in was overrated."

"How about a dance?" I suggest, standing and offering her my hand like we're attending a glamorous ball.

She cocks an eyebrow. "That's the best you can do?"

"Would it sweeten the pot if I promise not to act a fool on the dance floor?"

She considers this.

"Oh . . . no," I stammer, my voice transforming into a nasally-robot impression. "It. Is. Already. Happening . . . Initiating. Sweet. Moves." I chop my arms through the air mechanically, bending and twisting along to an imaginary beat.

I know it's silly, but what can I say? Old habits die hard.

"Oh God, please stop," Avery pleads, grabbing my arms, trying to physically restrain me. "I'll go, I'll go!"

"All right." I smile, dropping the act. "If you insist."

She finally takes my hand, and I squeeze it tight. But not as tight as I really want to.

Twenty-Six

The lodge has undergone a minor facelift, colorful string lights hung outside along with a large banner that reads **GOING-AWAY BASH**.

Campers file in, dressed to impress. Well, except Avery and me, mildly disheveled, her in a glorified T-shirt, me with small bits of forest clinging to most of my body.

Dennis greets us at the door with a respectful nod. "John. Avery."

"So . . . we're cool?" I ask, extending a hand. He doesn't take it immediately.

"That depends. You ready to admit I was right yet?"

I know what he's talking about, echoes of our heated argument the first night of camp bouncing around in my brain. He sized me up from the beginning, knew I needed this place more than I wanted to let on. And truth be told, I knew he was right all along.

"Let's just say I'm glad we decided to stay."

He smiles and shakes my hand, then steps aside lightly so Avery and I can join the party. The inside of the place looks like every awkward school dance I've ever been to, reminiscent of a cafeteria with lunch tables pushed hastily aside and limp party streamers hanging from the ceiling.

Its walls are lined with folding tables stocked with punch bowls and snacks. Somewhere in the middle, the bland carpeting has been covered with a cheap, temporary snap-together dance floor. The irony isn't lost on me that soon, Avery will be at a dance just like this with some cute boy or girl, and I'll be stuck at home, waiting until it's time to come pick her up.

A cacophony of music blasts from a stand speaker in the corner, hits from every decade in no particular order with no particular theme or progression. An old Backstreet Boys song comes on, and all the dads sing along with feigned sarcasm, but you can tell they really love it. Then an Olivia Rodrigo song and the girls erupt.

With all the commotion of the "hide-and-seek game gone awry" finally over, the authorities gone, and the other campers settled down, Avery and I nurse cups of punch in the corner, disco lights slicing across our bodies.

"So . . . what do we do now?" she says, looking around.

"Well, we're at the dance. Maybe we should . . . dance."

"I agreed to *one* song," she says. "If you want to use it up right away, that's your choice."

I tilt an ear up comically, as if straining to make out the song that's just starting. It's the Chicken Dance, naturally, a staple. To be followed closely, I imagine, by YMCA, the Macarena, and various slides (Cha-Cha, Electric, et al.). I promised not to embarrass Avery, and sadly that means depriving her and everyone else of my best moves. I want to make this one really count.

"Maybe we better mingle a bit first."

She nods enthusiastically in agreement.

Thank God.

And so we make a lap around the room. The dance floor is . . . weird. Mostly, people are just standing on it, talking to one another. Steve tries to get a dance circle going around himself, performing some kind of elaborate breakdancing routine, but no one seems interested. I'm just sayin', this party could really use some booze. *Real* booze.

We find Lou and Tam at one of the snack tables, shoveling pretzels into their little Styrofoam bowls.

"Hey, man!" I yell over the music, and Lou and I share a bro hug.

"I'm so glad you found your daughter!" he yells back, then: "I mean, like I'm glad she's not dead or something!"

"Yeah! Me too!"

"That came out wrong, but you know what I mean!"

I turn and see Avery talking to Tam, sharing some of her pretzels.

"I love your hair," Avery says to her. And I notice that it's braided beautifully down the middle and tossed around the front, draping along her neck. Like Elsa from *Frozen*. It even has little jewels and butterflies woven into it. A true masterpiece.

"Thanks," Tam says. "My daddy did it."

Lou beams.

"Do you want to maybe go dance with me?" Avery asks, and Tam nods excitedly. They take each other's hands and disappear somewhere on the dance floor, but not before Avery looks back at me one more time. I give her a smile and a nod and they fade into the crowd.

"GUYS, THIS IS A DISASTER!" a voice yells out, and Lou and I turn to see Ryan limping up to us in a tizzy.

"What's wrong?" I ask him.

"I took something, and I probably shouldn't have because I totally screwed it up. I'm so *fucked*. Listen, you can't tell anyone, but . . ."

He thrusts his hands out to reveal bright red polish on all ten of his fingers, applied with all the delicacy of a butcher. It's splotchy and too thick, and he didn't even manage to color inside the lines. It looks horrible.

"I don't get it," I say, laughing. "You said it was a disaster!"

"What would you call this!? Lou, you gotta help me. I just thought . . . I thought Jessie would like it. But it looks like crap, so can you fix it?"

Lou and I laugh harder, and right as our laugh begins to wind down, for whatever reason, it cranks right back up again, and we can't stop laughing. It's all so ridiculous.

"Don't make fun of me, assholes."

"Just relax," Lou says. "It will mean a lot to her that you tried."

"You think?"

"Definitely," I add.

At that moment, Jessie comes up to our little group and smiles at us. Her ears must have been ringing.

"You guys look nice."

Ryan clears his throat and puts on his stern-dad voice. One last look over at us for reassurance, and we both nod.

"Jessie, let me see your nails," he commands.

"What, why?" then, sheepishly, she sticks them out. "I just thought—"

"What did I tell you about all this girly stuff?"

She looks at him, wide-eyed, in shock. *Are you really yelling at me right now?* Then she hangs her head.

"Never, and I mean *never* . . . paint your nails without me again."

He displays his own hands so she can see his touching hack job of a manicure. Her frown flips into a massive smile, and she puts her fingers next to his, decorated in the same shade of red.

"We match," she says.

Some upbeat pop synth song comes on, and all the girls in the room squeal in unison.

"Go ahead and dance with your friends," Ryan tells her.

"Will you come, too?"

The lyrics flood the room, and it's all nonsensical, boy-crazed bubblegum. Not at all the type of music I picture Ryan listening to, but he sighs and allows Jessie to drag him off to the dance floor. Before he gets swallowed up in a sea of bodies, he turns to Lou.

"This is all your fault," he says playfully.

Lou and I stay behind and chug punch. I can feel it loosening me up a bit, even though it's nonalcoholic. Maybe it's the sugar.

Suddenly, I feel a tap on my lower shoulder, and I whirl around. There's Erica, looking absolutely adorable in a puffy white dress, something maybe leftover from her being a flower girl at a wedding, eating a SOLO cup full of Cheetos.

"Have you seen my daddy?"

I haven't, so I take her hand (covered in orange dust as it is) and we do a lap around the room together. No sign of him by any of the snack or punch tables, on the dance floor, or in the bathroom.

We step outside on the deck and there he is. On his phone.

"Yes, sir," he says, noticing us and holding up a *Just a second* finger. "Yes . . . yes, I understand. I understand . . . All right."

I'm still holding Erica's hand, and I can feel her body slump as she watches her dad yammer away. There's a resignation about her, like she's been through this a million times before and she knows there's no use fighting it.

She gives my hand a tug and says, "Come on, let's go back inside."

"Baby, wait," Booker cries out from the other end of the deck. He pulls the phone away from his face and approaches her gently, making a show of hanging up the call.

"I'm done, see? I'm putting it away."

She frowns at him.

"I'm sorry," he says, kneeling down to her. "I'm sorry it's always like this."

"It's OK," she says quietly.

"No, it's not. Tonight is all about you and me, I promise. I just had to make one last call."

She nods, not remotely convinced.

"Don't believe me? Here"—he grabs her right hand and puts his cell phone into it—"I don't need this anymore."

"Really?"

"Really."

Her face lights up. "You quit?" she says with a grin. "You really quit?!"

"Well—"

Not waiting for an answer, Erica cocks back and hurls the phone like a baseball. It hurtles off into the night and makes an audible *CRACK* as it collides with a tree somewhere out in the darkness.

"ERICA!"

"You said you didn't need it."

"Tonight! I didn't need it anymore *tonight*!" Booker stares into the darkness after his phone and raises his hands to rub his temples.

"Oh." She frowns. "I'm sorry."

"It's OK, it's fine, I'll just—"

"I'll go look for it," I interrupt. "Don't worry."

They're on the edge of a precarious moment that could go either way, and I don't want to intrude. I give Booker a pat on the back and walk down the wooden stairs, stopping at the bottom to continue listening, obviously.

"I can't just quit my job, baby, you understand that," he says to her, and I see her nod slowly.

"Maybe I can look for a new one or try to make this one better, somehow. But that stuff takes time. And it's complicated. Your mom and I are gonna talk about it when we get home. But, hey, I figured something out this week," he continues. "I realized that no matter what I do, I'm going to end up letting someone down. Someone's going to be disappointed with me. What I figured out is that I never, ever want that person to be you."

She smiles and wraps him in a hug. He squeezes her back. And I finally let them alone, taking a few steps and quickly finding Booker's phone. Or, at least, the remains of it. It's all in one piece, but with a wicked spiderweb crack across the front now.

I bring it back to him and hand it over.

"Will your boss be mad?" Erica asks him.

"Definitely. But tonight, let's let him be mad," he answers with a smirk.

They squeeze each other again, showing no signs of letting go, Booker physically absorbing the warmth of every bedtime, every bath, every school play, every walk to the bus stop he's missed over the years. He soaks it up and his face glows. I decide it's best to let them alone.

Inside, as I predicted, the Macarena blares, its bass notes rattling the entire building. I position myself by a window and look inside, hands pressed up against the glass, feeling a little like Peter Pan watching Wendy grow old without him. Avery, at the fringes of the dance floor, and the rest of the girls bounce up and down, shrieking with laughter. None of them know the Macarena, but they give it an effort. An upturned palm here, the shake of a foot there. No, too derivative of the Hokey Pokey. I ought to go in there and teach them, I think, but it doesn't feel right to interrupt her fun.

And suddenly, Avery dashes away. I lose sight of her in the crowd, and can't seem to find where she's run off to. For what feels like an eternity, my eyes scan the dance floor, the concession table. Did one of the other girls upset her? Did something happen? And now someone's touching my arm. Avery. She's right here next to me.

"Come on, hurry," she says, yanking me inside.

As the door shuts behind us and a blast of cool air-conditioned air wraps itself around me, I hear a familiar shift in the music. A twang of guitar notes, that sliding metallic meow you only hear in country music. A slower beat. The lights stop spinning now, settling on a more somber rotation in muted blues and purples.

We come to a stop in the center of the dance floor.

"A promise is a promise," she says with a smile.

I take her hands, and we begin to rock slowly back and forth with the music.

"I love this song," I say.

"I know. I hear you listening to it all the time. 'It Won't Be Like This for Long' by Darius Rucker," she boasts.

"His name is Hootie."

"What?"

"Never mind."

As the lyrics—which trace the life of a baby girl being born to her father walking her down the aisle at her wedding in the span of about three and a half minutes—enter my ears and clump together in a big ball somewhere in my throat, Avery leans her head into my chest, just so, as if to ease the pain. Or maybe she's just tired, I don't know.

"Did you request it?" I ask.

"It's just someone's phone plugged into the sound system. I grabbed it, went to Spotify, bada bing." She laughs.

"And here I thought you were dreading this. Dancing with your dad is *sooooo uncool*," I groan.

"Shut up." She jokingly kicks me in the shin. "I just didn't want to miss the chance, that's all."

Around us, the other dads and their girls are hesitantly pairing up, no one quite sure how close to stand, where to put their hands. I lock eyes with Ryan, who gives me a knowing nod just over the top of Jessie's head. Lou, with Tam standing on his feet, the two of them waddling along like a giant penguin, gives me a huge smile. Booker and Erica finally come in from outside, and he grabs her and whirls her around, like an ice dancer, adding a flourishy dip for good measure. She giggles and giggles, smiling at us while hanging upside down on her father's arm.

"Are you feeling ready for sixth grade?" I ask. "Only two more days."

"Oh my God, I completely forgot," Avery blurts. "The Adventure Box."

"Oh, yeah," I say casually, like I haven't been thinking about it every second of every day this entire summer.

"I didn't get you anything. I'm the worst, I know. Why didn't you remind me?"

"I was thinking . . . ," I say, and then a deep breath. It's time, I tell myself. It's definitely time. "What if we said goodbye to that tradition?"

She pulls back, looks at me like she's trying to figure out if I'm being serious.

"You're ready to have some adventures of your own. On your own. And besides, we can start a new tradition when we think of one."

"Are you sure?"

I laugh. "I think so."

"We'll still have adventures together, you know that, right? Middle school isn't the end of the entire world."

"I know."

"And if I ever end up on the travel team . . ."

"When. *When* you end up on the team."

"I'll still need someone to come with me sometimes. To stay in hotels and make sure I get to practice and games on time. Going to new cities and random towns together . . . That's pretty adventurous, right?"

"Yeah." I smile. "I guess it is."

I see the box in my mind now, me stuffing it away in Avery's closet somewhere when we get home. I try to imagine the journey it

will go on over the next couple decades. Getting packed and unpacked in various homes if we ever move, relocated when we decide
Avery's room needs a nuclear-level deep cleaning. Maybe collecting
cobwebs in the garage for a while. Then me dropping it off on Avery's doorstep when she's grown and has a family of her own, stuffed
in a bigger box with trophies and other relics from her childhood.
And she'll pull it out and remember all the good times we had, at
least, while I'm there. After I leave, she'll just be annoyed with me
now that she has to figure out where to put it in her own crowded
home, as I was when my parents pulled this move on me, and the
circle of life will be complete.

But enough of that. I snap back to Avery. *Pay attention*, I tell myself. *Block everything else out, just enjoy this moment. Bottle it up and
hold it tight. Maybe then it will last forever.*

But alas, it does not. Here come the spinning lights again, and
the yellows and oranges ricocheting off the disco ball. And the song's
final note rings out and just as quickly, here come the Village People.

Now Ryan throws an arm around my neck, screaming along
with the classic gay anthem. He's come a long way, this one.

Avery dances along, but of course she doesn't know the YMCA
dance, either. This generation is lost. Halfway through the song and
hopelessly flailing her arms around, Avery pulls her cabinmates to
the side of the dance floor, takes a deep breath, and begins speaking.
I can just barely make out what she's saying through a combination
of strained listening and lip-reading.

"I'm really sorry if I was a jerk," she tells them. "I'm not very
good at making new friends. Maybe we could start over."

Jessie leans in and gives her a warm hug.

"I turn twelve in a few months," Avery says now, the music pumping, and I'm just barely able to decipher, "Would you want to come to my bidet potty?"

Wait, that last part can't be right. Oh well. I've never been much of a lip-reader.

All I can think is how incredibly brave that was of her. To put herself out there like that, confront an awkward situation and be honest and vulnerable. And the way Jessie hugged her in response— thinking about it has me all verklempt.

I also wonder if maybe I missed out on something really special, not ever having to host my own men's group session. After the cabin-building marathon, we had all about had our fill of guy time—and then a lot of other crazy stuff happened, and it got lost in the shuffle. But the guys are all still here, I suppose I could round them up. But it wouldn't feel right to pull them away from their girls. Not now. And besides, there's something else I've been putting off that might feel just as good.

"How'd it go?" I ask when Avery comes back over my way.

"Good! Some of the girls found some bottles of silly string!" she strains over the music.

"OK! . . . Cool!"

"We're gonna go spray the boys' cabins!"

"All right! You go get 'em!"

She hesitates. "I could stay? If you want."

"No, you go," I say, feeling inspired. "I've got something I need to do anyway."

She gives me a quick hug, and the girls scurry along, sweaty-haired and flush-cheeked. I signal to the boys that I'm going to step out for a minute, but they're all having too much fun to notice. The air outside is sticky, but at least it's moving, and the walk back to my cabin is refreshing, if a little nerve-racking.

I walk in, and there's the stack of paper, and the pen, exactly where I left them.

JOHN

Dear Dad,

It's me, Johnny. How are you? How's the weather there? It's been perfect here, all clear blue skies and starry nights. A real Van Gogh painting. Can't complain one bit. Before we left for camp I heard you guys were in for a wet spell. Hope it hasn't been too bad. Unless of course you needed the rain! I can hear you in my head telling me how much the lawn needed it.

I've been a little out of touch here, a bit unplugged. I haven't had my phone this week. Well, most of the week. That's a different story altogether—I'll tell you over a beer next time you visit. Anyway, who's looking good in MLB? Like I said, I haven't been able to keep up with the scores. I don't know how you do it, tracking these tedious division races and who's gaining momentum for the Cy Young and all of that. I know you think phones and social media have broken my brain, zapped my attention span. I just think we're built a little different, you and me.

And speaking of baseball, Avery's doing great. She won her softball league this year. Wish you could have been there. And she's really excited for soccer in the fall. I'm sure she told you all about the travel team the last time you saw her on FaceTime. She's heading into the sixth grade, can you believe it? I know. Kill me—that was my first *thought, too. But you know what? I think I'm finally coming around on the idea.*

But I guess I'm not writing to talk about Avery, am I? I'm writing to talk about us.

All right, all right. Unclench your butt cheeks. It's not going to be that bad.

(Though, admittedly, I put this off all week, myself. Real brave.)

First, I just want you to put everything I'm about to say in a giant set of parentheses, OK? You were a great dad. You still are. After all, I turned out OK, didn't I? I landed Evelyn somehow, no doubt through some form of osmosis while watching the way you treated Mom. Always the perfect gentleman, charmingly old-fashioned. Growing up, there were a lot of parents falling apart around me. But never you guys. And of course, there's Avery, whip-smart, hardworking, kind. I made her! I helped, anyway. I don't know how much credit I get to take for her, how wonderful she is, but whatever I do get, you're certainly owed a commission. You showed me how to be a dad. In your own way.

I am lucky to live such a great life. I have so much to be thankful for. But I've always felt like there was something missing, and it's you.

I have this one extremely vivid memory, our first visit to your house after Avery was born. She was maybe a year old, or just shy of, impressing everyone with her earliest steps, clunky and chaotic. Hoisting herself up constantly by grabbing onto coffee tables, legs, and doorways. Beaming, you commented on her amazing upper-body strength. I remember Mom's smile, too, and the way we teased her because her baby babble sounded vaguely Irish. That's always stuck in my memory. But despite all the joy of that day, I was struggling. I don't think I've ever told anyone this, but being Avery's dad was not coming easy to me. The sleep deprivation, the overstimulation and understimulation both somehow happening at the same time. Sometimes I was sad for absolutely no reason at all. I was having a really hard time with stress, anxiety, and what I would later learn was depression.

I was so excited to come see you then because I knew you would understand. I didn't need a fix, but I needed someone to listen. There was Evelyn, but she had plenty of her own issues to deal with after the pregnancy and the birth, and I felt like it was my job at the time to be there for her, not drag her down further. Who was I to complain, really? "Honey, I'm feewing a wittle sad!" I'd say, and she'd think, "Are you serious, dude? I just had my vagina torn in half."

She would have been wonderful, of course. I know that. But to be honest, I was ashamed. I couldn't tell her. All I had ever wanted was to be a father, and everyone had started calling me Super Dad—I loved that. So how could I tell anyone that sometimes I just wanted to run away? That I could barely get out of bed some mornings, and went to sleep with a knot of dread in my stomach most nights? We talked that night, you and me, by the fire there in the living room, Mom ushering us together and vacating the room, probably eavesdropping from the kitchen. And you . . . well you were such a dad. You had a solution to everything, didn't you? A retort. "Just have to get her on a better routine, that's all. Just need to focus on taking care of your wife. Are you drinking too much? Getting enough fruits and veggies?" Of course you were warm and kind. At first. But when I told you that I was really struggling and that these vague platitudes and easy fixes weren't going to help me, I remember you turning cold, turning to your favorite phrase. "You need to pull yourself together." I half expected you to slap me across the face, trying to knock some sense into me.

Before long, you stood up and walked to the kitchen, made me tea with a dollop of whiskey, and sent me off to bed like a child, assuring me that a good night's sleep would make things so much better. I felt so embarrassed, because you were right. Why was I sitting here feeling sorry for myself when I had so much to be grateful for, so many people to take care of now? But I couldn't sleep. I was still disappointed. I had been hoping to hear that you went through it, too. That I was normal for feeling the way I was. That there wasn't anything wrong with me.

Instead, I left your house the next morning feeling completely alone, and like my only option was to suffer in silence.

I came around eventually. Into the light. But the shame stuck with me for a long, long time. Still does, to tell you the truth. That's not all your fault. It's the world we live in. But I do want us to do better.

I want you to talk to me. I want to know you. I don't feel like I know you at all.

Come on, now. You're seventy-six years old. Surely you've got things on your mind. You've got to be a little freaked out about your skin turning translucent and spotty. You have to be worried about your memory, your vision, what will happen over the next ten, twenty, thirty years. It must bother you that you have to use the bathroom every seventeen seconds. You've got to be occasionally leaking a little pee by now when someone makes you laugh, I've googled it! You can't hide it from me, old man. So why don't you ever talk to me about it?

For a long time, the longest time, I just assumed it wasn't something you wanted. To be my friend, or at least my peer. To let me in. But I think I'm realizing now that you just don't know how. You haven't been taught. No, when you were growing up, men were men were men. When you turned forty-five you started getting your annual prostate exam and you took it like a man and never said a word about it to anyone, and then one day you died and you took all of your hopes and dreams and fears into the dirt with you and you liked it that way. Sound about right?

I'm begging you now. Don't take anything with you, Dad. We want it all here, with us. And I think you and me can learn together.

Next time we see each other, we'll give it a try. After we spend the obligatory fifteen minutes catching up on sports, obviously. But maybe you can tell me about something you're struggling with. I'll tell you my greatest fears if you tell me yours. If you resist, I'll be forced to break out the Man Cards (I'll explain later, but trust me, you don't want me to do that). And it will be awkward and extremely uncomfortable for both of us!

We might hate it at first! But we'll get better at it and one day, eventually, it will seem normal to actually talk about stuff and share things with each other. Sometimes, we can still talk about nothing (weather, films, busty women on TV) or sit in a comfortable silence. Those are good moments, too. Some of my favorites. But there has to be more to our relationship. I don't need the fatherly advice and stern lessons so much anymore, you know? Without those, I'm afraid there isn't anything left.

I've got to sign off now. But first, I'm going to say something we should be saying to each other way more often. Every day even. Ready? Here it goes.

I LOVE YOU, DAD.

SATURDAY

Twenty-Seven

I remember sealing up the letter, dropping it in the mailbox at the front of the camp, and walking back to the party. The rest of the night was a blur.

It felt a lot like a wedding reception, to tell you the truth. Not just a party, but a real celebration of something. The dads and I exchanging random hugs on the dance floor for no particular reason, throwing our arms around one another and forming impromptu dance lines. The girls huddling in a circle and screaming along to their favorite songs.

Something pretty incredible was coming to an end. But it also felt like the beginning of something completely new, and I think we could all feel it.

The girls had to be carried out of there after the final song, crashing hard from too much sugary punch and dancing—the parallels to a long night of drinking made us all laugh. I hauled Avery out the way I used to carry her when she was little, when she'd koala onto me from the front, legs wrapped around my torso and arms around my neck. I've given her a bunch of piggyback rides over the last couple of years, but I can't remember holding her like this in a long while. It was a little clumsy with her long limbs flailing all over the place—after all, she's about as tall as me now. She's also gotten a lot heavier. *A lot.* But I wasn't about to tell her she had to get down and walk. Not tonight.

I kept thinking about how they always say you never know when you're picking up your kid for the last time, so you better believe I soaked up every hamstring-burning moment of that walk.

And now it's the morning and, whether I like it or not, it's time to leave.

Avery's bag lands in my trunk with a thud, and then I chuck my own duffel in there and stare at it for a minute. I want to make this last, stretch this moment into forever, but I've already run back to the cabin about five times thinking I forgot something. The last two trips were fruitless. There's really nothing left to do but drive home.

All around us in the parking lot, dads secure luggage while girls hug each other goodbye and share phone numbers, email addresses, and social media handles.

Avery suddenly appears at my side and gives my shirt a tug.

"Hey, there you are," I say.

"You OK?" she asks. "You were zoning out there for a minute."

"Yeah, I'm good. Did you hit the bathroom yet?"

She pats her belly. "All empty."

"Gross. Come on, let's say goodbye."

"One sec," she says, digging through her pockets. "Before we go. I remembered I did get you something for the Adventure Box. Sort of . . ."

"I told you not to worry about that."

She produces an envelope and hands it to me, matter-of-fact.

"We had to write these." She shrugs. "I did it when I was super mad at you. I want you to have it."

"Aw, you shouldn't have," I tease.

"No." She laughs. "It's just . . . You don't have to read it. I already told you everything. I thought it was kind of cool that maybe we learned how to talk to each other better this summer. That seems like something, right?"

I kiss her on the forehead, mostly a cover so she doesn't see my eyes beginning to leak.

"Better get a move on." My voice cracks.

I scan the parking lot and find a few familiar faces across the way—Lou and Ryan engaged in deep discussion near the bed of Ryan's truck. I grab Avery's hand and walk her over so we can say goodbye.

"I still don't feel right about everything that happened, the things I said to you," Ryan tells Lou.

"Forget it. It's in the past."

"No, I said I would make it up to you, and I intend to." He pulls out a business card and hands it over. "If you ever decide to open that restaurant, give me a call. I can get you supplies, equipment, building materials, anything you need. All at cost. You'll save a fortune."

"You don't have to do that."

"It's either that or smash my face into a tree. Your choice."

Lou pockets the card, laughing. "Thank you."

"It's not much but . . ." Ryan shrugs.

They share a manly fist bump, then think better of it and wrap each other in a hug instead.

"I guess this is it," I say.

"We should stay in touch," Lou says. "You know, for the girls. I don't see why we couldn't get them on FaceTime every now and then."

"Yeah." Ryan clears his throat. "Jessie would like that, I bet."

"Will you assholes just loosen up, already?" Booker yells out, sneaking up on us. He throws Ryan and me in a playful headlock, one with each arm. We both laugh and eventually wriggle out.

"Here, I'll go first: You dudes are pretty cool, and I'm glad I met you," he says.

"Same," we all mutter in unison.

"Now, was that so hard?"

I finally get a good look at him and, honestly, he looks like hell. The bags under his eyes are worse than ever, and though his mood and energy are through the roof, his body looks like it's about to give out on him.

"Up all night with work?" I say to him, sidebar-style, while Lou and Ryan finish packing up.

"Something like that. I called home. Had some real big stuff to talk over with the wife. We were on the phone for hours."

"I hope you get a break soon. And some sleep, for crying out loud."

"I'll figure it out eventually. But right now, I think I've finally got my priorities straight."

"Just remember to take care of yourself," I tell him.

And just then, Erica runs up and nearly bowls him over with a hug. "I don't wanna go. Can we stay forever?"

He looks at me and winks. "Don't worry about me, I'm good."

The guys and I trade numbers and let one another go. We all have long drives ahead. And you know dads. We're always eager to get a move on.

On the way back to my car, I see Avery finishing up a hug with Jessie.

"You promise you'll text me back?" Jessie says.

Avery smiles and hugs her again with an emphatic and very teenage "Duh!"

When the two girls finally let go, Jessie gives me a friendly "See ya, Mr. C," and then she's off.

Now it's just Avery and Tam, little Tam, standing off to the side as cars back out and leave this place in the rearview. Ryan and Jessie pass us by in the truck, with a quick honk of the horn for good measure. Booker and Erica wave and follow suit.

I just stand and listen to the girls say goodbye. It looks like Tam is actually crying. I wonder if I should grab Lou or intervene myself, but Avery kneels down to comfort her, and I decide to just see what happens.

"We'll definitely see each other soon, I promise," Avery tells Tam. "You're coming to my birthday, remember?"

Tam sniffles. "It's not that."

"Then what's wrong?"

Tam suddenly opens her mouth wide, like a great white about to devour a tuna.

"I got my first wiggly tooth," she says, pointing it out with her finger and wobbling it back and forth.

"Oh, wow!" Avery says. "That's so exciting!"

"It's not exciting—it's scary!" Tam yelps. "Does it hurt when it comes out?"

"Not at all," Avery says. "And you know, when it finally falls out, the tooth fairy will come and visit you! You know about the tooth fairy, right?"

"A little," Tam says, skeptical.

"She's a magical fairy who comes while you're asleep. She'll take your tooth back to her palace and keep it safe forever and ever, and if you're really brave about it, she'll leave you money and cool stuff like that."

"What if you're not brave?"

"You don't have to worry about that, know why?"

Tam shakes her head.

"Because when you lose your last baby tooth, like me, the tooth fairy gives you special fairy dust you can give to other kids to help them be tough."

Avery reaches into her pocket and pulls out a pretend pinch of fairy dust, then sprinkles it in the air just over Tam's head.

"There. You feel any better yet?"

Tam wiggles her nose, thinks for a second, and finally says, "Yeah, I think I do!"

I'm about to explode in an ugly sob, but I manage to choke it down before I think, *Ah, the hell with it*—and I let a few tears escape. Then I feel a squeeze on my shoulder and see Lou standing next to me, openly crying. He just gives me a smile while Avery and Tam hug goodbye.

And then they're off, and it's just me and Avery left with a few stragglers. "You ready?" she says.

"What about Megan, did you say goodbye to her yet?"

"Yeah, we said bye."

"You two gonna stay in touch?"

"Dad," she whines. "She's in college—she doesn't want to hang out with a little kid out in the real world."

"You're not a little kid. Go get her phone number. Seriously. You're gonna regret it if you don't."

She sighs and trudges off, but I can tell she's happy I gave her the push. While I wait, I take one last look in the trunk, our bags laid out side by side, the Adventure Box wedged in between them. I dig around in my pockets and find it—the small combination lock—pulling it out and rolling it around in my hands, its latch shimmering. I knew I kept it for a reason. For the first time, I'm really excited about the next chapter and where it might lead. Best to close up the box for good, before I change my mind.

Only . . . I don't know the combination.

"One-six-one-two," Dennis says, suddenly behind me, as if reading my thoughts. "It was my daughter's birthday."

"Was?"

He gives a peaceful smile.

"She used to help me out around here. When I wasn't too wrapped up in the work, too distracted, we made a lot of good memories. Everything here reminds me of her."

I think I finally understand why this place means so much to him.

"So, will we see you next year?" I ask.

"I'm afraid not."

I sink. Guess he won't be able to keep this place open after all.

"I'm gonna take some time off. Travel. Sail. See where the wind takes me."

"I'm glad."

"But don't worry. The camp will still be here. I'll leave it in good hands, I promise. For the first time in a while, I feel . . . hopeful."

"Me too."

We shake hands, and then he's gone.

Using the combination, I open the lock, and onto the box it goes. I thought it'd be harder, sadder, when this day finally came—to retire the Adventure Box. But instead, I can't stop grinning.

• • •

The car ride home is long but fun.

We stop on our way out of town to have the tire changed, collecting chips and sodas from the antique waiting room vending machine. On the road, we blast music and bicker over whose turn it is to pick a song. Avery and I sing along at the top of our lungs to the tunes we both know, which isn't many. We talk about the week and everything that happened, laughing at the awful food and my terrible archery skills and even about "Pee-Gate."

Eventually she gets quiet and closes her eyes, leaning her head against the window. I turn down the music so she can fall asleep. We're still about thirty minutes out from home, and I know she'll be bursting at the seams to tell Evelyn all about the trip the second we walk through the door. She needs her rest.

Suddenly, she bolts upright in her seat and slugs me in the arm, hard, with a balled fist. "Punch buggy no punch back!" she yells. It startles the bejesus out of me, and it's all I can do not to swerve off the road.

I look around and, sure enough, there it is. An old yellow beater of a Beetle, chugging along in the far lane.

"Hey, no fair. I thought you were asleep."

"That's what I wanted you to think." She smirks, closing her eyes again. "OK, now I'm going to sleep, for real."

"Hmm, how do I know you're not lying?"

"You'll just have to stay on your toes," she says with a yawn. She doesn't budge for the rest of the drive.

MONDAY

Twenty-Eight

Avery is eleven years old, and she's finally old enough that she's stopped tacking on "and a half" to her age. So have I. Avery is eleven. Just eleven.

We're driving in the car, the two of us. She looks out the window, and her head follows as we whizz past our street.

"Um, Dad, that was our turn."

"I know." I grin.

"I've had enough surprises for a while, I promise. Just tell me where we're going."

"Don't worry about it. I want to hear more about your first day."

She tells me, though she's distracted, eyes darting around and taking in the passing scenery, trying to spot landmarks and clues for where we might be headed.

With her head whipping around, the sun keeps bouncing off the bold, yet subtle, red streak she's added to her hair—with a little help from her reluctant mom. Avery entered negotiations wanting a laundry list of various piercings, and this is where we settled.

"Homeroom teacher's nice, a little boring. It's weird to have a homeroom and hop around to all these different classes, but I kind of like it. Um, I'm sitting next to Sarah in science. Remember her? We were in the same third-grade class."

"Oh, yeah, she was nice! Really into bugs and stuff, right? Carried that ant farm with her everywhere. Does she still have the ant farm?"

"Dad, it's been three years."

"Ants can live a long time," I say with a smirk. "You should invite her over."

Avery considers this for a second, still scanning every building we pass. "Maybe I will," she says, then, "Hey, I realized you never asked me whether or not I finished *The Lion, the Witch, and the Wardrobe*. You didn't quiz me on it or anything. I could have started the year off with a big fat zero."

I look over at her. *Come on.*

"OK, I finished it, like, the second day of camp."

"See. I didn't forget. I trusted you."

She grins.

"By the way," I add. "What did everyone think of the hair?"

She considers this for a second, then: "Don't know and don't care."

That's my girl.

We finally come to a stop in the parking lot of a small community college a little ways down the road from our house. It's all stained-concrete buildings with small lifeless windows. Nothing much to look at. But Avery's face lights up when we pull in, as I knew it would.

"I know this place. I've played here."

"Yep" is all I say, and then we both climb out, me carrying a small duffel bag.

She peppers me with questions, but I mostly ignore them as we weave our way across the campus, eventually making our way to a pristine soccer field, its bright greens almost stinging the eyes in comparison to the drab surroundings. We trot down a staircase and onto field level. Standing there by one of the goals is a woman wearing swishy joggers and a visor, barely five feet tall but looking like she could use every inch of her slight frame to take your ass down, if needed. She's got her arms crossed and nods as we approach. Behind her, a couple of other girls Avery's age or a little older dribble casually and take shots on the goal.

"Is that . . ." Avery trails off.

"It is."

"How did you . . ."

"I just asked really, really nicely."

She doesn't need to know that I begged and begged Coach Johnston for this tryout, and that Coach wasn't exactly thrilled with me ignoring her messages for as long as I did. But I came clean, told her how Avery never even knew what was going on and how she shouldn't have to suffer because of it. Coach Johnston agreed, though she doesn't have a very high opinion of *me*—partly because of my poor parenting choices, partly because I called her up at midnight and wouldn't let her off the phone until she came around.

But we're here now. That's what matters.

"I don't have . . ."

"Any of your stuff?" I say, holding out the duffel bag. Avery zips it open. Inside I've packed a brand-new ball (a size up from what she used last year), her cleats, socks, shorts, and a tank top.

Avery just stares inside the bag for a minute until I break her out of whatever thought she's stuck in.

"Go on, get dressed. Get out there."

"Dad. Thanks for doing this but . . . I don't know if I'm ready."

"I didn't do this. You did." Then . . . "Avery, you've been ready for this for a while."

She gulps and summons up the courage for a determined nod. A ferocity I've seen countless times flashes in her eyes as she swipes the bag and jogs over to a bathroom on the side of the field to change.

When she's done, I stand back and watch. Coach puts her through a series of drills to see what she can do. Evaluating Avery's agility, speed, and ball skills—sprints, dribbling around cones, things like that. After a while, Avery and the other girls do some one-on-ones, Avery trying to get past a lone defender and take a shot on the goalie. In her first attempt, the defending girl suffocates her—a rare occurrence—and Avery's shot attempt sails well wide of the goal. On the next try, the other girl slide tackles the ball out from under her, sending Avery to the ground. Hard. On the third attempt, the other girl steals the ball easily in seconds.

Avery's face burns red. She's covered in mud, with what looks like a nasty skinned knee.

It takes every ounce of willpower in my body not to run out there and help her.

Instead, Coach takes Avery aside. I'm too far away to hear, but there's gesturing, and repositioning Avery's body to illustrate something, and finally, a reassuring pat on the back.

"I didn't miss it, did I?" Evelyn says, appearing beside me, slightly winded.

"They're still going. You made great time from the office this time of day."

Dads love making great time this time of day.

"I wasn't going to miss this," she says.

Evelyn unslings a couple of folding chairs from her shoulder and pops them open. We sit and watch in silence for a few moments, but the whole time I'm thinking about how we never finished, well, *talking*. The weekend was a whirlwind, between getting unpacked from camp and getting everything ready for school for Avery. This is the first semi-quiet moment Evelyn and I have had together since we've been back.

"I'm sorry," I say in a way that probably seems out of thin air to her.

"What for?" she says, stuffing a handful of trail mix in her mouth.

"I never really understood why you wanted to stop trying."

"Oh," she says, her voice muffled, realizing we're about to have a serious moment while her mouth is completely full of M&M'S and raisins.

"I mean, I supported it; we were always in it together. But I'd be lying if I said I really got it. To me, if you want something bad enough, you do whatever it might take to get it."

She finally swallows but doesn't yet speak.

"You were right, though. There is a lot more to life than only being a parent. And what I finally understand is that, weirdly, realizing that makes you an even *better* parent."

"It doesn't make any sense, right?" she says.

"Not a damn lick of sense."

She laughs. "You make it sound like I had this master plan all along. I was just scared and tired, same as you. We're both just figuring it out as we go."

"Well, it affected me more than I realized. I know I've been a little distant at times, a little too focused on Avery. I'm sorry for that."

"Apology accepted."

"Hey," I say, turning to face her. I grab her face in my hands and look deep into her eyes. "I love you."

On the field, Avery's got the ball again. Now drenched in some combination of wet grass and sweat, she dribbles toward the goal and suddenly jukes the defending girl out of her shoes. She's one-on-one with the goalie now, winds her foot back for a shot, and sends the ball right into the upper corner of the goal—just over the goalie's outstretched fingers.

She throws her hands up triumphantly and looks over at us, beaming with a whole new level of pride.

Evelyn and I yelp and stand to cheer, but quickly we realize that this isn't an actual game, and a controlled clap is probably more appropriate. The other girls tackle her in celebration, and Avery can't stop smiling.

BING. My phone goes off—a text message. I pull it out, and the name pops up big on my screen: JASON.

"Now there's a name I haven't heard in a while," Evelyn says, sitting right next to me and easily able to read the screen.

"We've been texting a bit since I got back. Good to catch up."

"Does this mean the magic club is back on?"

"I don't know yet. Maybe."

"What was the stage name you used to go by again?"

"I don't wanna say."

"Come on, what was it?"

"You know what it was."

"I know. I just want to hear you say it."

I sigh, then drop my voice a few octaves. "Collins the Captivating!"

Evelyn cackles.

"Happy?" I say.

She smirks and tosses another handful of trail mix in her mouth, speaking through crunchy bites. "You know, I always liked Jason. You can invite him for dinner sometime soon if you want. Maybe tonight even."

"Ah, I can't. Got plans tonight."

She cocks an eyebrow at me. "What plans?"

"I've got a date. I didn't tell you?"

"Tell me more," she purrs, her face glowing in a way that absolutely melts me on the spot.

"You'll see when we get home," I say.

"Ugh, you have to give me something!" she teases. "Just . . . blink twice if it involves that new sushi place down the street."

"I was thinking pasta."

"From?"

I hold up my hands and wiggle my fingertips—*Homemade, baby.*

Acknowledgments

I have so many people to thank for inspiring and supporting *Dad Camp* on the long, winding road from kernel of an idea to published novel.

My agent, Andrea Blatt: Your initial excitement, enthusiasm, and confidence in this story helped me see it in a completely new way. You saw the potential in it and the kind of effect it could have on all different kinds of people even before I did. Once I had you in my corner I truly believed anything was possible for this book, and it was! Also a huge Thank-You to Lucy Balfour, Sam Birmingham, Nicole Weinroth, Sanjana Seelam, and the entire hard-working WME team.

My editor, Cassidy Sachs: Thank you for helping this book become the best version of itself. From the very beginning, it was so clear to me that you knew exactly what I was trying to do and where I needed help doing it. I have no idea how you have time to read so many manuscripts, make so many brilliant edits, and hold your

Acknowledgments

authors' hands through this crazy, whirlwind process. You're a superstar. Or you have a doppelganger. Maybe both!

Everyone at Dutton: Christine Ball, John Parsley, Nicole Jarvis, Jamie Knapp, Erika Semprun, Tiffany Estreicher, Kristin del Rosario, Melissa Solis, LeeAnn Pemberton—thank you for turning my silly story into a real book.

All the authors I've met along the way who have been kind and supportive, and especially the ones who took time out of their days to jump on the dreaded "quick call" with me and answer my annoying publishing questions. Richard Roper, Shannon Carpenter, Elaine Kearns, Taylor Kay Phillips, Robbie Couch, Becky Chalsen, everyone in the 2024 Debuts group, and more. I seriously will never forget anyone who's offered a kind word or so much as a thumbs-up emoji.

Katelyn Dramis: Thank you for . . . literally everything? You are the best friend I could ever ask for and an amazing author, you know that. But you are also the biggest dreamer I know. No one sets goals that seem impossible and then makes them a reality quite like you. You're an inspiration. It has meant the world to me to be able to go through this journey with you.

My dad, who taught me how to write. He'd always say, *"Tell 'em what you're gonna tell 'em, tell 'em, tell 'em what you told 'em"* and spent many long evenings red-lining my terrible school essays. He was over the moon when I started writing for my college paper, found my way into writing jokes for *The Onion*, and began tinkering with screenplays. Really wish you could have read this book, Dad. Love you and miss you.

My mom, who has printed hard copies of everything I've ever written. Most of it deserves to be burned in a large fire, but it means the world to me that you kept it anyway. You're my hero—mean it.

Acknowledgments

My daughters, Hannah and Natalie, for the endless inspiration, laughter, and joy. I love you girls so much I can't stand it. Being your dad is my greatest accomplishment.

Will, Joe, and Martin: For showing me what male friendship looks like at its absolute best.

Carson and Lincoln: For being amazing brothers and somehow even better uncles.

Gaga: For serving multiple terms as the president of my fan-club.

Steve W. Possibly the very first reader of the earliest version of this book. Thanks, bud.

All the awesome dudes I know who are raising the bar for what it means to be a great dad or even just a good man. You guys rock.

And Sarah: My Elliott. My Pam. My Rachel, my Monica. *My Evelyn*. After all this time, I'm still into you.

About the Author

EVAN S. PORTER is a dad to two girls, a blogger, and a freelance writer. He runs the blog *Dad Fixes Everything* and has contributed to *Parents* magazine, *The Onion News Network*, *AskMen*, *The Good Men Project*, and more. He lives in Atlanta with his wife, two daughters, two dogs, and not much in the way of elbow room.